I0669146

The Adventures of DOC ATLAS

Airship 27 Productions

TM

The Adventures of Doc ATLAS
"The Riddle of the Sphinx", "Desert Shadows", "The Green Death" all © 2022 Michael A. Black and Raymond Louis Lovato

Published by Airship 27 Productions
www.airship27.com
www.airship27hangar.com

Cover and interior illustrations © 2022 Ed Catto

Editor: Ron Fortier
Associate Editor: Fred Adams Jr.
Marketing and Promotions Manager: Michael Vance
Production designer: Rob Davis

ISBN: 978-1-953589-30-9

Printed in the United States of America

10 9 8 7 6 5 4 3 2 1

The Adventures of Doc Atlas

by Michael A. Black & Raymond Louis Lovato

Contents

THE RIDDLE OF THE SPHINX

Yucatan peninsula, Mexico, Monday, September 22nd, 1947

Arthur Guffrey shone the light from his portable lamp over the inscriptions on the wall once again. He couldn't help giving in to the impulse to rub his fingers slightly over the chiseled hieroglyphics, especially the one that had made his heart leap as soon as he'd seen it. It was amazing that after all these years he had finally found the vindication he'd been searching for—- evidence that proved their theory beyond a shadow of a doubt. Now he'd show them. He'd show all of them. Some grit clung to his fingers and he rubbed them together, studying it. Then he heard Audrey's voice call to him from farther up the tunnel.

"Father, are you coming?" she asked. "It's beginning to get dark."

"I'll be along shortly," Guffrey said. "Just want to try to make a few more notes."

"But we'll have the photographs for that."

He noticed the persistence in her voice and thought how much it reminded him of her mother. She never cared about his penchant for poking around in old dank tombs either. But now it had all come full circle. Now he finally had the indisputable facts. He sighed, regretting that his late wife would not be able to witness his vindication and greatest triumph.

"You go ahead, dear," Guffrey called. "I'll be along in a few minutes. You just take that film to be developed immediately."

He heard her "Oh, Father" exclamation as her footsteps grew fainter. Good, she was gone. He took out his notebook and made some more preliminary sketches in the dim light of the portable lamp. The face of the Sphinx-like figure seemed almost to stare back at him as his gaze rose again to the wall.

"Why have you suddenly appeared, my ancient friend," Guffrey said aloud, "giving me another riddle to solve?" He examined his fingers again, then wiped them on his pants.

He heaved a long, slow sigh and closed his notebook.

Perhaps it was time to go up to the surface, he thought, shining the weakening lamp on his wristwatch. But as he turned, he heard the first sounds of the scraping noises. Stones rubbing against stones, and then he felt the rumble beneath his feet. He held the lamp up at arm's length so it shone directly down the mouth of the tunnel. The light at the end

5

was fading from view, as if someone were drawing a dark curtain across the entranceway. Guffrey felt the surge of panic and he tried to force his obsolescent legs to sprint down the stone pathway. But before he could manage to take one step he felt the hand on his shoulder, and the room was plunged into total blackness.

New York City, early afternoon, three days later

The tall, blond man stood with his hands clasped behind his back as he looked out the bright windows on the 87th floor of the sumptuously furnished library. A folded telegram lay on the polished mahogany table a few feet behind him, and the man turned his tawny colored eyes on it. His face had a chiseled, handsome look to it, although it seemed completely devoid of emotion. The powerful sweep of his shoulders and arms made his physical prowess obvious, even in the expertly tailored brown business suit that he wore. His eyes moved to the door and moments later it opened as three people, two men and a woman entered. The woman, whose dark-hair hung around her shoulders in a soft, curling wave, was strikingly beautiful. Her head tilted slightly back with laughter. The man on her left, was tall and handsome, with carefully combed brown hair and a well-trimmed mustache. Impeccably dressed, he carried a long, finely crafted cane, as he walked with a barely noticeable limp. He looked amazingly like Errol Flynn. He was laughing as well. The other man was shorter and older than either of them, but powerfully built. The sleeves of his garish sport jacket were pulled tight over huge biceps and his large hands protruded from each cuff.

"Very funny, Ace," the shorter man said, wiping at his face with a handkerchief. "Very funny."

"My pleasure," Ace said, nodding to the man by the window. "I was just showing Mad Dog here my new carnation, Doc." He stuck his hand in his pants pocket and suddenly a misty spray shot from the flower on his lapel.

The woman giggled again, and Thomas "Mad Dog" Deagan, the shorter man said, "Aww, come on, Penny. It ain't that funny. What if he'd a done it to you?"

"And ruin my makeup?" Penelope Cartier said. "Ace knows better than that."

"Indeed I do," Ace Assante said, making a show of gallantly pulling a chair out for Penny to sit down. He glanced up and asked, "What's going on, Doc?"

The tall blond man pointed to the folded paper on the table and turned back to the window. Assante glanced quickly at the others and unfolded it and spread the paper out flat on the table top for everyone to read.

TELEGRAM: WESTERN UNION
TO DOC ATLAS, EMPIRE STATE BUILDING, 87th FLOOR, NEW YORK CITY, USA
FROM MISS AUDREY GUFFREY, SANTA MERIDA, MEXICO
NEED HELP STOP CONCERNS RIDDLE OF THE SPHINX STOP FATHER MISSING STOP NO ONE ELSE CAN HELP STOP PLEASE COME IMMEDIATELY STOP
AUDREY

Assante's brow furrowed as he looked at the others who seemed as baffled as he.

"What's this all about, Doc?" he asked. "And I don't understand this reference to the Riddle of the Sphinx."

As Doc Atlas turned toward them, the sunlight streamed in through the windows backlighting his powerful torso. "Professor Arthur Guffrey was a former associate of my father," Doc said. "At one time he was a world-renowned archeologist specializing in Egyptian artifacts and studies."

"I recall reading about him before the war," Assante said. "He was known as a man who was outstanding in his field."

"Yeah, I remember seeing him standing out there, too," said Deagan. "Only I didn't know it was his field."

Penny burst out laughing and smacked Deagan playfully on the shoulder while Assante shot him a scowl.

"Your dad was quite the expert in that stuff, too," Deagan said.

"He was at that, Thomas," Doc said, smiling briefly. "And at one time he and Dr. Guffrey were close friends."

"Is that where this Sphinx business comes in?" Penny asked.

Doc nodded. "I'm sure you all are aware of the Riddle of the Sphinx. What is the only animal who walks on four legs in the morning, two legs at midday, and three legs in the evening?"

Deagan scratched his head. "Don't sound like no animal I ever seen."

"You idiot," Assante said.

Penny laid a hand on Deagan's arm, smiling.

"It's supposed to be a reference to the different ages of man," she said. "A baby, a mature adult, and an older person."

"With a cane," Assante said, holding his up and twisting it to show the razor-sharp blade housed within. "Care for me to sharpen your wits a bit?"

Doc went to the chalkboard on the far wall and began writing.

"As you know, the traditional belief is that the Sphinx, as well as the pyramids, were built around 2520, B.C., during the reign of Khafre, as a self-tribute to the pharaoh. My father went on an expedition to Egypt in 1939. He was accompanied by Professor Guffrey. Together they explored the tomb of King Fhatid. My father and Professor Guffrey were friends at the time."

"At the time?" Ace said, giving Doc a questioning look.

"They had a falling out shortly thereafter," Doc continued. "Upon their return to New York with their artifacts, Guffrey became associated with a certain radical theory espoused by a charlatan named K. C. Edgar."

"I've heard of him," Penny said. "Don't they call him the Sleeping Prophet, or something?"

"The Transcendental Prophet," Doc said. His lips twitched with a hint of a smile. "I believe Edgar's unofficial title was carefully fashioned by him to deflect scrutiny of his theory that the Sphinx was built long before the reign of Khafre." He wrote another date on the board. "In fact, Edgar theorized that its origin predated the construction of the pyramids. In 7000 BC."

"Were the Egyptians that advanced of a civilization then?" Penny asked.

Doc shook his head. "It's dubious, but in Edgar's vision the Sphinx wasn't created by them." He drew a symbol on the chalkboard. It looked like the face of the sphinx with a star-like aura around it. "He credited its creation to the pilgrims from the lost city of Atlantis."

"Huh?" Deagan said.

Assante shook his head. "It's unbelievable that someone would believe that malarkey, much less an educated man like Professor Guffrey."

"Hey, I dunno," Deagan said. "I seen this movie serial once about Atlantis. They was supposed to be pretty far advanced."

"Oh Mad Dog, come on," Penny said.

"As I said," added Assante. "Only a moron would subscribe to such tripe."

"Regardless of the worth of the theory," Doc said, interceding in his group's customary good-natured banter, "it caused the aforementioned rift between Dr. Guffrey and my father. They never spoke again. Guffrey always blamed my father for not supporting him publicly. He lost his affiliation with the museum, and subsequently his job at the university. His wife died soon thereafter, and Guffrey took his young daughter with him searching for proof of the theory."

"Old K.C. Edgar seems to be making a living off it," Deagan said.

"He preys upon the weak minded," Assante said, tilting his cane toward Deagan's head. "Perhaps you'd like to join his flock?"

"Keep that fancy stick away from me or I'll take it and shove it—-"

"Thomas," Doc said in a quiet tone. "Will you see to the preparation of the Athena?"

"Sure, Doc."

"And see that it's fully fueled. I've estimated the quickest route will be to fly over the Gulf to the Yucatan peninsula." He looked at Assante. "Ace, can you file the necessary flight plans? I would like to leave this afternoon. We'll probably need to refuel again in Houston."

Assante nodded as he got up.

"I'll need time to pack," Penny said, standing up and grabbing her purse.

"Unfortunately, you won't be accompanying us this time," Doc said.

"What? You can't keep me away from a story like this," she said, placing her hands on her hips.

"There's been an outbreak of smallpox in the area, Penny," Doc said. "It's far too risky for you." He walked over to her.

"But what about you guys?"

"We've all been vaccinated," Doc said. "You have not."

"You weren't vaccinated?" Ace asked.

Penny shook her head quickly. "My parents didn't believe in it."

"Well," said Deagan, slapping his left shoulder. "Our Uncle Sam did, before we went overseas during the war."

Ace raised his eyebrows and affected a sad-looking smile as he nodded.

"Hey I sure hope that Audrey gal doesn't get the pox," Deagan said. "I remember that time I met her back when she was a kid. She was a real sweetie."

"She signed the telegram Audrey," Ace said. "Do you know her well, Doc?"

"We've known each other since childhood," he said, "although she is five years younger than I."

"Bet she had a crush on you, too, huh?" Deagan said, grinning.

Doc said nothing.

"Where can I get vaccinated?" Penny asked, looking worried.

"Come on," said Doc. "Let's go to the laboratory. I've already prepared one for you."

"Then I *can* go with after all?" she asked.

Doc shook his head. "I would want you to stay for at least 72 hours to assure that the vaccination had developed the proper antibodies. I'm afraid we can't afford to wait the necessary time."

"This just isn't fair," Penny said, pouting. "You guys get to have all the fun. Not to mention the great story I'll be missing out on."

"Aww, don't worry none," Deagan said, laying a commiserating palm on her arm. "I'm sure Ace here will take a lot of notes for you so you can still write your article and then one of them pulp novels where you always make me look like the monkey's uncle."

"If anything is written to depict you as closer to your hirsute origins," Ace said caustically, "I'll be glad to assist. Though I'd hardly call it a novel."

Santa Merida, Mexico, Seventeen hours later

Doc and Deagan stood in the hot, dry air and stretched as Ace negotiated with the owner of the small airfield. Displaying a smile interspersed with glints of shiny gold, he gladly agreed to watch Doc's plane for the rather generous offered price. He smiled again as he looked over at the silver metallic body of the big DC-4 gleaming in the early morning sunshine. After having flown all night, Deagan and Assante looked and felt exhausted. Only Doc appeared unaffected, although he'd spent nearly all his time at the controls, spelled only occasionally by Ace.

"Make sure you tell him half now and half when we get back," Deagan said, wiping his face with a handkerchief.

"What kind of fool do you think I am?" Ace shot back.

"I ain't gonna answer that one," Deagan said, grinning broadly. "Let's just say it's a good job for a mouthpiece."

Assante looked at him sternly for a few seconds then turned back to the Mexican and began talking again in rapid Spanish. Doc looked on, monitoring the conversation, but letting Ace do all the talking. Although he was fluent in several languages, including Spanish, it was Doc's customary preference not to demonstrate to others that he could speak and understand their languages.

"He says that won't be a problem," Ace said.

The Mexican's eyes grew large as Doc removed a large roll of Pesos from a brown money-belt and counted out the agreed-upon amount.

"Ask him where we might rent some vehicles to travel to the interior," Doc said.

As Assante began the new inquiries, Doc turned to Deagan.

"Thomas, make sure the Athena is properly secured and bring each of us sidearms."

"Gotcha, Doc," Mad Dog said, ambling toward the plane.

Ace continued his discussion with the other man, who was leaning over his desk drawing a map of sorts.

Assante straightened up and showed the paper to Doc.

"He says we can probably rent some motorcycles at this place," Ace said. "It's doubtful whether we'll be able to find any cars that would make the trip. I asked him about the area near Santa Merida. It's rather mountainous with heavy foliage. There's a macadamized road that goes there, but it's very dangerous."

Doc nodded.

"Tengo cuidado, senõr. La caretera es muy peligroso," the man said. "Hay muchos bandidos alla."

Just then Deagan walked up and handed Doc a Colt Government Model forty-five and a holster. The Mexican's eyes widened. "What'd he say, Ace?" Deagan asked.

"He said to watch out for bandits," Ace said with a grin.

Deagan smiled too, as he pulled out the forty-five and chambered a round. "Well, we got plenty of *bandidos* where we come from, too, partner," he said, trying his best to imitate John Wayne. "In fact, a lot of times we eat 'em for breakfast."

The vehicle shop turned out to be little more than a run-down looking barn composed of rotting wood and ill-fitted corrugated aluminum sheets. The owner spoke, sitting under the shade of an overhang, fanning himself as he continued to sweat profusely. Finally, after several minutes of sometimes heated conversation, Ace turned back to Doc and said, "He says he only has two motorcycles available for rent at this time."

Doc surveyed the area beyond where the man sat, which was littered with automobile parts of all shapes and sizes.

"Very well," Doc said. "Tell him we'll look at them."

With that decided, the man rose ponderously from his chair and motioned for them to follow. He led them through a fenced-in area and through stacks of boxes. At the end of the aisle the man pulled a large canvas tarp that had been spread across two Army model 841 Indian motorcycles, one of which had an attached sidecar. Both of the machines looked to be in good condition.

Deagan let out a low whistle, running his hand over the white star on the gas tank.

"Wow," he said. "This is swell. I ain't had my keister on an Indian since 1939."

The man said something in Spanish to Ace, and grinned.

"What'd he say?" Deagan asked.

"Believe me, you don't want to know," Ace said. He turned to Doc and told him the price. Doc reached in his money belt and removed the roll of bills again.

"Come on, Ace," Deagan said. "What did this guy say about me?"

Assante smiled and shook his head. Doc paid the man and went to the motorcycle with the sidecar.

"It seems two of us will have to use this one," he said.

"Ha," Deagan said. "And I know who it ain't gonna be." He turned his thumb toward his chest.

"Ask him the way to the local constable, Ace," Doc said. "I want to check on the status of Professor Guffrey before we leave."

Ace spoke to the man again as Deagan went over to the other motorcycle and ran his hand over the curve of the gas tank.

"She's a beaut, Doc," he said. "Good condition, too. How about we take her with us when we leave? I'll pay you when we get back to New York."

Doc smiled. "We'll see, Thomas." He punched the kick-starter as Ace came back over to them.

"Okay, I got the directions," he said, then turning to Deagan, added, "You really want me to tell you what that guy said before?"

Deagan nodded.

"He asked if your short legs would reach the pedals," Ace said, grinning.

"What?" Deagan snorted. "Pedals?"

Ace laughed as he held his hands out, palms up. "Hey, Mac, I'm just the messenger."

"Oh yeah?" Deagan said, marching over to the Mexican whose large grin began to fade as he saw the advancing American. The man started a quick trot down the aisle with Deagan in steady pursuit. Doc called out to him, but Deagan continued until Ace shot by him on the motorcycle, waving and laughing. Deagan's lower lip drew up and overlapped his upper, and he removed his hat and threw it on the ground. Doc pulled up next to him on the motorcycle with the sidecar.

"The man really said, 'Looks like your friend likes it,'" Doc said.

"That dirty son of a..." Deagan began to say, looking in Assante's direction.

"With Ace's leg the way it is," Doc said, strapping his goggles in place, "it might have been problematic for him to assume the rather cramped position in the sidecar, Thomas." Deagan seemed to consider this for a moment, then nodded, getting into the truncated seat without further comment as he, too, slipped on a pair of goggles.

The town was a ramshackle collection of buildings and houses. Most of them were one story brick stucco with ornately tiled roofs. A few of the more prestigious institutions, like the bank and the jail, were solid brick, but the main road bisecting the small hamlet was unpaved. As they rode down the dusty street, following Ace's clearly visible tracks and residual dust cloud, crowds of small children rushed to look at them and point.

When they got to the constable's office, Ace was already in a heated conversation with two men in uniform. One of them was large and very obese. He had captain's bars on his starched cap, but was wearing a sweat-soaked tee shirt. The other man was smaller and wore a tan shirt. It, too, was soaked through with sweat, and on the sleeves were upside-down sergeant's chevrons. A tag on his shirt above his left pocket said GARCIA. The heavy man sat down in a chair in the shade and began fanning himself with some papers.

Deagan gave Ace a dirty look as he and Doc dismounted, but said nothing. Ace came over to them looking rather drawn.

"I'm afraid I might have rubbed the local constabulary the wrong way," he said pointing to his side. "They took my gun away."

"Leave it to a lawyer," Deagan said.

The obese man glanced at them and said something in a low voice.

"*Senōres*," the sergeant said. "*El capitan* requests that you surrender your firearms immediately."

"Listen, bub," Deagan said. "I ain't gonna give up my—-"

Doc gently laid a hand on Deagan's shoulder, while at the same time removed his own weapon and handed it toward the policeman.

"I assume we will get receipts to reclaim them upon our return?" he said.

The little sergeant withdrew the sleek black-barreled Colt from the holster and held it up, smiling.

"Ah, it is a beautiful *pistola, senōr*. I will be very happy to hold it for you."

"Just don't forget the receipt, pal," Deagan said, handing his gun over as well. The sergeant holstered Doc's weapon and carried them both inside.

"Have you asked about Professor Guffrey?" Doc asked.

"Yes, he has, *senōr*," the large man said. "I am *Capitan* Cruz. The daughter of the *profesor* has already made a report about his absence."

"I see. And has your investigation yielded any more information as to his whereabouts?"

Captain Cruz canted his head and smiled slightly.

"*La senōrita* is very worried. But some of my men went with her to search the ruins and the area. I told her that her father must have wandered off in the jungle."

"La selva es muy peligroso," Sergeant Garcia said, coming back through the door with a paper. "Here is your receipt, *senōr*. You may pick up your *pistolas* when you leave Santa Merida."

"Thank you," Doc said. "Has anyone from the camp been in town today?"

"*Si, el profesor egipcio* and his *guia*," Garcia said, pointing to the building across the street. An open-topped jeep sat in front of the building, which had a peeling yellow sign with black letters that said *TIENDA, MERCADO Y TELEGRAMAS*. A swarthy looking man with dark eyes and hair pulled back into a ponytail sat in the front seat eyeing them. He was carving a piece of wood into some sort of totem with a long, flat knife. Several small children watched in awe as he finished the carving, held it up, and tossed it to them. The children fought over the gift, until one emerged victorious and ran off with the others in hot pursuit. The man spat in the dust and began cleaning his fingernails with the knife.

Doc turned to the Captain and asked, "Do you have any theories on Professor Guffrey's disappearance?"

Cruz licked his lips before he spoke. "You know, like my *sergento* told you, the jungle, it is a very dangerous place." He sighed heavily. "My guess is that he became confused and wandered off. It is my hope that some of the natives found him."

"Natives?"

"*Si*. There are *muchos indios* who live around the ruins," Cruz said. "They are a very secretive people. It is *posible* that they are caring for him in one of their remote camps. My men are checking daily for any news.

But," he shrugged and shook his head, "to be quite honest with you, the longer it goes…" He left the sentence unfinished.

"I see," Doc said. "Could you please spread the word that I'm offering a substantial reward for any information leading to the safe return of the Professor?"

Cruz raised his eyebrows. "And how much would that be, *senōr*?"

"Let's say, fifty thousand pesos."

Garcia let out a low whistle and grinned. "*Senōr*, you offer that kind of *dinero*, I will go out looking for the body of Cortez himself."

Doc looked across the street at the shop and saw another man exiting with two locals carrying a large box of provisions. The man was short and heavyset, with a rotund physique, looking rather soft in the middle. He was as darkly complexioned as the man in the jeep, but he did not have the look of a Mexican. The two local men placed the boxes in the back of the vehicle, and the short man got in. The two men held out their hands as he tossed them a few coins. The swarthy man in the driver's seat said something to them in a low, guttural voice. The dialogue continued, out of earshot of Doc and company. The man in the jeep jammed the knife into a leather sheath on his belt and snarled something at the two men. They both looked across toward the jail, then hurried off.

Doc strode across the street toward the jeep, the man behind the wheel eyeing him carefully. The high cheekbones and obsidian eyes suggested more than just a trace of Indian blood, Doc decided, as did the silver and turquoise-stone necklace the man wore.

"I'm Dr. Michael Atlas and these are my associates, Misters Deagan and Assante," Doc said, holding out his hand. "Are you by chance with the Guffrey expedition?"

The driver ignored Doc's outstretched hand, but the smaller man immediately got out and rushed around to shake it. Doc noticed flecks of gray in the man's black hair and mustache.

"Ah, yes, Dr. Atlas," he said, placing his other hand on top of Doc's as well. "I am Dr. Mohammed Rabbat, Professor's Guffrey's partner. We met some time ago in my country, Egypt. This is our local guide, Carlos. We were just in picking up supplies and checking to see if there'd been any word from you. I'm surprised you were able to get here so quickly."

"Professor Guffrey was a friend of my father. Is Audrey here as well?"

Rabbat steepled his fingers and grunted slightly.

"I am certain that she would have made the trip had she known you were arriving," he said. "But she has seldom left the encampment since her father's disappearance."

"There's been no news?"

Rabbat shook his head sadly. "We've searched the ruins several times, thinking that he possibly got trapped in an unexplored room. But it is as if he simply vanished."

"What about the Captain's theory that he's lost in the jungle?"

Rabbat's breath hissed out in a derisive rush.

"Ah, that man has already made up his mind that the Professor will never be found," he said. "His efforts to assist us have been ludicrously inefficient."

"Well, Doc just sweetened the pie a bit by offering a reward," Deagan said. "Money talks, especially south of the border."

Rabbat looked at him with a grim smile. "I'm afraid, sir, that we have already tried that ourselves. It has met with little success."

"Perhaps it would be beneficial for us to see the area where Professor Guffrey disappeared," Doc said. "Can you show us the way to the camp?"

"Of course," Rabbat said. "If you will follow us?"

He went around and got in the jeep. Doc exchanged glances with the man behind the wheel. Carlos pressed the starter button, and the jeep's engine sputtered to life.

Ace turned quickly to check Deagan's whereabouts, but saw Mad Dog already cramming himself into the sidecar.

"You look good in there," Ace said as he walked to his motorcycle.

"Don't push it," Deagan said. "I'm still taking that thing for a ride before this is through."

"Not if I can help it," Ace said, snapping the starter with his boot.

Rabbat told them the ruins were perhaps 15 kilometers southeast of the town. "The road is passable almost all the way," he said. "We will wait for you at the juncture where the trail to the ruins begins if you wish."

Doc nodded.

"You will perhaps not wish to ride too closely behind us," Rabbat said, smiling and showing a set of small teeth inlaid with gold. "The dust can be very unpleasant."

Doc adjusted his goggles as they watched the jeep pull away Doc Deagan looked up from the sidecar, "That guy kind of reminds me of a fat Peter Lorre. Professor Rabbat, huh? You ever heard of him?"

"Only by reputation," Doc said, kicking the starter. "But I wasn't aware that he subscribes to the K.C. Edgar theories. Still he's considered one of the preeminent Egyptologists in the world today."

"Another guy who's outstanding in his field, huh?" Deagan said, pulling his goggles down and slapping the top of the sidecar. "Man, this thing was made for a man half my size."

At the outskirts of the town they passed some women squatting by a stream washing clothes. More groups of half-naked children came to watch the progression of vehicles as they passed. Perhaps thirty yards beyond the last buildings the foliage began to swell up with a scattering of dwarf-like trees and rows of cactuses. The farther inland they went, the more verdant the landscape became. Rabbat's jeep was a hundred yards ahead of them leaving a cloudy turbulence in its wake. Doc backed off the accelerator slightly creating more distance and keeping the speed under thirty miles per hour. Ace pulled up along side and shouted at Deagan.

"How you enjoying the trip?" The sandy dust covered the lower portion of his face and his mustache.

"I used to ride sidesaddle when I was in the army," Deagan said. "But it was hard to find a lawyer to do my driving in them days."

Doc smiled at the banter as he scanned the road ahead. The jeep rounded a turn, and suddenly something whipped sinuously across the dusty surface like a big serpent. It took Doc a split second to realize what it was, and he immediately cut the handlebars to the right, steering toward Ace's motorcycle. Deagan looked up as the two vehicles abruptly veered toward a near collision, then he heard Doc yell, "Thomas, duck!" With that said, the Golden Avenger jumped upward and out of the seat of his motorcycle, traveling over the top of Deagan in the sidecar, and plowing into Assante.

Reacting instinctively to Doc's warning, Deagan hunched forward. Doc simultaneously grabbed Ace, ripping him completely off his bike, then spun in midair so that when they landed on the rough surface seconds later, Ace's thinner form was spared much of the impact. Ace's motorcycle twisted onto its side and began rotating in a circular motion for a few seconds as the rear wheel continued to spin. Doc's motorcycle continued forward, slowing to a stop. Deagan hopped out and began running back toward his two fallen partners when he was abruptly knocked backward with a violent jerk.

"What the?" he started to say as the first shot rang out. Doc was already up on his feet, carrying the unconscious Assante on one shoulder and scrambling towards the now fallen Deagan.

Another shot whizzed past Doc's head and he dipped slightly to his side, brushing the ground with his left hand for balance. He reached Deagan with two more hurried steps and grabbed him by the collar, using his momentum to push all three of them into the thick shrubbery alongside the roadway.

Deagan began scrambling along in a low crouch as Doc released his collar.

"Was that what I think it was?" he asked in a hushed, breathless tone.

"Piano wire," Doc said, not bothering to add that he'd seen the wire rising from the dirt moments after the jeep had passed. They heard voices off to their right.

Deagan accepted Ace's still limp form from Doc and continued thrashing through the underbrush, muttering curses as he was attacked by a myriad of thorns and cactus needles. Doc quickly withdrew two small sphere-like objects from the back of his money belt and angled off to the right. More voices filtered toward them. Doc flattened out as he heard the sounds of at least two men approaching.

"Fueron alla," one of the men said. He held a large revolver with an extended barrel at his side. The other man, who was holding a similar weapon, grunted and began pushing some stray branches out of their way as they moved forward.

Doc twisted the first sphere with a quick, deft motion, then rose to his knees. With a powerful and accurate throw, he sent it hurling toward the two men, clipping the first man between the eyes. The man was obviously stunned, but the second man caught Doc's movement and grinned malevolently as he raised his pistol.

"You throw stones, huh, hombre?" he said. "Now you die."

But before he could fire, a terrific explosion erupted, sending both men flying pell-mell through the sea of undergrowth as a result of the concussive wave. Doc, who had immediately flattened and covered his ears after tossing the miniature grenade, rose quickly and shot forward. Both assailants were dead. He retrieved their weapons and checked the cylinders. One pistol had two rounds expended; the other still had a full load. Placing the fully loaded weapon in his belt, Doc moved forward with the second one held in front of him. Moments later he heard a voice yell in Spanish.

"*Manuel, que paso?*" the voice said. "*Que causa la explosion?*"

The third man came through the bushes holding a long barreled pistol in one hand and an army walkie-talkie in the other. His eyes looked sinister under a red bandana that had been tied over the top of his skull.

"*Halto,*" Doc said, leveling his pistol at the man. "*Suelte su arma.*"

But instead of heeding Doc's command to drop his weapon, the man began to raise the pistol and aim it. Doc squeezed off two shots striking him in the chest and the forehead. He was dead before he hit the ground.

As the cloud of dust from Rabbat's jeep began to dissipate, the five men stood along the side of the road and looked at the three bodies. Doc had placed them in supine positions on the ground.

"When we heard the explosion," Dr. Rabbat said, "we immediately turned around. We never imagined..." He let the sentence trail off as Carlos went over to the first body.

"*Bandidos*," Carlos said, using his boot to raise the limp head of the dead man.

"Allah be praised," Dr. Rabbat said, steepling his fingers. "As I said, we never imagined they would dare attack you, Dr. Atlas. We've gone to and from the town so many times without incident."

"Do they look at all familiar?" Doc asked.

"I saw them back by *la tienda*," Carlos said. "They must have seen you take the *dinero* out of your belt."

"Obviously you seen it, too," Deagan said, scowling.

Carlos looked back at Deagan with a vapid expression, his dark eyes shining like obsidian.

"I must say," Dr. Rabbat said. "I find it simply amazing that you were able to subdue your assailants with such aplomb. You must have been in the military, yes?"

Doc nodded.

"And those miniature explosives. May I see one?"

Doc glanced at the Egyptian momentarily, then removed one of the two remaining spheres from the special pouch on his belt.

"Amazing, simply amazing," Rabbat rolled it in his hand. "And you activate it how?"

"It requires a certain amount of manual dexterity," Doc said, pointing to the clearly marked sections, "but you merely twist the halves in opposite directions. The delay fuse is approximately four seconds."

"Then boom," Deagan flipped his huge hands up in an explanatory gesture.

"Ingenious," Rabbat carefully handed the sphere back to Doc. "It is little wonder that you were able to prevail."

"We've been in a lot tighter spots than this," Ace grinned.

"And you activate it how?"

"Whaddya mean 'we?'" Deagan retorted. "If it wasn't for me and Doc carrying your limp keister all over these damn woods, you'd a been back there wearing a French necktie."

"A French necktie?" Rabbat asked.

"That's what we used to call 'em in the War," Deagan said.

"The French resistance used to stretch piano wire across the road at throat level to decapitate Nazi motorcyclists," Ace explained. "Say, Doc, we'd better report this little encounter to the authorities. Especially since they made such a production out of confiscating our weapons."

"That is not necessary," said Carlos. He spat on the nearest corpse. "As I told you, these men are bandidos. No one cares if they live or die. There is no need to notify la policia."

"Just the same, the incident needs to be reported," Doc turned to Dr. Rabbat. "Would you mind if we used your jeep to transport these men back to town?"

"But of course," Rabbat said. "But I would prefer to deliver the supplies to the camp first." He glanced at Carlos. "They will surely be going nowhere, eh?"

Carlos smiled.

"Very well," Doc concurred. "We'll proceed to the camp. Then you and Thomas can go back to speak to the authorities, Ace."

Assante nodded. His head swiveled around as Deagan began walking across the road toward the fallen Indian motorcycle.

"Hey, where do you think you're going with that?" Ace questioned.

"Nowheres," Deagan picked up the motorcycle and righted it by using only one arm. He looked at Ace and held his hand out in a magnanimous proffering gesture and grinned. "At least not yet, anyway."

The road wound sinuously through the ubiquitous forest for a few more miles, at which point the jeep turned left down a secondary dirt road. This road seemed well traveled, but recently cut bushes hung limply on each of the edges. It was as if a caravan of laborers had just finished hacking the path through the dense vegetation. Ahead of them Doc and the others saw a huge pyramid-like structure rising above the canopy of trees in symmetrical fashion. The tapering pattern of the rich brown bricks narrowed to a flat peak, dwarfing the verdant forest. The closer they got, the more immense the structure appeared. Suddenly rows of stone walls sprung up on either side of the road, along with a series of smaller buildings in various stages of dilapidation. Much of the construction had been done with heavy limestone although the buildings seemed to have been fashioned out of the same brown bricks as the pyramid.

A small encampment of perhaps a dozen tents scattered among the ruins came into view, with several stacks of wooden crates in between them. Two men, obviously both local natives, stood at the edge of the road with rifles. As they saw the jeep they perked up. Doc saw Carlos stop and talk with the men, gesturing and pointing. Then he turned back toward Doc and waved.

As they drove past, the sentries came to attention and saluted, then collapsed into a mocking laughter.

"I'd like to take those rifles away from them and show them what to do with 'em," Deagan muttered from the sidecar.

Doc pulled to a stop beside the jeep and dismounted.

"Is it necessary to have armed guards here, Dr. Rabbat?"

"Ah," Rabbat smiled somewhat sadly. "Unfortunately, there is a contingent of rather unfriendly natives in the region. Mayan descendants. Although they have not caused us any unpleasantness, they hold these ruins to be very sacred. The guards are perhaps our insurance that we will be allowed to complete our excavation unmolested."

"Michael, thank God you've come," Doc heard a female voice say. He turned in time to see Audrey Guffrey running from one of the nearby tents. Her long auburn hair trailed behind her like a reddish flame. She was in her late-twenties and voluptuously built. Deagan gave out a low whistle as she literally threw herself into Doc's arm, pushing her head onto his powerful chest.

"Hey, she makes Rita Hayworth look like your grandmother," he said to Assante.

"Now I'm really getting worried," Ace shot back. "We've found something we agree on."

The Guffrey girl's sobs were quieted by Doc, who ushered her off to one of the tents, keeping his arm around her waist in an avuncular gesture. They went inside the tent, and moments later Doc emerged and went back to Deagan and Assante.

"I need to confer with Audrey at this time. You two go back to town and report the confrontation with the bandits to the police."

"Roger-wilco, Doc," Deagan said. "And this time, I'm taking the Indian."

"Over my dead body," Ace smiled.

"Hey, that can be arranged," Deagan shot back with an equally broad grin.

"Ask Dr. Rabbat's man to accompany you," Doc ordered. "He seems to have a thorough knowledge of the countryside." He pointed to an old army truck with a canopy parked near the adjacent tents. "Perhaps both of you had better ride in that with Carlos. It should offer more ballistic cover than a motorcycle, and it's dusk now. It will surely be dark upon your return." Doc smiled. "And it might be problematic trying to carry three corpses on the motorcycles."

Deagan snorted and the smile faded from Assante's face. But both men trudged wearily over to the truck. Doc went back to the tent and stepped inside. Audrey Guffrey sat on one of the two cots, the mosquito netting pushed to one side, her face in her hands. She looked up at Doc, and he saw the twin trails of tears streaming down from her eyes.

"Oh, Michael. I'm so afraid for Father. I just know something terrible has happened to him."

Doc sat down on the cot across from her, removing his handkerchief and holding it toward her.

"Please, tell me everything," he said. "Start at the beginning and leave nothing out, no matter how insignificant it may seem."

Meanwhile, early evening in New York City

The artificial lighting glowed in the morgue office of the New York Times as Penny's nimble fingers sped through the files marked "G, for Guffrey." She had already found numerous articles on the distinguished accomplishments and discoveries of Professor Arthur Guffrey. She'd even found one detailing the famous Egyptian excavation that involved Doc's father, as well as another article describing the bitter feud that had developed shortly thereafter. Neither disturbed her as much as the scrawled handwritten notation at the bottom of the card saying: See society page, 06-10-41. Audrey Guffrey escorted to Radcliff graduation dance by son of Dr. Victor Atlas.

It couldn't be Doc, could it? she wondered, rapidly searching the files for the society section. Not her Doc escorting some other woman to a dance?

Penny reached the end of the files in the folder and tossed it aside, immediately digging into the next one.

Ah, relax, she told herself, trying to conjure up a laugh. *She's a bookworm. Some professor's daughter. Majored in anthropology, for crying out loud. Probably looks like Elsa Lanchester in The Bride of Frankenstein, only with glasses.*

She pursed her lips and blew some errant hairs away from her face. The itching resumed again on the burgeoning scab on her left shoulder, and she rubbed her fingers gingerly over the Band Aid.

Yeah, she thought. *Real thick glasses. Doc was probably ordered to do it by his father, and he probably hated every minute of it. I'll bet he was bored out of his mind.*

And then she found the file marked SOCIETY, and popped it open. The stunning picture of Doc in a tuxedo, smiling, and the gorgeous creature next to him, her head tilted back in a half-laugh, half-smile, her full lips parted ever-so-slightly, the sensual curving sweep of her breasts beneath the elegant evening gown, made Penny's heart skip a beat.

No, this wasn't fair, she thought. *That can't be her. It isn't possible.* Her fingernail traced the caption under the photo and she dreaded each word as she read it.

Dr. Michael G. Atlas, son of prominent scientist and inventor, Victor Atlas, and Audrey S. Guffrey, daughter of renowned archeologist Arthur Guffrey, seem oblivious to the well-publicized feud between their fathers and they make a great couple at the Radcliff graduation dance. Miss Guffrey plans to begin a course of study to become a physician, just like her escort, Dr. Atlas.

A great couple, thought Penny. *That settles it. I'm going to Mexico if I have to beg, borrow, or steal my way down there.*

Doc placed the last picture down on the cot and was about to speak when he heard the honking. Audrey looked up at him with a perplexed expression.

"It must be my associates returning earlier than expected," Doc stood and flipped open the tent flap in time to see the beat-up old army truck pulling into the encampment. Carlos was at the wheel, but Deagan was leaning over pressing the horn.

Doc strode over to the vehicle as Ace and Mad Dog piled out.

"Hey, Doc, guess what?" Deagan began.

"A problem with *habeas corpus*," Ace added.

Deagan frowned. "We went back to find them bodies and take 'em to town like you told us—"

"But they were gone," Ace finished the sentence.

Deagan shot him another disparaging look.

"Any idea who might have taken them?" Doc asked, directing his gaze toward Carlos.

The man shrugged slightly and spat in the dirt.

"I don't know," he said. "Maybe it was some of the big jungle cats. Panteras. There are many of them in this area."

"Huh?" Deagan said. "Some cats drag off three bodies?"

Carlos smiled slightly. "Senõr, you haff never seen our cats."

Deagan frowned.

"What do you want us to do now, Doc?" he asked.

Doc seemed to consider this for a moment as he looked around. The sky was already beginning to darken.

"What time does the local constabulary's office close?" he asked Carlos.

"We might be able to find them at *la taverna local*," he said.

Doc looked at him, and then to Ace, who translated, "The local tavern."

"It's getting dark," Doc said. "Perhaps the matter can wait until morning."

"Swell," Deagan rubbed his hands together and pointed toward the center of the encampment where a man was placing a pot on a grill over a large campfire. "I don't know about the rest of you, but I'm getting pretty hungry."

"Dangle the thought of a banana in front of a gorilla," Ace smiled at Audrey while pointing to Deagan, "and he'll forget the task at hand in favor of satisfying his baser instincts."

"I got some basic instinct for ya," Deagan balled up his fist.

"Are you two always like this?" she asked, a faint smile tracing her lips.

"Nah, we're usually a lot worse," Deagan said. "But it's good to see those pretty eyes of yours smiling. You might not remember me, but we met way back when you was just a kid. You see, I've known Doc and his father for a long time."

"I'm sure she remembers her first trip to the zoo," Ace stepped up and looped her arm through his. "Come, let us depart to the dining area for some civilized conversation."

"You two get along as well as Fred Allen and Jack Benny," Audrey said, smiling.

As the trio moved away, Doc studied Carlos. The man's eyes followed Audrey momentarily, then snapped back toward Doc, as if some preternatural instinct had told him he was being watched. A hint of smile twitched at his lip.

Doc nodded and began walking toward the campfire.

Deagan was already pointing to the carcass of a bird roasting on a spit.

"What is it, bud?" he asked. "A chicken?"

The cook shook his head and furrowed his brow. Ace started to speak, but Audrey said something in fluent Spanish and the Mexican smiled and nodded.

"Pavo salvaje," he said. "*Y frijoles.*"

"Wild turkey and kidney beans," Ace translated. "In case you're interested."

"Oh, you speak Spanish, Mr. Assante?" Audrey asked.

"Please, call me Ace," he answered with a dashing smile. "All my friends do."

"And I won't tell you what else we call him," Deagan grinned. He clapped his hands together and rubbed them vigorously. "Say, fellas, after we eat, what do you say to a little game of five card stud?"

The group of Mexicans looked perplexed.

"Hey, Ace," Deagan asked. "How do you say poker in Spanish?"

Ace smiled and said, "*Mi amigo dice que necesita los articulos de tocador.*"

The cook, who was standing over the simmering pot, looked at Deagan with a frown and pointed to the edge of the forest.

Deagan's brow furrowed. "Huh? What's over there?"

"I'm afraid that's not an accurate translation, Mr. Deagan," Audrey smiled. "Your friend told him you needed to go to visit the latrine."

Deagan scowled at Ace. "I shoulda known better..."

"Is that what I said?" Ace grinned and shrugged. "My Spanish is a little rusty."

Audrey laughed and quickly added, "But we'll hardly have time for card games, I'm afraid. We'll have to prepare some sleeping quarters for the three of you as soon as possible. You'll need mosquito netting, or you'll literally be eaten alive."

Deagan slapped his forearm.

"Yeah, I did notice them little critters. Seem to be getting worse now that the sun's going down."

"They can be unbearable," Audrey said. "I have some insect repellent in my tent."

"You don't need to worry about me, none, ma'am. I spent enough time in the infantry to be able to sleep just about anywheres. And as for mosquitoes, they couldn't be no worse here than they was in the Philippines, right, Doc?"

"Wasn't that where you caught malaria?" Ace asked caustically.

"Well, at least I made it over to both theaters, buster," Deagan countered. "Instead of playing Mr. Fancy-pants lawyer in Europe after the dirty work was done."

"Hey, it was my bombing runs that helped end that dirty work, remember?" Assante said.

"Do you have a spare tent we could use?" Doc asked.

Audrey nodded as she turned to Doc. "Michael, you might as well sleep in my tent. Father's bunk is empty and I'd feel safer with you close by."

Doc nodded slightly, showing no emotion.

Deagan shot a quick glance at Ace, then raised his eyebrows.

"Your two friends can stay in that one," she pointed to a tent to the left. "The men who were using it left unexpectedly today."

"Oh really?" Ace queried. "For what reason?"

"Indios," Carlos said, suddenly stepping over to the stew pot and sipping from the ladle. "They were afraid of los indios after the professor desaparece."

Deagan looked grimly at Ace, and then at Doc. The big Mexican's words needed no translation.

"So what ever happened to your plans to attend medical school?" Doc asked Audrey as they walked down the pebbled trail toward the large pyramid.

"Well, I finished my nursing courses," she turned her face to smile at him. "But I felt compelled to go with Father on an expedition. The next thing I knew, we were traveling to another location. And then another." She looked down. "I'm sorry I wasn't there for you when your father died."

Doc nodded.

"But at least you caught the men responsible, right?" she pointed to the entrance that was only about twenty yards away. "Perhaps it gave a sense of justice or closure?"

Doc shook his head. "Justice is often elusive. Closure perhaps even more so. It's given me some solace to try and continue his work in certain areas."

Audrey led them down the intricate tunnel, light from her portable lamp bouncing over the rough stone walls as she walked. The passageway was capacious, perhaps measuring seven feet by twelve. Doc was close behind her, his lamp held steady, followed by Deagan, Assante, and Dr. Rabbat. Deagan started to whistle until the dust from the earthen floor rose up to his face. He coughed a few times and stopped.

"Now I finally understand the significance of Buck's *The Good Earth*," Ace said.

Audrey turned to Doc and smiled slightly, but it was a tense smile. "It veers to the left just up ahead," she said. "I was right about here when he called to me."

Doc nodded, his chiseled features seemed unperturbed, but also cognizant of everything. He directed the beam from his lamp toward the ceiling and walls as they walked. The corridor narrowed to about six feet across. Doc and Assante had to stoop a bit as the ceiling slanted downward slightly as it met with solid looking rocks ahead. Audrey turned to the left and as they followed they saw that the corridor had expanded back to its normal spacious width.

"The room is down here," she said. "About thirty more feet."

The beam of her light swept over another set of pillars crossed by a heavy stone lintel. It obviously led to another, larger space.

"Wait until you see it, Dr. Atlas," Rabbat said. "It will convince you beyond a shadow of a doubt."

Doc said nothing, but merely followed behind Audrey, pausing periodically to touch the sides of the corridor.

As they passed between the pillars the passage opened into an enormous room with high ceilings and two enormous segmented support beams in the center. Doc estimated that they were near the center of the pyramid. Audrey shone her light over the walls, which were covered with intricate hieroglyphical markings depicting cryptic figures and symbols.

"There," Professor Rabbat grunted, his light centering on a leonine body with the flaring crown and humanoid face on the opposite wall. The figure was surrounded by a seven-pointed star. "You are familiar with the Pyramid of Khafre, are you not? This carving is virtually a mirror image of the Sphinx. You will notice, too, the crescentic flourishes around the edges of the surrounding star... the positioning of this symbol above the others. Everything points to its significance." His voice became almost animated with excitement. "It is just as it was described in the prophesies of K.C. Edgar. Professor Guffrey had been very excited about its discovery. He called it the Western Sphinx. It is believed to be the first such hieroglyph of its kind found on this continent."

Doc moved forward to examine the wall. He held his beam near the intricately carved figures.

"Exactly when did you become familiar with this theory, Professor?"

"Several years ago. In my country."

"Is that when you met Dr. Guffrey?"

"Why, no, it is not. Actually, we met for the first time here. But we had corresponded previously. I was familiar with his endorsement of the Atlantis theory, and contacted him." Rabbat continued speak in a rapid excited voice.

"It is the theory of K.C. Edgar that the Sphinx is much older than the pyramids themselves, having been built by the original ancestors of the lost continent of Atlantis," he said. He moved over and traced his fingers across some drawings on the adjacent wall. "You see here, this obviously depicts a large body of water, does it not?"

Deagan and Assante moved forward to study the section.

"Looks like it could be just about anything to me," Deagan said.

Professor Rabbat's head jerked as if he'd been slapped. He shone his light over another section. "But, if you please, look here. This is most definitely an homage to Horas, the Serpent King of the monument at Abydos."

Deagan's features scrunched up and he squinted. "I'd say it's a bird. Seen quite a few of 'em on the way here, too."

"I'm starting to get worried again, Doc," Ace confessed. "Mad Dog and I are agreeing on something again."

Rabbat huffed loudly.

"But the prophecies predicted the discovery that the two cultures would be ultimately linked." Rabbat's hand fluttered as he spoke. "Surely you cannot dismiss all of the theories of a man of such genius. Why if we had the time, I would gladly give you a lecture on just how many of his prophecies have indeed come to pass."

"Yeah?" Deagan said. "Don't forget the Nazis were great for quoting that one old French guy that it was prophesized that they were gonna win the War, too. What was that old frog's name, Ace?"

"Nostradamus," Assante replied. "But like most prophets, the accuracy of their predictions is almost always directly proportional to the skill and artistic license of the person who interprets them."

"Leave it to a lawyer to resay in twenty words what I said in ten," Deagan said.

"I've seen enough," Doc declared turning and heading out of the room. "We must get back to camp and get some rest. We'll explore this further tomorrow."

The others glanced at each other briefly, then turned to follow him.

The hushed tones of the voices carried to him over the incessant chirping of a myriad of insects and Doc immediately snapped awake. He didn't move, but began to soak in the surroundings with all of his senses: Audrey's soft breathing on the cot to his left, the heavy humidity that seemed to encompass everything like an invisible blanket, the ubiquitous insects..

And then he heard it again, and the chirping stopped. It was a grunt of pain followed by more hushed tones. Doc's arm swept upward to push away the mosquito netting and he moved his legs cautiously off the cot. He reached for his boots, tapping each one at the heel and turning it upside-down before inserting his foot and lacing it tightly. Deagan had always called it a "scorpion check" when they had been on their special missions in the Philippines.

Doc stood and glanced down at the still slumbering Audrey before refastening the netting around his cot and noiselessly slipping out of the tent. The air was silent, which meant that the insects were still in a heightened state of alert. He proceeded in the direction he'd heard the last noises, moving quietly through the ruins toward the base of the pyramid.

Another muffled grunt of pain floated toward him, followed by the harsh, whispering voices: at least two disparate tones, both of them familiar.

"Do not incapacitate him to the point where he cannot tell us where it's at."

It was Rabbat.

"Shut up. I know what I am doing."

Carlos, Doc thought. Then the same voice continued in a language that was totally foreign, full of harsh sounding clicks and fricatives.

"Ask him," Rabbat directed. "Ask him about the idols."

Doc's fingertips gently pushed aside a few leaves so he could survey the three figures without revealing himself. Professor Rabbat stood off to one side while Carlos held a small, slumping figure by the back of the shirt. The third person was slightly built, with long hair braided into a ponytail, and his arms were bound securely to a stick wedged horizontally across his back. His clothes were in tatters, and his bare feet were tied to a hobble fashioned from some rough looking rope. The dark head drooped toward his chest, but shot upward and emitted a sharp cry of pain as Carlos stepped around and hit him in the stomach, saying something in the strange, guttural language.

Doc could see that the captive was young, no more than a boy in his teens. He pushed aside the branches and stepped forward.

"What is going on here?" he asked.

The heads of both Carlos and Rabbat twisted toward him in surprise. Doc held them in a steady gaze.

"Why, Dr. Atlas," Professor Rabbat said nervously. "How did you come upon us?"

Doc did not answer. Rabbat's face jittered slightly before he continued. "We didn't hear you approach. You startled us."

"Obviously," Doc gestured toward the captive. "Who is he?"

"*Un asesino*," Carlos replied reaching his right hand down by his belt. "I caught him sneaking around our camp." His right hand came up with his long-bladed knife and he raised it to the boy's throat.

"He is from one of the local Indian tribes," Rabbat said quickly. "We were questioning him about the disappearance of Professor Guffrey. I'm convinced this man knows the whereabouts of our friend."

"Man?" Doc said. "He looks more like a boy. And if he is a criminal, he should be turned over to the authorities, not beaten and tortured."

"But we have no time," Rabbat countered. "The Professor's life is at stake."

"I will make him talk," Carlos pressed the sharpened edge of the blade against the flesh. The metal glinted in the moonlight as a few drops of blood seeped over the shiny surface. The boy hissed in pain and terror.

Doc moved forward and seized Carlos's wrist. The muscles of the other man's arm tensed up, but the knife slowly was pulled away from the boy's throat. A thin slash, trickling crimson, was now visible under his Adam's apple.

"Let me go, *Yanqui*, or I will keel you," Carlos spat through clenched jaws, his lips curled back from his teeth in a feral snarl.

"Not with this," Doc extended his thumb up over the back of the other man's right hand and twisted, causing Carlos's fingers to immediately open up. The knife slipped from his grasp. Doc caught it with his free hand, but continued the pressure.

"Release him," Doc commanded, exerting enough force to put Carlos on his knees. He grunted, but complied, freeing his grip on the boy's torn shirt. Doc held the wrist immobile for a few seconds more. The boy looked at them, his dark eyes darting from figure to figure, then he tried to run for the thicker underbrush at a quick sprint. Doc's boot stomped on the dragging loop of the hobble and tripped the boy before he could get two steps. Rabbat's features distorted into a grimace.

"Atlas, you fool," he spat. "You almost let him get away."

Doc released his hold on Carlos and allowed the man to get to his feet.

"Give me back my *cuchillo*, senõr," Carlos rubbed his wrist with his left hand.

"I think not," Doc flipped the blade into the air, catching it by the tip. He then turned abruptly and threw the knife with incredible force at a tree several yards away, burying it almost to the hilt. "Perhaps by the time you can work it free, you'll have cooled down."

He looked into Carlos's angry dark eyes momentarily and then turned and picked up the fallen Indian boy. He started back to camp with the boy in tow.

"If we're in danger of attack," he said over his shoulder, "we should post some guards. My associates and I will assist."

Doc gently shook Deagan awake, and then Ace. Both men had been in the deep sleep that sheer physical exhaustion brought, but did their best to shake off their fatigue. Doc held a finger to his lips to indicate silence, then pointed to the boy.

"Looks like we got company," Deagan whispered.

Doc held up his backpack. He removed one of the pistols that they'd taken from the slain bandits and handed it to Ace. Then he removed his wireless signal transmitter and a small portable generator. They moved with practiced stealth out of the tent and into the bushes.

Doc quickly surveyed the area, then leaned close to his two friends. In hushed tones he explained their objectives.

"Ace, you watch the base. Thomas and I will climb to the top." He indicated the captive. "Keep your eye on him, too. He may know the whereabouts of Professor Guffrey."

Ace doubled the rope of the hobble around his left fist while holding the pistol in his right. They all began a careful and quiet trip toward the pyramid with Doc in the lead. It took them perhaps ten minutes to reach the stone base. Doc paused and held up his fist to indicate a stop. He spoke with subdued deliberation again.

"We can't risk any lights being seen here. Ace, I suggest you take up a position over there." He indicated a dense patch of shrubbery. Ace nodded and moved toward it with the boy. Doc turned to Deagan.

"Thomas, use caution on this ascent. These steps are particularly hazardous."

"Gotcha, Doc," Mad Dog said. "I'll follow your lead."

Doc adjusted the backpack and began moving up the steps of the pyramid. Each one was about eight inches high, but only five to six inches deep. The slant of the structure made the upward climb possible, but tedious. Doc moved on all fours, and Deagan followed suit, but not at Doc's fast pace. Several times Doc had to slow and wait for the shorter man to catch up to him. Finally, after several minutes of hard work, they reached a flat section on top of the massive, man-made formation.

Doc quickly slipped off the backpack and removed the generator and wireless. He handed the generator to Deagan.

"Give me a minute, will ya, Doc," Deagan's breathing coming in gasps. "Too many of those Havana stogies."

Doc nodded and took the generator back. After attaching the wires, he set the transmitter on the surface in front of Deagan and began twisting the handles of the generator himself.

"I'll do this portion, Thomas, if you'll send the code."

Deagan nodded. "Shoot."

Doc spun the handles around in alternating circles, creating the necessary current to power the transmission. As he did this he dictated the message that he wanted sent. Deagan's nimble finger pecked out the words in Morse code with expert acuity. When they had finished Doc continued to spin for power while they waited for an acknowledgement. When it came moments later, Doc released the handles and let them slow to a stop. He and Deagan sat under the black velvet sky as he repacked the equipment in the backpack.

"Man, this is high," Deagan commendted. "I'll bet you could see almost to Mexico City in the daytime, huh?"

"Probably not too likely," Doc said.

"Hey, Doc, why do you think they built something like this way out in the middle of nowhere?"

"Most likely as a tribute to some Mayan king. A tomb to house a deity."

"Tomb? You mean there's somebody buried inside this thing?"

Doc nodded, and he heard Deagan's laughter in the darkness.

"Hey, Doc, I just thought of something. Who'd a thought that you and me would be up on top of the world's tallest tombstone in Mexico, sending a message that my girl Polly's gonna read in New York later today?" He laughed again. "It's too bad we'll never be able to thank him for the use of his oversized abode."

Doc allowed himself a rare smile before they began their descent.

As they reached the bottom Doc saw Ace emerge from the brush with the captive Indian in tow.

"Hey, Doc," Deagan asked. "What we gonna do with that guy?"

Doc considered this for a moment, then said, "Ace and I will watch him. He has a wound that needs attention. Thomas, I need you to go guard Audrey's tent, but don't wake her just yet."

New York City, Several hours later

Penny watched as Polly St. Clair, Doc's chief secretary, finished the last of her soup and wiped her lips with the napkin.

"Thanks for taking me to lunch, Penny," Polly said. "I was really famished, and it's been a while since we got to catch up on our girl talk."

"Don't mention it," Penny lit a cigarette and blew a stream of smoke away from the table. "So have you heard anything from Doc?"

"Yeah. In fact, he sent one of his coded messages last night." She patted her folder.

"Really? Well, what did he say?" Penny asked.

Polly smiled. "You know he doesn't like me to talk about anything, but I guess he wouldn't mind you knowing. He's asked me to check on some Egyptian professor. I've got to finish the research and send him a reply at midnight tonight."

"What? You mean he's somewhere close to a telegraph office?"

"No," Polly placed her fingers on Penny's arm. "Doc maintains a network of ham radio operators and telegraph offices all over the country. Pays them a stipend to monitor our emergency frequency in case he needs to contact me about something." She picked up her cup and drained the last of her coffee. "Say, that reminds me. I have to send out some checks before the end of the month."

Penny looked at Polly before speaking. "Did Doc say anything about meeting an Audrey Guffrey down there?"

"Audrey? You know about her?" Polly's eyes widened.

"What is it I'm supposed to know?"

"Just that her and Doc were," she paused and shrugged. "Childhood friends, I guess."

Or childhood sweethearts, Penny thought.

Polly stood. "I gotta go powder my nose. You want to come along?"

"Nah," Penny picked up her own coffee cup. "Let me finish this first." She took another drag on her cigarette as Polly grabbed her purse and moved away from the table. As soon as she had disappeared, Penny quickly stubbed out her cigarette and flipped open the folder. She paged through several sheets until she found it.

POLLY, NEED YOU TO CHECK ON THE CREDENTIALS AND WHEREABOUTS OF A DR MOHAMMED RABBAT, PROFESSOR OF EGYPTOLOGY FROM THE UNIVERSITY OF CAIRO. WILL MONITOR FREQUENCY FOR A REPLY AT MIDNIGHT TONIGHT. PLEASE EXPEDITE. THOMAS SENDS HIS REGARDS. DOC

Thomas sends his regards, Penny thought. *Isn't that sweet. Wonder why he didn't even tell her to say hello to me?* She flipped the folder shut with a slam just as Polly came out of the ladies' room.

Penny stood and took two bits out of her purse, plunking it on the table for the waitress. Polly looked at her as she reached the table.

"Guess lunchtime's over, huh?" she asked.

"Yeah," Penny grabbed the check. "I got an appointment with my editor."

Lou Stoner sat behind his desk with his hands clasped on the crown of his head. The huge cigar in his mouth glowed as he alternated prodigious puffs with equally prodigious draws. He cocked his head and glanced at Penny who was standing in front of him.

"Look, kid," Stoner said. "I can sympathize with you wanting to go down

Mexico way to see your boyfriend, Atlas, but every time I go out on a limb for you on one of these wild goose chases, it ends up getting sawed off."

Penny placed both of her hands on his cluttered desktop and leaned forward. His eyebrows perked up at the sight of the lacy edges of her brassiere, which was suddenly visible due to the top two buttons of her blouse being undone. Penny acted as if she hadn't noticed it.

"I mean," Stoner said, "I'm all for romance, but..."

"Look, boss, romance has nothing to do with it. There's a story here, chief. I can smell it."

"Ah, I dunno," Stoner released his hands from his head and swiveled forward in his chair. He looked away and puffed on his cigar.

"This has something to do with the disappearance of this guy Dr. Guffrey," Penny continued. "And some Egyptian professor named Rabbat. I got that much."

Stoner tapped some ash into the tray, and glanced at her again. She leaned forward some more, causing the loop of her blouse to droop considerably.

"Anyway, Doc wouldn't have sent a secret message to his headquarters in the middle of the night unless something big was brewing. If you let me look into this, we can scoop every paper in town."

"I dunno," Stoner's gaze narrowed on the lacy edges and spilling cleavage before him.

Penny's gaze seemed to follow his, then she quickly straightened up, placing her palms over her breasts and opening her mouth in a look of total shock and embarrassment.

"Mr. Stoner!" she gasped, quickly fiddling with her buttons. "Why didn't you tell me my blouse was undone?"

She turned around, hoping that something akin to a crimson blush would creep up her neck.

"I ... ah, I'm sorry," Stoner sputtered. His cigar sent a spray of ashes into the air in front of him as he reached for a pad of papers inside his desk drawer and quickly signed one. "Here," he said. "There's your damn travel voucher. Go down to payroll and get the advance money you need. Then go ahead and take off to pack."

"I already am packed," Penny snared the voucher as she still fiddled with the last button. She smiled and said, "Thanks, Boss."

Worked like a charm, she thought on her way out.

✪ ✪ ✪

"Every time I go out on a limb for you it ends up getting sawed off."

The Yucatan, mid-morning

The eastern sun crept upward in the sky, casting the section of the ruins in shadow. Audrey watched as Doc carefully removed the bandage and examined the wound on the boy's throat while Deagan held the Indian's arms. They had untied his upper body earlier, but he still wore the hobble. Doc reached into his backpack and removed a tube, squeezing some cream onto his fingertips and applying it to the wound-site.

"It's a good thing he doesn't need stitches," Audrey said. "In this primitive wilderness, there'd be no one to remove them."

"This anti-bacterial ointment should prevent infection," Doc said.

"But Doc has these neat disposable stitches he uses, too," Deagan said. "They just disappear on their own. Used 'em on me a couple times."

"That's hardly a ringing endorsement," Ace grinned.

Deagan frowned. "Actually, Doc has all kinds of inventions. A camera that develops the picture by itself, a small radio receiver we can wear on our belts, special goggles so you can see in total darkness… All kinds of stuff. Ace gets patents on all of them for him."

"If Doc wasn't already rich," Assante said, "he would be."

Audrey smiled and looked up at Doc.

"Have you retained your nurse's training?" Doc asked.

"As many times as I've been in the field?" she replied. "You bet."

"Then could you apply the bandage, please? I want to repack my kit." He stooped and began replacing his equipment.

Audrey moved forward and cut a swath of gauze.

"I didn't know you was a nurse, Audrey," Deagan said.

"Actually, at one time I was planning to go on to medical school," she affixed the gauze with tape to the boy's neck.

"Why didn't you?" Deagan asked.

She smiled winsomely. "Too many trips around the world with my father, I suppose." Her gaze shifted to the ground. "If only I knew what happened to him. Where he was…"

"You think this guy knows something?" Deagan applied a bit of pressure to the Indian's arms.

The boy grimaced.

"Thomas," Doc snapped. "You can release him now."

Deagan looked surprised, but complied. The boy jumped away and stared at them with a wary expression, his dark eyes finally centering on Doc.

"Do you speak any of the Mayan dialects?" Doc asked Audrey.

"Only a few words. My father taught me some. But Carlos does. Should I find him?"

Doc shook his head. "I don't completely trust Carlos." He removed his knife from its sheath, and knelt, cutting the rope restricting the Indian's feet. The dark eyes flashed in amazement, but instead of fleeing, he merely nodded and began working the knots around his ankles loose.

"Do you know the word for 'father'?"

Audrey shook her head "I'm not sure I could pronounce it even if I did."

"Perhaps you have a picture of your father then?" Doc suggested.

Audrey reached inside her heavy khaki blouse and removed a small locket that was suspended around her neck by a delicate gold chain. She popped open the clasp and held it up displaying facial photos of a man and a woman. "My parents," she said.

Doc took the chain from her neck and held the locket toward the Indian boy.

"We are looking for this man," he pointed to the picture of Professor Guffrey. "Have you seen him?"

The Indian looked at the picture, but gave no indication that he understood. Doc pointed again, then gestured at the surrounding jungle questioningly.

The Indian appeared contemplative for a moment, then stood up, dropping the unknotted ropes. He looked again at Doc, who made a gesture indicating the boy was free to leave.

"We letting him go, Doc?" Deagan questioned.

Doc nodded.

The boy started to run, then stopped, looking to see if they were pursuing him. When he saw they weren't, he stopped and looked at them again. Finally, he pointed to his neck, and gestured for them to follow. They followed him to the base of the pyramid entrance.

"We going inside, Doc?" Deagan asked.

Doc halted and looked around. There was no sign of Carlos, Rabbat, or any of the other men.

"We may have prying eyes. You and Ace stay here by the entrance." He took a thin, but extremely powerful flashlight out of his utility belt. The Indian boy went inside and Doc and Audrey followed. The boy led them down the same pathway to the room with the high ceiling. He began gesticulating and speaking Mayan. Doc swept the beam of his flashlight over the walls, but could make little sense of the boy's words. He shook his head.

"If only we knew what he was trying to tell us," Audrey said.

Doc moved forward and pointed to the Sphinx-like figure.

The Indian stared at it intently, then his lips curled back in and he said something. He motioned for them to follow, and left the decorated room. Instead of heading in the same direction they'd come, he turned and proceeded down a passageway that went deeper into the pyramid.

"When did your father become associated with Professor Rabbat?" Doc asked.

"He contacted us about three months ago in New York. He was familiar with my father's series of articles, and mentioned the discovery down here that seemed to tie them together. We came almost immediately."

The boy paused in front of them and spoke quickly. He pointed toward the wall, and then past them in the direction they'd just come. Doc and Audrey looked behind them as a grinding rumble enveloped them. Doc brought his flashlight up in time to let the beam sweep up over a slab of stone that was moving out in perpendicular fashion from the wall, blocking the passage.

"Oh, my God, Michael," Audrey said. "What's happening?"

"Obviously this section of stone was fitted into the wall to provide some sort of closure," Doc said. He shone his flashlight toward the Indian, who was pressing on a flat portion of rock near the base of the wall. The boy rose and gestured to them again. The area before them had opened up displaying a previously secret darkened hallway.

"Have you ever gone down this one before?" Doc followed the Indian through the opening.

"No," said Audrey. "We didn't even know it existed."

The passageway was very narrow, and full of cobwebs and dust. The walls felt cool and gritty to their touch, and the air seemed to have taken on a heavier consistency. Doc had to turn sideways several times because it wouldn't accommodate the width of his shoulders. The ceiling sloped downward as well, causing them to go on all fours.

"Michael, I'm not sure we should be doing this," Audrey cautioned. "What if he's leading us into a trap?" The strain in her voice was evident.

Doc considered this for a moment, but he did not slow down. He had switched off his light to save the battery just in case they did find themselves lost, but he felt comfortable that he could negotiate the return should it become necessary.

"Let's keep going," he said.

The passage narrowed further and angled downward, forcing them to crawl. The Indian was squirming ahead of them, and Doc suddenly wondered if perhaps the space would become too small for his massive physique.

"Audrey, are you all right?" he asked over his shoulder.

"Yes," she coughed slightly. "But this is terrible."

Doc had completely lost sight of the Indian boy. He thought about pausing to try and pull out his flashlight again, but realized the light would destroy whatever visual purple his eyes had developed up to this point. Plus, stopping might alarm Audrey.

He pressed on, using his elbows to propel him. The area ahead was totally black now, yet a sudden coolness teased his face. The tunnel ended and a new passageway abruptly opened up, allowing him to stand. He heard Audrey's labored breathing, removed his flashlight again, and shone it down at the hole, stooping to help her through the opening and to her feet.

"Oh, thank heavens we're out of there," she brushed some of her long auburn tresses away from her face. "I must look a sight."

"We both do," Doc smiled as he looked at her dirt streaked face and clothes.

Blinking to adjust his eyes, Doc saw the Indian boy standing a few yards away. The cavern was immense. Enormous tapering stalactites hung suspended above them, met with corresponding mirror images extending upward from the floor, and the air was musty smelling.

"Is this another part of the pyramid?" Audrey wondered. "I've never been in here before."

"We're below ground here," Doc surmised. "It must be some underground cave, probably caused by a subterranean river."

They began following the Indian boy again down another huge corridor that made several sinuous twists and turns. The sandy bottom seemed to bear out that the path had been forged by rushing water, and was now a dry basin. But several times they passed through shallow pools of standing water. Finally the Indian stopped, said something in Mayan, and pointed. Doc looked at the stone wall in front of them. It felt solidly in place, and he doubted that any system of fulcrum and balances, no matter how sophisticated, could move it. The breeze licked at their faces again, and the boy smiled. Doc looked upward and saw the cuts in the limestone that formed a primitive ladder.

The Indian boy scurried up first, followed by Audrey, who was boosted up by Doc. He then brought up the rear. The wall canted slightly allowing them to climb upward without much effort. A perpendicular juncture was at the top, and they had to crawl once more, but this time a small square of light was visible at the far end, holding the promise of sunlight and an exit to the outside.

✪ ✪ ✪

Assante was looking at his watch again when Deagan tapped him on the shoulder and said, "We got company."

Ace looked up and saw Dr. Rabbat, Carlos, and several of their men heading toward the pyramid entrance. They were a rough-looking bunch and a couple of them carried rifles.

"Good morning, gentlemen," Rabbat greeted. "We wanted to speak with Dr. Atlas."

"Him and Audrey went into this stack of stones," Deagan gestured with his thumb. "They ain't come out yet."

"Ah, yes," Rabbat said. "Do you perhaps know the whereabouts of the suspected killer?"

"Killer?" Ace queried. "And who might that be?"

"That Indian youth," Rabbat clarified.

"He's in there with Doc," Deagan said.

"Then there is great danger." Rabbat placed a hand on his forehead. "Carlos is convinced that he was not only here last night to do us harm, but that he was also behind the attacks against you on the road."

Deagan and Assante exchanged glances.

"It had to be los indios," Carlos said. "No one else could have taken the dead *bandidos*."

"I thought you said it was jungle cats?" Ace reminded the guide.

Carlos shrugged. "I thought it might be at first. But mis hermanos just got back from there. They found no tracks *de los gatos grandes*."

"Don't you see," Rabbat argued. "The Indians regard this place as sacred ground, much as my own people once regarded the great pyramids as sacrosanct. It makes perfect sense that they would want to strike back at Professor Guffrey for violating their sanctity." He steepled his fingers. "Please, we must try to find Dr. Atlas and Audrey before some harm befalls them."

Deagan puckered his lower lip.

"I don't guess it'd do any harm for us to mosey on in there," he relented. "How about it, Ace?"

Assante shook his head. "I have an aversion to dark places," he took out his cigarette case. "I'll wait here if you don't mind."

"As you wish," Rabbat handed Deagan one of the portable lamps and they went inside the structure. Ace offered a cigarette to Carlos who grunted *gracias*, and accepted Ace's lighter. Assante knew Deagan was more than capable of handling Rabbat, should the occasion arise, and the solidness of the pistol stuck in his belt gave him a sense of reassurance as well. The feeling vanished, however, when Deagan hurried out several minutes later with a worried look on his face.

"Ace," Mad Dog said, "Doc ain't anywhere to be found in there."

Beams of sunlight streamed into the front of the cave through the hanging tendrils of roots from a denuded tree. The Indian boy pushed them aside and scrambled down the slanting embankment with a practiced ease. Doc studied the terrain as he helped Audrey negotiate the earthen slope down to the basin floor. They appeared to be in some sort of large sinkhole that was perhaps fifty feet across and thirty feet deep. Pools of standing water were at various places in the large depression.

"What is this place, Michael?" Audrey asked.

"The ground beneath us was eroded away by the underground river long ago," Doc said. "This portion collapsed down to the limestone base, unlike the cave from which we just emerged."

"Ohhhh, that water looks so clear. What I wouldn't give to be able to take a quick bath, or even just wash my face." She smiled self-effacingly. "I must look a fright."

Doc smiled. "No amount of surface dirt could mar your natural beauty."

The Indian boy was perhaps twenty yards ahead of them now. He turned and waited, pointing at the opposite embankment. Two other Indians, dressed in more traditional native wear, stood there holding long spears. Several more came up to the edge and stood looking down at them. Doc felt Audrey's hand grip his.

"Don't be afraid, Aubrey. I have a weapon, but I don't believe they intend to harm us."

As they walked farther the top line of the embankment began to fill with more figures, men, women, and children, all pointing and talking in their strange clicking tongue. Audrey's other hand touched Doc's arm, but she said nothing. The Indian boy had reached the other side of the hole and began climbing the lattice-like network of exposed tree roots. As he neared the top, some of the natives reached down to help him over the cusp. He spoke to them, gesturing back at Audrey and Doc, then motioned for them to join him.

Doc boosted Audrey up on the tangled skein of roots and followed closely behind her. Outstretched hands helped her as she climbed to the top, and Doc quickened his pace and swung his legs over the embankment at the same time as Audrey. It was clear to all that he needed no assistance.

The forest, although still densely vegetated, opened into a small clearing. Several sets of primitive-looking huts with straw roofs were visible, as was a smoldering campfire. The crowd began opening as the Indian boy moved toward the camp with Doc and Audrey following. More natives, mostly women in brightly colored skirts carrying infants, were standing by the huts, their dark eyes staring intently at the new visitors. A bare-chested man with high cheekbones and a regal look emerged from a hut and looked startled at the intrusion until he saw the boy. He hurried forth and smiled, stopping to hug the youth with both of his arms.

They spoke in the harsh sounding language again, with the boy gesturing and pointing to his throat. The other man stared at Doc and continued to listen. Doc surveyed the surroundings, taking in everything from the dimensions of the settlement to the approximate number of people present. Suddenly he saw a pale figure with gold spectacles rise from a log in front of a far hut. He touched Audrey's arm gently and pointed. She looked and gasped, the tears already starting to stream down her dust covered cheeks.

"Oh, my God," she gasped. "It's Father!"

Doc watched as she ran forward, meeting Professor Arthur Guffrey in the center of the camp. They embraced and Doc saw that the old man was crying as well.

A fortuitous reunion, he thought.

He walked up to them and placed his hand on the professor's shoulder.

"We're glad that you're all right, Dr. Guffrey."

The old man looked up at him and smiled.

"Michael. Thank God you're here. I kept praying that somehow you'd come. When the Mayans told me of a tall man with Herculean proportions at the pyramid, I knew that Audrey must have contacted you."

"Father, we've been so worried. Where have you been these past few days? What happened?"

Professor Guffrey patted his daughter's arm and gestured toward the boy. "Balam approached me that day inside the pyramid, when I was alone, and brought me here. This man is Balam's father, the chieftain, Ahaw Sahal. But there's no time to explain that now." They were joined by the boy and the older man, who said something to the professor. Guffrey turned to Doc. "Michael, come with me. There's a great need for your abilities and very little time."

Doc's brow furrowed slightly, but he let the old man lead him to the entranceway of the closest hut. Doc peered inside. In the cool darkness a small boy of perhaps five or six lay shivering on a straw mat, seeming to float in and out of consciousness. Beside him were a woman and an old man, his hair hanging in long gray braids down in front of his shoulders.

"That's Saknik, the spiritual leader of the tribe," Professor Guffrey said. "A shaman, or holy man. His grandson is very ill. I've tried my best to comfort him, but I'm afraid he needs someone with more medical expertise than I have."

Doc went in and knelt beside the boy, placing the back of his hand on the child's forehead. He probed various parts of the boy's body with his fingers, centering on the right side, which when touched elicited a moaning cry. Standing, Doc went back to the doorway.

"Are you fluent in their language?" he asked.

"Hardly," Professor Guffrey answered. "I mean, I can communicate in the basic sense, and a few of them speak some Spanish." He smiled weakly. "I have learned quite a bit during the last few days, but it's been anything but fluent."

"The boy has acute appendicitis," Doc diagnosed. "He needs immediate surgery. There's a significant chance his vermiform appendix will rupture, in which case the resulting peritonitis will surely be fatal."

"Oh no," Audrey said. "But you can't possibly do anything here. It's so primitive."

"If only I had my medical kit," Doc glanced back inside the hut. "He won't survive unless we act now."

"They were telling me of a legend," Professor Guffrey said. "It came from a vision of the holy man. It said a tall stranger from the north, adorned with gold, shall arrive and perform a miracle." His fingers touched his gold-rimmed spectacles. "I think they saw my glasses and assumed it was me. That's why they abducted me that day in the pyramid."

Doc's amber colored eyes were already surveying the camp. He went over and grabbed some metallic pots that had been stacked alongside one of the huts. "Have someone fill these with water," he directed. "I'll need more. Start heating them immediately." With that said, Doc went to the edge of the camp and squatted down to examine some vegetation. After a few minutes of searching, he uprooted several plants and brought back an assortment of digitate leaves to the hut. "If they will grind these into paste, and mix it with water, it should serve as an anesthesia." He went to one of the women and eyed the hem of her long dress.

"Professor, can you ask them about the needles they use to sew their dresses?

Guffrey came over and spoke a few words, gesturing emphatically. At first the woman's face showed no sign of comprehension, but then she smiled and nodded. She went to a hut across the encampment and returned moments later with several needles and some dark thread. The professor took it and hurriedly showed it to Doc.

"Will this do?"

"It may suffice for the exterior stitches," Doc took the needles and examined them. He went to the fire and held each into the flames briefly, then bent them into circular curves by using the wooden spools of thread. He looked around. "We'll need something less coarse for the internal stitches. Something fine."

"What about my hair?" Audrey offered.

Doc shook his head. "Human hair is too brittle."

"They have some long horse hair wound around one of their spools," the professor said. "I saw it earlier."

"Get it at once. We'll have to boil the hair to sterilize it," Doc looked at Audrey. "Do you feel able to assist me?"

"Michael, you can't be serious," she drew her hands to her mouth. "This is insane. To attempt surgery under such conditions... How can you possibly succeed?"

Doc placed both of his hands on her shoulders and looked into her eyes.

"There's a slim possibility we can make a small incision and remove the infected appendage and stitch up the organ," he explained. "The surgical site will have to be closed in at least two layers, deep inside and then closer to the skin. I'll need your to help stanch the flow of blood among other things. Do you remember your surgical training?"

"It's been so long, since college."

"But Audrey," her father said, "you used to be very good at fixing injuries during our expeditions."

"But this is so different. I don't know, Michael. I just don't know."

"Come, let's wash ourselves and prepare," Doc removed his knife from its sheath and handed it to the professor. "Please see that this, as well as the needles and hair, are sterilized."

Audrey stood immobile, her gaze fixed on the boy in the hut. Doc reached out and took her hand gently in his. Her eyes turned toward him and he pulled her close.

"We're that boy's only chance. We must make the attempt. And I believe in you."

Deagan tossed down Doc's backpack and placed his hands on his hips. "Dammit, Ace! If we only knew where Doc went to."

Assante brought his cigarette to his lips and nodded. He'd been watching the activity by Professor Rabbat's tent. Carlos and several of his men were loading their rifles and talking among themselves.

"What they been saying?" Deagan followed Ace's gaze.

"They're forming a search party to go look for Doc and Audrey."

"Well, we can't afford not to go along, can we?"

"They're talking about raiding the Indian village."

"So the question is, do we lick 'em or join 'em, huh?" Deagan did a quick head count. "Too many of 'em to try and lick here. What we got between us, ten rounds of ammunition?"

"Eight." Assante grinned. "This weapon had four rounds expended, remember?"

"Well, I don't think Doc would approve of us tagging along with 'em while they massacre indigenous personnel. Even if we were trying to rescue him.

"Plus, it'll be getting dark soon, and I don't know about you, but traipsing around in the jungle at night with those guys doesn't seem too prudent."

Deagan scratched his jaw and nodded to Carlos as he looked up. The big Mexican nodded back, then said something in Spanish to his associates.

"We may not have to after all," Ace said. "It sounds like they're not sure exactly where the village is at. Maybe we can forestall any searching tonight by telling them we'll help them in the morning."

"You got something there, Ace. Besides, I'm thinking if Doc was in real trouble, he'd have activated his emergency beacon." He picked up the backpack again and removed a black directional finder about the size of a camera. It had a compass attached. "But just the same, you and me better take turns sleeping tonight."

"And keep an extra eye on our friends there, too," Ace blew out a cloud of smoke and began stripping the butt of his cigarette.

Somewhere just outside of Mexico City

Penny watched the sun disappearing beyond the distant trees of the horizon as the train rumbled forward at what seemed like an interminably slow pace. The car was full of people, all chatting in Spanish and pleasantly ignoring her. Her suitcase sat between her knees, and she felt the slow trickle of a drop of sweat roll down the back of her neck as more hot air blew in through the open windows.

If this damn train would pick up some speed, she thought, maybe it would cool us off. I'm going to need a bath and a clean dress before I go looking for Doc, too.

The train seemed to slow somehow, and more unpleasant smells from a passing farm wafted in mixing with the pervasive scent of human body odor that seemed to be hanging inside the packed train car.

Penny licked her lips and thought she'd give anything for a drink of cold New York water. A man sitting across the aisle unscrewed the cap of a hip flask and took a slow pull. Upon seeing her watching him, he smiled, showing a gap of several missing teeth, and held the flask out toward her.

Penny shook her head and turned away.

Oh swell, she thought. A Mexican masher and I can't even tell him to go jump in the lake because he wouldn't understand me.

The train jerked abruptly a few times, then slowed to a stop, its wheels making a screeching sound against the metallic rails. The conductor came to the end of the car and called something out in Spanish. Some people across from her got up, and Penny did also, figuring she'd at least move to another car, away from the masher. As she neared the door, lugging her suitcase in front of her and bumping into people standing and sitting in the aisle, she looked back to see a mix of people scrambling into her seat. More people got on and began showing their tickets to the conductor, who chatted with them rapidly.

"Excuse me," Penny said, trying to look over the man's shoulder into the next car for an open seat. She saw none. "How far is it to Santa Merida?"

The conductor repeated Santa Merida and several people standing in the area between the two doors laughed. He was a rather short, heavyset man, with a drooping black mustache.

"*Lo siento, senōritia,*" he said. "But that is a very long, long way to go yet."

"That man back there was bothering me," Penny cocked her head in the direction of the car.

The conductor nodded, and held up his hand. "I will try to find you a seat in another car after the next stop. Pero, it will take most of the night before we reach *el estacion del cambio.*"

"Is that where Santa Merida is?"

"No, *senōrita,*" the conductor smiled again. "That is where you must change trains."

Doc and Audrey emerged from the hut as darkness had begun to descend upon the village. Professor Guffrey followed them and gave his daughter a hug. Then he turned to Doc. His hands and arms were covered with bloodstains, and his face was dappled with speckles of crimson.

"Michael, that was the most amazing piece of surgery I've ever seen," Guffrey said. "I would have never believed it possible."

Doc smiled. "Your assistance was invaluable, Professor, but I must commend Audrey. Without her I would never have been able to do it."

The old shaman, Saknik, came over and placed his hand on Doc's arm in an obvious gesture of gratitude. The old man smiled, showing the gaps in his teeth, and then faded away into the darkness.

"He is pretty amazing, isn't he, Father?" Audrey kept staring at Doc. She was almost as bloodstained as he.

"How on earth did you learn such unorthodox techniques?" the Professor asked.

"Because of my medical knowledge, and my other skills," Doc said. "I was placed with a special insertion team in the military. Our experience in the Philippines was under the worst conditions. Fortunately, I learned a lot about battlefield surgery techniques with minimal equipment."

Professor Guffrey placed his hand on Doc's shoulder and shook his head. "You're an extraordinary man."

"We'd better wash up," Doc moved toward the pots hanging over the campfire.

"What I really need is a bath," Audrey said. "But I guess that's out of the question here."

"Not necessarily," Professor Guffrey said. "There are several pools in the basin that the natives use for bathing purposes. They're spring-fed and actually quite nice, but the largest one is about twelve feet deep."

"Oh, then I can go for a swim?"

"That would not be advisable," Doc warned. "Remember that Carlos spoke of large feral cats in the area."

"They howl at night sometimes," Professor Guffrey agreed. "But mostly they go after these large rat-like animals called *esquintla*. Besides, once my daughter has her mind made up about something..." He smiled as he let the sentence trail off. "She reminds me so much of her mother."

"Fiddlesticks," Audrey retorted. "I'll be fine. And if you're so worried, Michael, perhaps you could come along to guard me. You have a pistol there, don't you?"

Doc said nothing for a moment, then began heading through the camp. "Very well," he said over his shoulder. "I'll grab us a torch to light the way."

After planting the burning torch securely in the earth at the edge of the edge of the sinkhole, Doc helped Audrey descend the tangle of dried roots.

"It's almost like a ladder," she joked as they climbed down. Once on solid ground, Doc removed his small flashlight and shone it around. The batteries were almost used up since they had continuously focused it on the surgical area once the natural light had begun to fade. He pointed to the largest of the three pools.

"That must be the deep one your father spoke about."

"Let's go then," Audrey snatched his flashlight and began to run. He caught up to her almost immediately, but purposely stayed a few steps behind. At the edge of the water she stopped abruptly and they almost collided.

"Here's your flashlight, Michael. Now I'll thank you to turn around."

Doc's brow furrowed.

"Unless you're going to watch me get undressed, that is?"

Doc immediately turned around and replaced his flashlight in its holder.

"Mmmm, the water's delicious," Audrey said.

Doc began to turn. "Don't drink any," he said, then heard her soft laugh.

"After all the countless expeditions to some of the most primitive countries on earth, do you really think I'd take the chance on catching typhoid fever drinking some unpurified water?"

"There's a danger of hepatitis, too," he suddenly felt a splash of cold water sprinkle over his back.

"Okay, I'm in," Audrey said. "You can turn around now. Or better yet, why don't you join me?"

Doc considered this for a moment, then began unbuttoning his shirt. He removed his boots and socks next, followed by his utility belt. After emptying all his pants pockets, he stood and walked to the edge of the pool, stepping over the tangled heap of her clothes.

"You can undress all the way, Michael. I promise not to look."

Doc smiled. The pale light of the full moon shone down through the void in the trees, lighting the outline of her body in the clear water.

"These pants will dry quickly," he waded waist-deep into the water. He immediately began to scrub at his hands and face. Audrey kicked her way into the center of the pool, using an even breaststroke. Doc admonished her not to go too far.

"Swim to me, Michael."

Doc stood and watched her body gracefully cut through the water. He raised his arms and dove under the surface, propelling himself with powerful strokes, until he surfaced and swam near her. She splashed some water at him again. Doc turned over on his back and swam around her, circling her form.

"How deep do you think it is here?" she asked breathlessly.

"Deep enough that we should return to shallower water," he began swimming back toward the edge. He stopped where the water was waist-deep again, and listened to make sure he could hear her smooth kicks behind him. But he heard nothing. Doc turned, and saw only the ripples from his body breaking the smooth surface of the water.

"Audrey," he called. And then she surfaced behind him, her arms encircling his waist, her smooth body pressing against his back.

"Don't move, Michael. I just want to hold you like this for a minute."

He could feel her breasts pushing against him as the rapidity of her breathing began to lessen.

"That was so wonderful, what you did, saving that boy's life. And to think I was actually part of it."

"You did well," Doc was suddenly thankful that he was waist-deep in cold water. "But the danger's far from over for him. He still has to make it through the night."

He felt her arms squeeze him tighter.

"So do we, Michael. So do we."

Deagan snapped awake at the first sound of the buzzing. The first thing he did was to immediately raise his pistol and survey the area. But only the bright glints of sunlight cresting over the eastern top of the pyramid and the ubiquitous chirping of the insects greeted him. He glanced over at Assante who was still sound asleep, and then toward the tents that housed Carlos and Rabbat. The flaps of their tents were closed, but several of their men lounged around in haphazard fashion, snoring, probably from the vast quantities of tequila they had consumed after the agreement to postpone any search for Doc and Audrey.

The proposed search party had been put off until morning principally because Ace and Deagan had explained that Doc possessed a special miniature beacon that, once activated, would lead them to his position. "Alls he has to do is trigger the switch," Deagan had told them, holding up Doc's backpack, "and this will show us which direction to go in."

And now the alarm on the directional finder was buzzing.

Deagan quickly turned off the audible part of the alarm and gently shook Ace awake, holding his finger to his lips to indicate silence. Assante blinked twice, then sat up, staring intently at the backpack. Deagan nodded and they both began a quiet extrication from the tent.

"Which way?" Ace whispered.

Deagan looked at the compass and pointed. They headed through the lower ruins and into the forest. Assante glanced behind them, but it appeared as if Carlos and his bunch had not stirred. He held a thumbs-up to Deagan, who grinned.

"So far, so good," he said in a low voice.

Doc checked the boy's pulse and respiration rate. The color had come back to his face and torso, and he appeared to be sleeping comfortably. Audrey stood by his side watching, her hands roaming up his arm. The old Indian holy man stood on Doc's other flank, his dark eyes peering down at the boy. The old man said something in Mayan and patted Doc's shoulder.

"Do you think you'll be able to remove these stitches after ten to twelve days?" Doc asked.

"I'm certain I can," Audrey said. "You've already done all the hard work."

Doc nodded. "You'll also need to apply some special topical ointment to prevent any inflection to the subcutaneous tissue."

He glanced over toward the tents that housed Carlos and Rabbat.

"Special ointment?"

"My associates should be here shortly. They'll be bringing my backpack with my medical supplies."

"But how will they know where to find us?"

"My dear," Professor Guffrey interjected. "Haven't you realized by now that Michael here has the situation well in hand?" He reached out and slapped Doc on the back. "Your father must have been very proud of you, son."

Doc made one last examination of his patient, and straightened up.

"When Thomas and Ace get here, I believe I also have some herbal tea in my pack. Perhaps we can begin to boil some water."

"That will be a welcome treat," Professor Guffrey said. He walked toward the campfire and said something to one of the women. She jumped up and grabbed an old, blackened metallic pot and began filling it with water from a nearby barrel-like container.

"Professor," Doc asked, "I need to ask you about your findings here in Mexico."

The professor's mouth stretched downward at the corners.

"What is it you need to know, Michael? How much of a fool I've been?"

"Father!" Audrey gasped.

Guffrey sighed heavily, and licked his lips. His gaze was fixed on the ground.

"When did you realize that the carving of the Sphinx enclosed in the star and crescent was a fake?" Doc asked.

"It was obvious from the beginning," Guffrey confessed. "Or at least it should have been." He sighed again. "I was simply too stubborn to admit to myself what I should have known all along. The day Balam took me from the pyramid..." He looked up at Audrey, "when you called out to me, that's when I finally realized it. I'd just reached up and touched it..."

"And that's when you discovered the graphite on your fingertips?" Doc filled-in.

Guffrey nodded.

"Someone had smeared the carving with it to give the illusion that it had been there as long as the other hieroglyphics," Guffrey went on. "I suppose I hadn't noticed it before because I was so eager to believe that I'd finally found the proof I'd been searching for. That and I believed the assurances of Professor Rabbat."

"You mean he lied to us?" Audrey asked. "But why?"

"I suspect it had something to do with obtaining your father's funding and reputation to get this expedition started," Doc deduced. "Had you met him before? In Egypt perhaps?"

"No. We'd corresponded," Guffrey said. "I was actually very flattered that a man of his rather distinguished reputation would agree to join me in this venture."

"I'm afraid all is not as it seems with him, too," Doc said. "I have reason to suspect that he is not actually the real Professor Rabbat."

Guffrey's jaw seemed to visibly drop.

"I became suspicious when after our initial meeting in town," Doc elaborated. "He mentioned that he'd met you before in the Middle East on an expedition. Then he insisted that we follow him at a distance to the camp, ostensibly to avoid the dust of the road. The bandits who subsequently attacked us had been lying in wait, and I have no doubt the passing of Rabbat's jeep was some sort of pre-arranged signal. Otherwise, they would not have known we'd be passing along that road at that particular time. He also changed his story after we arrived in camp, denying that you'd ever met. Then I caught him and Carlos torturing that boy as to the whereabouts of some idols."

"Yes," Guffrey said. "The Mayans do have a treasured shrine. They've kept it within a series of caves near here for thousands of years. It's been passed from generation to generation. It's a closely guarded secret. A legend of sorts, but I've been privileged enough to see it."

"You have?" Audrey asked. "What does it look like?"

"It's beautiful, my dear. Two magnificent jade totems with jeweled eyes on a base of gold. Well, not exactly—"

His description was cut short by an explosion of ascending birds from the tree-line surrounding the village, followed by Deagan's loud, whooping yell from across the campground. He and Assante had emerged from the forested area near the far side of the large sinkhole and had begun to traverse the rough shrubbery. Doc waved over to them and smiled.

"I believe the infantry has arrived," he chuckled.

The villagers came forward, some carrying spears, bows and arrows. A few had ancient looking rifles. Doc rushed forward and greeted Deagan and Ace more profusely than was his custom.

"Jeeze, what a reception committee," Deagan esclaimed, looking at the array of heavily armed Indians.

"I would have thought you'd be used to dodging the slings and arrows of outrageous fortune by now," Ace said. The tension in his voice was obvious.

Audrey and Professor Guffrey approached Doc, and Audrey smiled at Deagan.

"I hope you gentlemen brought Michael's medical kit," she said.

Deagan held up the backpack and then grinned.

"Hi, Audrey. Don't tell me this is your dad?"

"It most certainly is," she said. "Father, may I introduce you to two of the finest gentlemen I've ever met."

"At least one of the finest," Ace corrected, reaching across Deagan's chest to shake hands with the professor.

The Chief, Ahaw Sahal and Balam came forward and Doc asked Professor Guffrey to complete the introductions. Doc took the backpack from Deagan and headed back to the hut, motioning for Saknik, the shaman, to accompany him.

"So old Peter Lorre's a phony, huh?" Deagan said as they sat around the campfire drinking the tea Audrey had prepared. "I never did trust that guy. Too creepy looking."

"What's our next move, Doc?" Ace asked. "I'm certain they didn't follow us here."

"He's certain," Deagan cocked his thumb toward Assante. "Only because I kept insistin' that we circle back and wait, then erase our trail."

"If you'd been alone," Ace chided, "it probably would have been easier for you to swing from tree to tree."

Before Deagan could reply, Doc spoke.

"Professor Guffrey, we need to warn these people of the imminent danger. I'm certain now that their primary intention all along was to gain possession of those idols you spoke of."

The professor considered this for a moment and nodded.

"They probably are worth a lot of money to some," he said. "But the Mayans have been dealing with people who have tried to steal from them for centuries." He raised his eyebrows a bit. "On the other hand, many of the Mayan treasures have been pilfered through the years…"

"And from what I saw when Rabbat and Carlos had Balam," Doc recalled, "they will spare no mercy to obtain what they're after."

The professor rose and set his drinking mug by his feet.

"They've managed to keep the idols safe by moving them to various locations periodically," he said. "The shrine is never left unguarded. Come on, I'll show you where it's at now."

He went to Ahaw Sahal and Balam and spoke haltingly, using extensive gestures. The chief nodded and gestured for Doc and the others to follow. They moved to the edge of the sinkhole and began climbing down, one by one. Doc descended quickly, then waited to assist Audrey and then Ace, although he took pains to not make it obvious. Deagan was able to climb down with little trouble, showing an incredible nimbleness. Professor Guffrey and the shaman were the last to descend.

Balam led them across the basin floor, past the large pools of water, and into the mouth of a small cave. He waited and let the shaman and his father enter first. Professor Guffrey held out his hand. "We're probably the first outsiders to have been granted this privilege in quite a while."

As they walked into the cave the air temperature seemed to cool noticeably and the musty smell increased. About one hundred yards ahead light flickered from a pair of burning torches. A man stood near the torches armed with a large club. He did a ritualistic salute when Ahaw Sahal and Saknik approached and then stepped aside. Behind him they could see it in the center of a small enclave perhaps fifteen feet square.

The idols were perhaps two feet tall, their cool, mint green color almost coquettish in its translucence. The two figures were mirror images of each other, except the face of the one of the left was frowning, while its counterpart had what could only be described as a smile of mirth. Both statues held a smaller figure against their torsos, the faces of which corresponded respectively to the expressions of the larger physiognomies. Their greenish glow shimmered in the torchlight, as did the brilliant yellow base upon which they were mounted. The base had a lustrous shimmer, and seemed to be formed from solid cubes of gold.

"Oh, it's so beautiful," Audrey said.

"From what I can gather," Professor Guffrey said, "they're supposed to represent the duality of man. Good and evil. The similarity to the various incarnations of Buddha in the Eastern depictions is startling."

"Much like the collective unconscious that has been discussed in the works of Carl Gustav Jung," Doc added.

"Collective what?" Deagan queried.

"Unconscious," Ace said. "Like we all wish you were most of the time."

"It's a theory based on the similar themes that run through disparate cultures," Audrey said.

"We must take proper precautions," Doc started to say.

But a sudden staccato crack of gunfire echoed through the cave, accompanied by distant screaming.

"What the hell? That sounded like a Thompson," Deagan wrinkled his brow as he glanced at the others.

Doc, Assante, and Deagan rushed forward, their guns drawn, only to see Carlos, Rabbat and several others standing near the mouth of the cave holding a group of Mayan women and children at gunpoint.

"Hola," Carlos said, his teeth a flash of white under his dark mustache. "It was nice of you to finally lead us to the right cave, gringos." His smile twisted into a scowl and he raised the military style walkie-talkie to his lips and spoke something in Spanish. Then he turned to Doc menacingly. "Listen to me. More of my compadres are outside the cave with los ninos y muheres. We haff a machine-gun, and we know how to use it." He hung the radio on the handle of his holstered forty-five automatic and grabbed a small child by the hair, pulling the screaming child close. In a silver flash the knife appeared in his hand and he pressed it against the child's throat.

"You are too far away this time to grab me, right, *hombre*?" he looked straight at Doc. "Now, throw me your weapons or I will cut this little *latoso's* neck like a chicken's."

Doc stood silently, not moving.

"Do it!" Carlos shouted.

Professor Rabbat walked down next to Carlos and held up his hand.

"My friend is a very ruthless man, Dr. Atlas," Rabbat said. "I fear that you know only too well that he is capable of carrying out what he said." He shrugged and smiled, but Doc could see that Rabbat's face was wet with sweat. "All we wish is for you to comply. We are only after the idols, and once we have them, we shall leave here peacefully. Now tell me, doctor, are they worth this child's life?"

The small boy screamed as Carlos drew the honed metal across a section of his neck, leaving a crimson smear.

"Do I finish the job or not?" his voice rasped.

"We'll comply," Doc said, "but you'll never get out of here alive."

Rabbat smiled. "We are more than willing to take that chance. Now toss your weapons over there." He pointed with his pistol to the side wall farthest away from them. "And do not forget to remove your famous utility belt also, Dr. Atlas."

Doc's nostrils flared. Not trusting Rabbat or Carlos in the least, but knowing not to obey would mean the certain death of the child; he tossed the pistol away, then removed his belt. Deagan and Ace relinquished theirs also.

"Now release the child," Doc said.

Rabbat's low chuckle reverberated in the cave.

"I'm afraid you are in no position to put forth demands," he held up his pistol and pointed it at them. "Nonetheless, I do not wish to shoot you. As I said, our only interest is in obtaining the idols. Now, move back, if you please."

Doc and the others backed up slowly, hands raised. Balam, his father, and Saknik stood at the opening to the treasure room along with the guard. Ahaw Sahal pushed Balam away and centered himself in the doorway, speaking directly to Carlos in Mayan.

Carlos sheathed his knife and, still holding the boy's hair in his left hand, grabbed his pistol with his right. His arm straightened and the corresponding explosion was deafening in the confined space. The guard's hands clutched his chest as he tumbled forward. Carlos grinned, adjusting his aim, and fired two more shots. Ahaw Sahal collapsed next to the guard as the ejected rounds popping back over Carlos's shoulder. Balam rushed forward to his fallen father, tears streaming down his face. Doc quickly moved to assist, pressing his palm against the wound site as the dark blood began seeping through his fingers.

Rabbat brushed past them as Carlos transferred his aim toward the others.

"You dirty son of a—" Deagan cursed. "Shooting an unarmed man like that."

"Maybe I shoot some more, un?" Carlos said. Then to Rabbat, "Hurry up. Traiga los."

"I can't manage it myself," Rabbat called out. There's too much here."

Carlos pointed his gun at Deagan.

"You look very strong, monkey man. You go help my friend move them out here, eh?"

Deagan's lips curled up into a growl, but he moved toward the room. Carlos whistled at Audrey. "Help him, senõritia, or I will shoot *su padre* next."

Audrey, her face awash with silent tears followed Deagan into the room.

Doc glanced after them and saw Rabbat filling his pockets with the golden cubes. His pant legs bulging grotesquely, he licked his lips and began filling his backpack with more of the lustrous metal. Deagan hoisted the two idols from their base and held them toward Rabbat.

"You carry them over to Carlos and we'll give you the child," Rabbat grabbed Audrey by the arm and pushed her out in front of him. "Do not try to interfere if you value this woman's life."

Audrey stepped cautiously over the splayed legs of the fallen Ahaw Sahal, followed by Deagan.

"Michael, can you save him?" she asked.

Before Doc could answer Carlos smashed Deagan's head with the barrel of his pistol and roughly shoved the child hostage forward. He snatched Audrey's arm, pressing the barrel of the pistol against her temple as the idols fell to the dirt floor. Rabbat stooped and picked them up, carefully brushing them off, before handing them to one of Carlos's men. Rabbat readjusted the heavily laden backpack.

"Now we haff three treasures, eh?" his free arm snaking around to draw Audrey close to his body. "Come on. Let's go." He began pulling her toward the entrance. "She will come with us so you won't shoot in the backs, eh?"

"That's more your style," Ace helped Deagan to his feet.

Rabbat rushed to follow, his legs pumping in an almost exaggerated fashion due to the extra weight.

"Carlos, wait," Rabbat called. "Wait for me. Help me carry some of this. We'll be rich men."

Carlos smirked.

"You can carry it yourself," he replied. "We haff what we came for, no?"

Doc felt Ahaw Sahal's ragged breathing cease. He glanced to Balam, who knelt beside him in stunned disbelief. Standing, Doc turned and began moving toward Rabbat, who turned and fired his pistol. The round went wild, but it caused Doc and the others to duck. Rabbat fired another round that ricocheted off the walls.

"I advise you not to advance," he warned breathlessly. Then he stooped and picked up Doc's utility belt, digging frantically into one of the pouches. "I have something for you, Dr. Atlas."

Doc's face showed alarm as he rose quickly and began pushing the others farther back into the tunnels. Rabbat fired his weapon several more times, the reports sounding more and more distant in the enclosed walls. The shooting ceased and the small sphere came bouncing off the walls, the hollow pocking sound being punctuated four seconds later by the powerful echo of the explosion. Clouds of dust billowed toward them as the sections of walls and roof collapsed. Doc continued to herd the others into the deeper recesses of the cave as the heavy rumbling continued. Unable to breathe, they fell to the ground gasping in the inky blackness, the damp soil offering them no shelter or relief.

✪✪✪

The entrance of the cave had erupted outward with a hoard of frightened bats shooting up into the sky accompanied by the effluvial billows from the preceding explosion. Several of Carlos's henchmen looked shocked and the one holding the Tommy gun paused to cross himself. Then they heard coughing, accompanied by voices and Rabbat, Carlos, and Audrey emerged covered with dust. Carlos was practically dragging her, pausing to slap her face at her non-compliance. Two of his men followed, one of whom carried the jade idols.

"You got 'em, huh, boss?" the man with the machine-gun asked.

Carlos threw Audrey down to the ground and told them to tie her hands.

"She's coming with us."

"We're wasting time taking her," Rabbat argued. "We have more than we anticipated, and she will only slow us down. Leave her here."

"Have you forgotten she can identify us?" Carlos brushed some of the dust from his shirt.

"Very well," Rabbat conceded. "Shoot her then. But let's go."

Carlos smirked at him, then looked at Audrey with a sinister hunger in his eyes.

"I've been watching la *senōrita* all these weeks," he grinned. "Now I do not intend to give her up until I tire of her. Besides, I do not think that the famous Doc Atlas will be following us now."

"And what about the rest of the natives?" Rabbat asked. "We've got a long way back to the camp."

Carlos turned to the man holding the machine-gun. "Joaquin, fuego la."

Joaquin nodded and raised the Thompson, sending a burst in an arcing motion into the surrounding trees.

"Those *hinchapelotas* haff never seen a weapon like this one," Carlos glanced down at the two men binding Audrey's hands behind her back. Apparently satisfied that she was sufficiently secured, he looked at the group. "*Vamanos, mis hermanos.*" The man carrying the idols headed into the forest as well as the two pushing Audrey. Carlos dropped back and waited for them to pass him, then he too started walking at a rapid pace. Joaquin, with the machine-gun, fell in behind him.

"Wait," Rabbat pleaded. "I need some help with this gold."

"Gold? You can keep that for yourself," Carlos' voice lowered into a harsh sneer. "Like I tol' you, I haff what I came for."

✪✪✪

Doc checked each of them after their coughing subsided. The dust had seemed to roll past them, but left a grainy feel to the air. The old shaman spoke in Mayan, and Doc heard Professor Guffrey's voice.

"Michael, he's asking if you have any fire."

"Will this do?" Ace took out his Zippo Storm King lighter. His thumb rotated the wheel against the flint and the flame illuminated the cavern.

Balam and Saknik looked around and spoke.

"They're trying to figure out where we are," Guffrey explained.

"Doc, you think there's a way out of here, or should we start digging?" Deagan asked.

"Let's trust in the judgment of our hosts," Doc pointed toward the two Indians.

Balam held out his hand in a manner that requested the lighter. Ace gave it to him. Then the youth started walking down the tunnel. The others followed. After a few minutes they came to a fork in the path. Without hesitation Balam led them down the one to the left. After a few more circuitous turns, they felt a coolness to the air and the passageway opened up into the massive underground cavern that Doc had been through before. Balam went to one wall where a piece of wood lay on a rock. He felt the end, and then held the flame of the lighter to it. It burst into flame and he handed the lighter back to Ace.

Doc reached out and placed a hand on Balam's shoulder.

"Professor," he said. "Tell him that we need to get back to the pyramid as soon as possible."

Guffrey spoke in halting fashion, gesturing copiously as if to compensate for his lack of vocabulary. Finally Balam seemed to understand, and nodded. He pointed to his right and began a quick trot, the fire of the torch whistling in the coolness of the subterranean ambiance.

"Where we headed, Doc?" Ace asked.

"There's a passageway that will take us up through the pyramid," Doc said. "I have no doubt that's where Carlos and Rabbat are going. We might be able to make better time than they, since we're less obstructed down here. If so, we should arrive first and have the element of surprise."

"It's called out flanking 'em," Deagan said. "In case you didn't know, fly-boy." He strode past Ace, who hurried to keep up.

✪✪✪

Rabbat had barely been able to keep them in sight as the trek progressed. His pace slowed measurably, and despite his panting and calls for the others to slow down, he kept falling farther and farther behind. Breathing in gasps from the unaccustomed exercise and the heaviness of the load he carried, he paused to wipe his forehead.

A snapping sound came from behind him and he drew his pistol. The heavy drooping vines and scrawny trees were all beginning to look alike to him, but he saw no one. A bird burst from one of the branches and he foolishly fired off a round.

"Carlos," he cried out. "Where are you?"

No answer.

Rabbat started moving again, but his sense of direction seemed thrown off. Was the camp this way? All at once he wasn't sure. The detritus of the forest crackled loudly under his boots, but he was suddenly certain that he heard someone approaching from his rear. He whirled and fired, seeing nothing but the vast wall of verdancy.

Panting he turned and began to trudge onward again. He paused to loosen Doc's utility belt from around his waist. He still had one of the miniature grenades left. That would be his trump card should he need it. *Let those stupid savages come*, he thought.

Then the first arrow struck him in the left calf. The pain shot up his leg and he reached down to remove it. But the slightest touch caused him to double over in pain. He twisted to the ground, firing off the remaining rounds in his pistol at the area behind him.

The jungle seemed quiet except for the sound of his own ragged breathing.

Reload, he thought. Must reload.

He turned, fishing in his shirt pocket for more ammunition, but as he turned the light filtering through the trees seemed to darken momentarily. When he looked up the sunlight glinted off the metallic point of the spear.

Doc watched as Balam gave the torch to Deagan and reached out toward the stone wall. He knelt, feeling his way down, then pressed several of the large blocks. The familiar grinding noises started and the wall in front of them began to move.

"This is the same passage that closed before me the day I was taken,"

Professor Guffrey said.

"Well I'll be a monkey's uncle," Deagan said.

"Don't belabor the obvious," Ace moved by him.

Deagan's lower lip thrust out, but he held his hand out for the others to pass through before him. Doc quickly assumed the lead. The opening of the pyramid was just ahead, the massive stone lintels framing the brightness of the sunlight. At the entrance to the pyramid he paused, edging up to the vertical stone to sneak a look at the campsite. Through the ruins Doc could see Carlos carefully directing his henchmen to wrap the two idols in a large canvas tarp. As they began securing it with ropes, two others stood guard, including the one with the machine-gun. Another was holding Audrey, who was still bound, next to the jeep. The military field radio still hung from Carlos's belt.

"There are at least six of them," Doc said, holding his fingers up toward Balam as he spoke. "They're heavily armed, and they still have Audrey. I don't see Rabbat with them."

Professor Guffrey covered his face with his hands.

"Oh, my God, what have I done, bringing her here?" he sobbed.

Balam said something in Mayan and placed a hand on the professor's shoulder. Guffrey straightened up and translated. "He says that he's certain his people are on the way."

"If we don't act now, they may not arrive in time," Doc said. "We can't let them leave in those vehicles."

"What's the plan, Doc?" Deagan asked.

"We'll have to move quickly while we still have the element of surprise. We need a diversion."

"Leave that to me and Ace. Come on, fly-boy. Think you can hot-wire that truck?" He pointed to the old military half-ton that was perhaps fifty feet from where Carlos and the others stood. "We might be able to work our way around this wall to them trees to get to it."

Ace grinned. "Lead on, McDuff."

"That's McDeagan to you," Mad Dog said as they began a crouching trot behind the lower walls ringing the pathway to the pyramid.

"Professor, you and Saknik stay here," Doc motioned for Balam to follow him, and moved in the opposite direction from Deagan and Ace. They ran through the scattered ruins, moving between the concentric rings of low walls until they were near the edge of the camp. Doc cautiously peered around the wall toward the closest tent. It was more than thirty feet away. It was certain death if they were seen running toward it. He looked toward the truck. No sign of Deagan or Ace. He debated taking the initiative, but he was still too far from Carlos and his men to have a chance.

Suddenly he heard the sound of gunfire, but at a distance. Carlos appeared startled as well, and he raised his radio and spoke. After listening he yelled, "*Tenga prisa. Los indios vienen.*" The two men holding Audrey placed her in the rear seat of the jeep and began heading for the truck. Carlos pushed the men away from the canvas package and carried it to the jeep himself. He was just placing it the passenger seat next to him when the old half-ton army truck roared to life and began driving toward them. The henchmen rushed the truck, their weapons raised. The truck continued, with no one discernable behind the wheel.

Doc placed a calming hand on Balam's shoulder, then pointed to himself, and then the nearest set of tents. He indicated for the boy to remain there. In an instant, Doc was off, moving so quickly that he reached the tents in a matter of seconds.

Several rounds erupted from the Tommy gun, shattering the truck's windshield, but still the vehicle moved forward. The machine gunner continued his spraying, and bullets hit the radiator and blew out the front tires. His compadres yelled at him to stop firing, but he continued until the Thompson ran out of ammo. Two of the other men rushed the vehicle, which had limped to a stop a few feet away from them, and ripped open the door, guns drawn, revealing a drooping group of hastily knitted wires and a large branch wedged between the seat and the gas pedal.

The man at the driver's door turned around with a quizzical look on his face, only to jerk and clutch at the large knife, buried almost to the hilt, suddenly protruding from his chest. The other man whirled as Doc was upon him, hurling one of the sharpened tent stakes. It pierced the shoulder of his gun arm, and he fell forward curling up in pain. Doc reached the man with the Thompson just as he was attempting to lock in a new magazine. He brought the solid wooden butt of the weapon up toward Doc's face in a sweeping arc, but the Golden Avenger dodged it with accomplished ease. His fist slammed into the man's jaw, seeming almost momentarily to separate the henchman's head from his body.

Doc grabbed the machine-gun, but a bullet whizzed by his head. He instinctively dropped and continued to try and rearm the weapon.

The two other men who had rushed the truck were firing their handguns at him. One of them smiled and steadied his aim, apparently confident that he had Doc in his sights. But before he could fire Deagan and Ace jumped from the rear bed of the truck. Deagan threw himself forward in a flying tackle, knocking the gunman's arms upward before he was roughly brought to the ground. The second man turned, pointing the long muzzle of his revolver at the now prone Deagan, but a shot rang out the gunman's head exploded in a crimson mist. As he twisted to the ground, Doc saw Assante crouching by the truck with one of the dead henchmen's pistols.

A primal cry sounded from the other side of the compound as the forest seemed to spit forth a hundred Indians brandishing weapons of all sorts. Two of the last of Carlos's bunch ran a few yards in front of them, but they were quickly overtaken. From the screams and the accompanying chopping strikes, Doc knew that these two crooks were no longer a threat.

He turned his view back to the immediate scene in time to see Carlos and his sole remaining confederate, who was trying to scramble into the jeep. Carlos raised his pistol and shot the man in the back of the head, pushing the slumping body out of the way as he got behind the wheel of the jeep and started it up. Doc could see Audrey's face recoil in terror as the jeep bounced over the uneven ground toward the macadamized road.

Balam ran down to join them and the surging crowd of Indians continued forward. As the group came upon Doc and the others, Balam jumped in front of them, yelling in his native tongue. The Indians stopped, looking at Doc and the dead henchmen. Several of them carried items taken from the men already killed, and one held Doc's bloody utility belt.

Doc grabbed the belt and began running toward the center of the camp.

"Thomas, Ace," he yelled. "The motorcycles."

Deagan and Ace ran forward, each trying to get to the Indian first. Deagan managed to outrun Ace's limping pace, but just as he got there, Doc shot past him and jumped on the seat.

"I'll need you two to take the one with the sidecar, Thomas," Doc ordered. "I'll draw his fire and you get Audrey." His foot kicked down the starter. The motorcycle roared to life and Doc sped forward after the jeep.

Deagan nodded and turned, but as he did so he saw that Assante had assumed the driver's seat in the two-man cycle.

"Let's go," Ace grinned as he revved the accelerator.

Deagan quickly sandwiched himself into the sidecar and Ace tore out after Doc.

Doc could barely see in the cloud of dust left in the jeep's wake. Nonetheless, he pressed onward, trying to listen for the other vehicle over the high-pitched whine of the motorcycle's engine. The dust cloud thinned slightly and he caught a glimpse of the jeep. Carlos was leaning back over the seat and a red glow erupted from the gun his fist.

Doc banked to the side and hoped that Deagan and Ace were not in the bullet's path. Seconds later they appeared beside him, Ace smiling brightly. He'd taken the time to place his goggles on his face, as had Deagan. Doc indicated that he'd go right and they crisscrossed the gravel road. Twisting the accelerator, Doc shot closer to the jeep as Carlos fired another shot.

Dropping back, Doc zigzagged again, coming up to the left side of the jeep. Carlos twisted, trying to turn, but Doc adroitly steered the motorcycle right again. As Carlos turned to level his weapon at Doc, Ace and Deagan roared up to the left rear of the jeep. Deagan had wedged his short legs into the top portion of the sidecar, and was stretching the rest of his body outward. Ace veered in closer to the jeep and Deagan snatched Audrey in his powerful arms.

Ace immediately slowed, allowing the jeep to continue hurtling forward. Carlos glanced quickly at them, and then raised his pistol at Doc, who was immediately alongside on the right, and fired just as Doc grabbed the canvas covered idols.

The muzzle flash of the point blank discharge looked like a small explosion to Ace and Mad Dog.

"Did Doc get hit?" Deagan yelled, still holding Audrey across his lap in the sidecar.

Ace's lips pulled into a grim line as he saw Doc's motorcycle careening out of control before him, skidding across the road in a sideways skid, leaving a thick gouge in the surface gravel as it went.

But suddenly Doc seemed to regain control of the machine, his feet splaying outward for stability. In a split-second he stopped the cycle, dropped the canvas covered totems, and ran forward down the road. He was reaching into his utility belt as he ran. The jeep was at least sixty yards away from him now, but Doc's right arm cocked back then shot forward in a flash. The miniature grenade spanned the distance in four seconds and detonated just as Carlos had swiveled in the seat to fire another round.

Everyone stared at the brightness of the blast, then shielded their eyes from subsequent percussive wave. As the cloud of dust rolled past them, Ace, Deagan, and Audrey looked up, searching for any sight of Doc, but couldn't see him. Ace drove forward slowly, while Deagan untied Audrey's hands. The Indian motorcycle lay on its side in the middle of the road.

"Doc," Ace called, coughing slightly. "Where are you? Are you all right?"

"I am," Doc announced.

Through the powdery mist they saw him emerging from the side of the road carrying the canvas-wrapped idols.

"That last round was point blank," Deagan said. "Did he hit you?"

Doc held up the canvas to show them the perforation of the bullet hole. He undid the ropes securing the tarp and laid the package on the road and began flipping it over and over. After several rolls the two jade idols were at the end of the canvas trail. The left leg of the frowning idol had been completely shattered just below the hip.

"But I'm afraid our dour friend here sustained a rather grievous injury," Doc smiled as he looked at Audrey. "But I don't think any emergency surgery will be in order this time."

Hours later, Deagan and Ace came through the camp with a group of natives following. Doc, Professor Guffrey, and Audrey stood up and waved. As they neared Doc the Indians dropped back, as if in awe. Deagan rested the Thompson on his shoulder and held a black backpack in his other hand.

"This'll make a nice addition to our arsenal, won't it?" he said.

"Any sign of Rabbat?" Audrey asked. "I'd hate to think that he's out there somewhere watching us."

"No need to worry about that," Ace said.

"They led us to his body," added Deagan. "It looks like an old fashioned pin cushion. He ain't gonna be bothering nobody no more."

"We saw to a quick burial," Ace finished. "Figured it would save explaining that these people were only defending themselves after being attacked."

"I've buried those killed by the Indians as well," Doc reported. "The others we'll notify the local authorities about."

Deagan grunted in approval and held the backpack toward Doc.

"Looks like Rabbat fell behind the others because he was weighted down with this."

Doc opened the pack and took out several of the lustrous yellow cubes.

"The lure of gold," Ace commented. "As old as mankind itself."

Doc tested the weight of the metal in his hand, then took out his knife. The sun glistened off the stone as he held one of the cubes up and scraped it with the blade. Deagan's face broke into a wide grin as he saw the yellow flakes. Ace looked questioningly.

"He was actually weighted down with a whole lot of nothin'." Deagan smirked. "That's fool's gold, ain't it?"

"Also known as pyrite," Doc said. "One of the most common metallic substances found in the earth's crust. With its luster, it's often mistaken for gold, but is significantly less dense and much more brittle."

"It's why the Spaniards left the Mayans," Professor Guffrey said. "They had no gold to steal."

"Add the Egyptians to that list now," Ace nodded with a grin.

Several of the natives moved forward now, behind Saknik and Balam. They carried the two idols. Balam spoke to Professor Guffrey and gestured at Doc.

"Michael. They want to give you the idols for saving the chief's son and routing Carlos and the others."

"Professor," Doc protested, "please tell them I'm very grateful, but I can hardly accept such a gift."

Guffrey leaned closer.

"Remember, son," he smiled. "I've spent quite a bit of time with them these past few days. Not to accept their offering would be considered an egregious affront."

Doc was silent for a moment.

"Then I will take this one," he reached out for the broken statue whose twisted frown now looked like a grimace of pain. He held it up and smiled. "It not only saved my life, but perhaps its removal will signal an end to evil in the area. Also tell them that I will make sure that it is kept in a place of honor."

Guffrey did a rough translation and the Indians began a collective cheering. The old shaman placed a hand on Doc's shoulder and smiled.

The next morning the sun was rising over the village of Santa Merida as Doc and company were unloading a few medical supplies from the plane and placing them into Professor Guffrey's new jeep. Audrey stood by watching with a wistful expression on her face. Doc looked up and saw her, then smiled.

"Are you sure you won't come back with us now?"

She smiled and shook her head.

"I have to stay just a little bit longer. To help my father get set up for his new project. Besides, I have some medical work left to do. I'll have to remove that boy's stitches." She smiled as she gestured at the boxes of supplies. "We have a lot of people down here to vaccinate, and the means to do it, now."

"A book on the similarities between the Egyptian and Mayan cultures is a worthwhile undertaking for him. So when can I tell the medical school to expect you?"

"I'll be home for Christmas," she reached out and took his hand. "Michael, you've made such difference here. And for me, too. You've made me see that my true calling is medicine. How can I ever thank you?"

"You becoming a good physician will be reward enough."

Audrey's hand caressed his face, and she leaned forward to kiss him. Slowly, Doc's arms embraced her.

"Whoever that woman is, who's stolen your heart," Audrey's lips whispered close to his ear, "she's a lucky girl."

They continued in their embrace, oblivious to those around them, and to the approach of a slow moving taxicab down the main street of the town. The cab stopped abruptly. Doc and Audrey kissed again as the taxi's door slammed. Then Doc heard Deagan say, "Hey, look who's here."

Doc glanced over Audrey's shoulder to see a dark haired woman, looking rumpled and exhausted, approaching from a distance carrying two large suitcases. As the woman got closer, Deagan slapped Ace on the shoulder and pointed.

"What? Penny?" Ace said. "How the hell did you get all the way down here?"

"It wasn't easy," Penny let her suitcases drop to the ground at the sides. She glared at Doc and Audrey who were about twenty feet away. Doc had not acknowledged her arrival at all.

"Well, ain't you a sight for sore eyes," Deagan said. "We missed ya."

"Yeah, I'll bet," Penny snickered. "It sure looks that way."

"Aww, don't let that make you jealous," Deagan said. "Her and Doc are old friends."

"From way back," Ace said.

"I know that," Penny acknowledged, her face flushing. "And I am not jealous!"

Doc and Audrey were at the jeep now. He helped her into the seat and placed the final box in the back and pulled the canvas tarp tight around the load. She leaned forward and kissed him gently on the cheek.

"I'll call you when I get back to New York."

Doc smiled and nodded. "I'll be looking forward to seeing you there." He waved as the Professor put the jeep in gear and drove off. Then he turned and strolled over to Penny, his expression somewhat stern.

"Also known as pyrite..."

"Penelope," he began, "I believe I forbade you to come down here."

"And I can see why, too," she looked at the departing jeep.

Doc reached out for her arm.

"Let me check your vaccination," he said, but she immediately pulled away.

"Don't touch me!"

Doc stared at her for a moment, then turned away. "Very well. Thomas, could you see that her baggage is properly placed in the Athena. Ace, let's get the plane prepared. We have a long flight."

"Okay, Doc," Assante started to move forward, but Penny ran up to him.

"Ace," Penny reached out and touched his arm. "Do you remember when we first met, you invited me to the opera?"

"Yes, but that was a while ago, before—-"

"Well, is the offer still good?"

Ace looked to Doc, who said nothing.

"Well, is it?" Penny rereated.

"I ... I'll have to check my social calendar," Ace answered evasively.

"Good," Penny turned to Doc and added, "And why don't we make it a double date? You can ask Audrey?"

"Perhaps I shall," Doc walked toward the plane.

"Whooeee," said Deagan, lighting up one of his cigars and blowing out a prodigious smoke ring. "Better make sure that plane's A-okay, guys. I think I see a storm a coming."

THE END

Special thanks to Arthur C. Sippo, M.D., M.P.H., F.A.C.P.M. for his assistance

DESERT SHADOWS

July 7th, 1947

Near Roswell New Mexico

Robert Fielding adjusted the fuel mixture on his North American T-6 Texan single engine plane as he began the gradual slanting descent that would bring him down near the landing strip on his ranch. Being near the Roswell Army Air Field, he radioed the tower that he'd be descending from 4,000 feet and that his banking turn would take him close to their air space. Since he'd gotten the T-6 for a nominal sum from military surplus, he didn't want it mistaken for one of the military's planes.

"Roger, T-6," the voice said over the radio. We show you on screen. All looks clear for your descent. Over."

"Roger that, Roswell Tower," Fielding said into his own mike. "Thanks for the…"

He never finished the transmission. Something seemed to whiz by the front of his plane leaving a discernible wake. He grabbed the yoke with both hands to guide the small plane through the turbulence. The unexpected roughness didn't bother him as much as the tower having told him he was clear. After all, he was a former Army Air Corps flier himself, and hated the thought of another serviceman being remiss in his duties. If an air traffic controller would have broadcast erroneous information like that when he'd been on active duty, the guy would have found himself standing before a review board in a hurry.

"Roswell Tower," said Fielding, "you guys aren't flying any of those new fangled jet fighters up this way, are you?"

"Negative, T-6," the radio replied. "I say again, our screen shows you on a clear descent. Over."

Another wave of turbulence shook the small plane and Fielding grabbed the yoke once more. Something was causing the disturbance. Something like a plane traveling at a hell of a speed. He reached for the mike again.

"Roswell from T-6 Texan, I'm experiencing some high turbulence up here. Are you sure you guys don't show any other crafts in the area? Over."

"Negative, T.6. Do you need to set down on our field? Over."

Fielding was considering taking them up on their offer. The Air Base was closer than his ranch by several miles, and there damn sure was something causing these shears. The question was what? Then he saw a shining glint of something hovering in the sky to his left. Huge ... Circular. *What the hell is that?* He asked himself.

All at once he heard a strange whining sound. Like the whistle of an approaching artillery shell. It seemed to grow louder. Fielding glanced around the cockpit. No other aircraft in sight. The turbulence started again, but this time much stronger. He had to keep both hands on the yoke to maintain control, but even so he could feel the plane jumping and lurching like a yo-yo. Still he did not lose control, nor did he panic. After all, he'd flown 25 missions over Germany in worse than this. And he'd been copilot to the best. Fielding grabbed for the mike.

"Roswell Tower, this is T-6. Mayday! Mayday! I'm losing cont..."

But before he could finish the cockpit glass exploded sending a burst of a thousand needle-like shards over him. Wind seared his bloodied face. Trying to shield his eyes with one hand, he pulled back on the yoke with his other. Maybe if he could get above it... Suddenly he heard the sputtering of the engine as it faded out, and the howling noise increased, seeming to rupture his eardrums. Blood burst from his nose, then his mouth. Unable to breathe, Fielding tried to pull the nose of the plane up, but the noise continued to increase. He felt something pop in each ear, then the thundering roar of the plane as it spun into an almost vertical dive drowning out everything. Even the sound of his screams.

The cab pulled up the busy sidewalk in front of the Empire State Building at 34th and 5th. The man inside got out slowly, extending his long legs first, then bracing himself on the door and gaining purchase with a long, wooden cane. The cane had an ornately formed handle that seemed to fit easily into the man's powerful hand. As he stood and reached for his wallet, people passing by were taken by his startling handsomeness. He was a dead ringer for Errol Flynn.

As the cab pulled away, the man moved with slow deliberation toward the main entrance of the tallest of buildings. The doorman, a big dough-faced Irishman, touched the brim of his cap and said, "Good afternoon to you, Mr. Assante."

Edward "Ace" Assante merely nodded, which was a surprise to O'Bannion, the doorman. Assante was usually the cheerful picture of style and grace. But today he looked fatigued and saddened.

"Would everything be all right with you, sir?" O'Bannion asked. His permanent duty station as the doorman, and his assistance to Doc Atlas and his crew on several occasions, had given him something of a familiarity with the famous group.

Ace showed him a weary smile, then shook his head.

"I've had better days," he proceeded toward the express elevator that would take him up to the floor of the headquarters of Doc Atlas. Slipping his special key in the slot, Ace twisted it and waited for the express elevator to begin its quick ascent. He glanced up at the video monitor in case Doc or Polly, Doc's chief secretary, were watching to see who was inside. A special alarm sounded inside Doc's quarters whenever anyone used the express. The regular elevators did not stop at Doc's floors.

The doors whooshed open a few seconds later and Ace stepped into the hallway that led to Doc's main office. The heels of his shoes echoed against the highly polished marble. After pushing through the doors, Ace saw a pretty redhead sitting behind the large desk busily typing. She looked up and smiled brightly as Assante entered.

"Hi, Ace," she greeted. "They're in the gymnasium."Ace nodded and proceeded onward.

"Gosh, are you all right?" Polly asked.

Ace merely shook his head and continued through the door to the left, which he knew led to Doc's living quarters. Beyond that were his laboratory, equipment rooms, and gym. Doc's headquarters was so large that they took up the entire floor as well as the ones above and below. One of the floors contained a massive main-frame computer, the first of its kind, along with an entire staff of office workers. It was their job to feed information into the computer so that Doc could run projections for virtually any subject of which he had interest or concern. Often times the Government would contact him for assistance due to his incredible abilities and intelligence.

Assante continued down the hallway and through the doors that opened into the gymnasium. It was a long room with heavy mats lining the walls. Several rows of weightlifting equipment were stacked against one wall, and high jumping, pole vaulting, and parallel bars sat within an extended oblong track. Tables containing stacks of such eclectic items as bowling pins, baseballs, archery equipment, and fencing swords lay in organized groups. Twin ropes, thick as huge cables, were attached to a bare steel girder along the ceiling. And at the far end of the gym Ace could see two men near a maze of boxing equipment. One of the men, the shorter of the two, was holding a heavy bag that was attached to a metallic frame. Each blow caused the thick corded muscles of his arms to fan outward in bas-relief displaying a sense of power. The other man was a tawny haired Adonis. He was six-foot one and the muscles of his perfectly proportioned body seemed to bulge on his frame like bundled piano wire. Each blow that he sent whistling into the heavy bag seemed to practically lift the shorter man off his feet. And Ace knew that Doc was holding back with his punches.

Stopping a few yards from them, Assante felt in his pocket for his cigarettes and withdrew one from a fancy silver case. Taking his lighter, he flipped back the tip, but before he could flick the wheel to strike the flint, the shorter man yelled at him.

"Hey, Ace, what the hell you doing? You know that Doc don't allow no smoking here in the gym. Especially when he's working out. And you're wearing dress shoes, too, you knucklehead."

Assante merely held the lighter out and stared at it.

"You deaf, shyster?" the shorter man, Thomas "Mad Dog" Deagan yelled again. "I told ya no smoking."

"Thomas," Doc Atlas paused from his punching drill. "Ace seems a bit preoccupied."

"When ain't he preoccupied?" Deagan said. He waited for the customary caustic, but friendly reply that usually continued into an ongoing banter between the two old friends. But none came.

"Doc, if you have a minute, I'd like to speak to you," Assante still held the lighter in his fist.

"Certainly," Doc said.

"We still got another round to go," Deagan reminded.

"I'll wait for you in the library then?" Assante asked.

Doc nodded and resumed punching the bag.

Ace walked back across the polished wood floor and through the set of doors that led to the conference room. Inside, he removed his hat and sat at a table near the entrance. Grabbing an ashtray, he lighted his cigarette, pausing to watch the flame, then clipping down the lid. He read the inscription on the side of the Zippo as the tears welled up in his eyes.

TO ACE—
MAY GOD ALWAYS BE YOUR CO-PILOT
BOB FIELDING.

Assante was staring wistfully at the writing when the door burst open and a startlingly attractive woman came in. She had raven-black hair that hung about her shoulders, and features that were at once beautiful and symmetrically perfect. Her light blue suit showed the exquisite curves of her elegant figure, and she had begun unfastening the buttons of the jacket as she walked. Flinging the coat onto the tabletop, she set down the sheaf of papers she had and reached in her purse.

"Hi, Ace. Where's Doc?"

It took Penelope Cartier, top reporter for the *New York Times,* only half a heartbeat to tune in on Assante's melancholy mood.

"Ace, what's wrong?" she moved over to him and placed a hand on his shoulder with the familiarity of a close friend, or an old lover. "You look terrible."

"A buddy of mine was killed," Assante said. "We served together in the War."

"Oh, that's terrible. I'm so sorry."

Assante's thumb closed over the lighter and he put it in his pocket. Penny's hand lightly moved toward his neck.

"He was my co-pilot," Assante continued. "We flew 25 missions together, before I got hit. He managed to get the B-17 back to England, as chewed up as she was, and radioed for an ambulance as we were setting down. Probably saved my leg and my life."

Penny leaned her hip against him as he brought both hands to cover his face. Reaching down, she quickly plucked the smoldering cigarette from between his fingers and brought it to her own lips. Just then the door opened quickly and Deagan entered, wiping his face with a sodden towel.

"Man, if I coulda punched half as hard as Doc, I woulda been able to take on Joe Louis," he said. He glanced over at Assante and added, "What's the matter, shyster? Lose a big case, or something?"

"Mad Dog, leave him alone," Penny exhaled a smoky breath and shot him a reproachful glance. "He just lost a friend."

"Oh yeah?" Deagan gave his face a few more ineffectual wipes. "Anybody I'd know?"

"I doubt it," Assante replied. "He was from my old bombardier unit."

Deagan grunted. As a retired military man, he'd lost plenty of buddies himself, and knew the bond men shared after serving together. "Sorry to hear that, Ace."

Assante nodded an acknowledgment.

"His wife called me this morning. Wanted to know if I'd come out to the funeral. Be one of the pall bearers. I figured it's the least I could do. He practically saved my life once."

"Where's the funeral at?" Deagan asked.

"New Mexico. A little place called Roswell. But he crashed near an Army Air Base and the military's holding his body as well as the wreckage." Assante's brow furrowed as he looked at Deagan. "The family can't even cut through all the red tape to make the necessary funeral arrangements. I thought if you or Doc could make a few phone calls it might break the log jam."

"Sure, I'll do what I can," Deagan said. "You know the name of the base commander?"

Assante shook his bead.

"My secretary's been trying to get me reservations on a flight to Santa Fe or Albuquerque, but it seems that everything's booked up."

The door opened again and Doc Atlas strode in. Despite the towel around his neck, his body still gleamed with a fine sheen of perspiration that seemed to accentuate the powerful symmetry of his chiseled musculature.

"It won't be necessary for you to fly commercially, Ace," Doc said. "I've just called the maintenance crew at the airfield to prepare the Pegasus. We can fly directly there."

As soon as Doc Atlas entered the room, Penny quickly stubbed out the cigarette and discreetly removed her hand from Ace's shoulder.

"Doc," Assante looked up at the Golden Avenger. "I certainly appreciate it, but I couldn't ask you to drop all your own personal business."

"Actually, it will serve a double purpose," Doc said. "I've been asked by Washington to proceed out to Roswell Army Air Field to take part in an informal investigation. I was going to ask you to accompany me anyway."

"Investigation? What kind?"

"I'll brief you all on the plane," Doc said. "I must shower and prepare for the trip." He turned and abruptly pushed through the door to his living quarters.

Used to Docs tacit announcements, the others were not surprised by this. But as Deagan scratched his jaw, and Assante continued to look perplexed, Penny grabbed the newspaper she'd been holding and spread it out on the table top in front of them.

"Hey, guys, what do you want to bet it has to do with something about this?" she smiled triumphantly. The two men stared down at the block letters of the headline, and then back to one another. It read:

FLYING SAUCER CRASHES NEAR AIR BASE ARMY TO HOLD BRIEFING WITH DETAILS.

Deagan emitted a low whistle. "No wonder there ain't no room on any of the planes flying west."

The Pegasus was a Cessna UC-78 Bobcat Light Personnel Transport plane that Doc usually used for quick jaunts. His crew at the air-field had it fueled and set up for him upon arrival. Since Penny insisted on coming along due to the burgeoning UFO stories emanating from the area, Doc elected to delay the take-off until she had packed enough clothes for several days. Doc and Ace did the customary pre-flight inspection themselves while the crew fueled the plane. With Ace in the co-pilot's seat, and Doc at the controls, the Pegasus taxied to the runway and took off flawlessly into the strong northern wind. Once airborne Doc radioed ahead with his flight plan, which was practically pre-approved due to Doc's prominence.

After setting down in Chicago and Joplin, for refueling, Doc again took off toward New Mexico. Somewhere over Kansas he noticed Ace's eyes starting to droop.

"Ace, are you tired?"

Assante snapped awake.

"No. Why? Did I miss something?"

"Perhaps some adequate rest," Doc said with a rare smile. "Why don't you go in back and take a nap."

Ace yawned.

"Yeah, I guess I'm not doing much good up here, am I? Maybe I'll go back and test some of that awful coffee Mad Dog always brings along in his old thermos."

Ace left the cockpit and went back into the plane. Doc continued flying, his amber eyes scanning the horizon tirelessly. Presently Penny came forward holding a cup of steaming black coffee in both hands. Cautiously, she released her grip with one of her hands and gently touched Doc's shoulder.

"I thought you might like some of this, darling."

"Thank you."

Penny moved into the seat next to him and gazed through the glass windshield at the darkening sky.

"Oh my God, it's so beautiful up here. Look, those clouds are all in a row."

"They always are. It's just the curve of the horizon that makes them appear on different levels from the ground."

"Really? Just perception, or I guess people's misperceptions." She glanced back into the plane and smiled. "The two of them are back there chatting like long-lost school chums instead of arguing like they usually do. Ace is talking about all the missions he flew with that Fielding fellow."

"Beneath the surface of their bickering," Doc said, "lies a deep friendship between them."

"There certainly does." Penny's dark eyes slowly took in the powerful symmetry of Doc's well-proportioned, but powerful body. "So, have you seen any suspicious unidentified flying objects?"

"None."

"What do you think about all this brouhaha in New Mexico? Do you think it could be true?"

"I have yet to form an opinion. But it might not be prudent to subscribe to this current wave of hysteria too quickly."

"I suppose not. But the paper's printed a three thousand dollar reward for anyone who can find proof that a flying saucer really did crash there." She looked at him and sighed. "Do you think there actually are crafts and creatures from other worlds?"

Doc didn't answer, as was his custom with most hypothetical questions. Used to this, Penny continued.

"The first half of the century's almost over, and just look at how far we've come. Buck Rogers doesn't seem so far fetched anymore. We'll probably send a man to the moon by the end of the century, don't you think?"

"Perhaps," Doc agreed. "Perhaps sooner."

Upon landing at Roswell Army Air Field and securing the Pegasus in a section reserved for aircraft storage west of the main hanger, Doc, Ace, Deagan and Penny moved away from the airstrip. Although they had flown straight through two time zones, and it was only beginning to get dark here, their fatigue from the long flight was evident on all except Doc. He seemed tireless. An army sergeant with an MP brassard on his arm pulled up for them in a jeep. He glanced at Penny with a startled look and then smiled sheepishly.

"Sorry, ma'am," he said. "I wasn't told you'd be coming along. My orders just specified picking up the gents."

"That's okay, soldier," Penny hiked up her skirt so she could step into the back of the jeep. "It won't be the first time I hitched a ride where I had to sit on the back fender. Just get this crate moving so we can cool off."

The sergeant's eyes were glued on her shapely legs.

Ace slipped in next, followed by Deagan, who lowered the seat behind him. Doc got in the front passenger side and turned to the sergeant.

"If you would be so kind as to drop Miss Cartier off by the officer's club, then take us to see the base commander," Doc said.

"Yes, sir."

The jeep took off with a start, spinning away from the parallel twin airstrips and heading toward the cluster of Quonset huts and buildings.

Ace, Deagan, and Doc were ushered into a Spartan looking office with a large gunmetal gray desk opposite the door. Three chairs had been set up in front, and the blades of a large fan blew through a metallic cage circulating the hot air. Both Deagan and Ace had removed their suit jackets and loosened their ties. Doc had worn his usual tan utility shirt and dark pants, but even he seemed to be feeling the effects of the hot, dry desert heat.

"Quite a change from July in New York, eh?" Colonel William Blanchard said as he and another man walked into the room. The other man was tall and dark. His uniform shirt seemed to hang loosely on his lanky frame. Blanchard sat in the chair behind the desk and grinned broadly at Deagan. "It's been a long time, Mad Dog."

Deagan rose and shook Blanchard's extended hand.

"You're right about that, Butch," Deagan said. "What you been doing since the end of the War?"

"Keeping the peace," the Colonel said. "Hell, it's been a while hasn't it?"

"A while since we were young?" Deagan grinned. Blanchard's eyebrows lifted, then he shook his head.

"Yes, I think so," he said. "This is Captain Rod Seals with MCI. Military Counter-Intelligence."

Seals moved forward and shook hands with Doc, Ace, and Deagan. His dark eyes seemed to linger on Doc longer than usual, as if he were sizing up the Golden Avenger.

"I just got off the phone with Secretary Forestall," Blanchard took out a handkerchief and wiped his forehead and upper lip. "He explained that he wanted you out here as part of an informal investigative committee."

"That is what he expressed to me also," Doc said. "What can you tell me of this crash incident?"

"Not much," Seals answered standing near the Colonel. He removed a pack of cigarettes and said, "Colonel, may I?" Blanchard nodded and handed him an ashtray. Seal first offered the pack around, but no one took any. After extracting one and placing it between his lips, Seals said, "This whole thing's been blown totally out of proportion.

"How's that?" Deagan asked.

Seals lighted his cigarette, shook out the match, and dropped it in the ashtray.

"There never was any flying saucer wreckage recovered. The press grabbed an unsubstantiated rumor and ran it like it was fact."

"Well, if it wasn't a flying saucer, what was it?" Ace was leaning forward, both hands resting on the top of his cane.

"Simply put, gentlemen," Seals said, "it was a weather balloon."

"Huh? A balloon?" Deagan said. "But didn't you guys already say it was some kind of alien craft?"

Colonel Blanchard cleared his throat. "This whole matter has been one confusing SNAFU after another. Captain."

"The actual crash that the papers are raving about now happened last month sometime," Seals added.

"Last month?" Ace said.

"Right. One of our local ranchers, a Mr. Mac Brazel, noticed some sort of strange wreckage out on the range on June 14th about 85 miles north of here." He went to a section of maps along the far wall. "The wreckage was strewn over about two hundred yards along here. Brazel didn't think much of it until the newspapers started running stories about all these supposed UFO sightings."

"UFO?" Deagan asked.

"Unidentified Flying Objects," Seals explained. "Little more than people seeing lights in the sky. We surmise that somehow Brazel got wind of some radio or newspaper offering a reward to anyone who found a flying saucer, as they've been calling them, and he saw a chance to get rich quickly."

Seals took a long drag on the cigarette and let the smoke envelope him as he lifted a large leather briefcase onto the desk.

"On July 7th Brazel dropped off some of the wrecked stuff he'd found at the local sheriffs office. The next day the *Roswell Daily Record* printed this." Seals reached into the briefcase and withdrew a folded newspaper. Holding it in both hands, he spread it out in front of them. The headline stood out in bold lettering:

RAAF CAPTURES FLYING SAUCER ON RANCH IN ROSWELL REGION

Seals folded the paper and replaced it in the case. The tip of his cigarette turned to crimson ash.

"This debris, I might add, weighed about five pounds and was composed of wood, tinfoil, and metal. It was the remnants of a high altitude weather balloon. Unfortunately, when one of our overzealous officers in Intelligence recovered the material from the sheriff, he made some outlandish statement about the wreckage being from a flying saucer." Seals frowned.

"Major Marcel is being dealt with appropriately," Colonel Blanchard said.

"Marcel was the man who received the material from Sheriff Wilcox," Seals clarified. "Apparently he convinced our press officer to go along with his wild theory."

"Where is this wreckage?" Doc asked. All eyes turned to him. "I should like a chance to examine it myself."

"Why, I'm afraid that isn't possible, *Major* Atlas," Colonel Blanchard said quickly, stressing Doc's former military rank. "Everything was transferred to Brigade HQ in Ft. Worth. By order of the General."

Doc turned to Deagan. "Thomas, tomorrow make the call to General Ramey."

Deagan smirked and nodded. Blanchard's lips seemed to stretch into a thin line.

"We also have another matter to attend to," Doc turned back to the Colonel. "I believe that you are holding the remains of a crashed civilian airplane along with the pilot?"

"You're talking about Robert Fielding?" Seals asked, the ash of his cigarette turning bright orange again. "How the hell did you hear about him?"

"He and I flew missions together during the War," Ace said. "His widow called me."

Colonel Blanchard exhaled slowly. "Yes, regrettably we are holding his remains. Our base doctor wanted someone to assist him with the autopsy due to some… irregularities he noticed. We didn't feel comfortable releasing him or the wreckage until we'd had a chance to go over everything with a fine-tooth comb. Then this flying saucer thing hit the papers and everything got fouled up."

"Sir," Assante said, "do you have any idea how stress-filled this has been for his family?"

"Indeed I do, Captain Assante," Blanchard showed that he'd also taken the time to research Ace's former military rank. "Believe me, I wrote plenty of condolence letters home during the War, so I know all about a family's grief."

"With all due respect, sir," Assante reminded, "we are not at war now."

"Perhaps," Doc offered, "if I may be allowed to examine the body, and the wreckage, I could expedite the matter."

"Why, that would certainly help, Major Atlas," Captain Seals said. He'd taken out another cigarette and was flicking open his Zippo. "But like we told you, we're waiting on the arrival of another qualified physician."

"You can call him Doc," Deagan popped a large wooden kitchen match with his thumbnail and holding it in front of the Captain's nose. Seals shifted his eyes to Deagan, then flipped the cap to his lighter closed.

Penny draped her coat over the rear of the bar stool and took a small sip of her martini. A bit too heavy on the vermouth for her tastes, but it was cold and at this point that's all that counted for her. She closed her eyes and leaned her head back, feeling the warmth of the liquor trickle down the inside of her throat. Two large fans, each encased in a crisscross of steel wires, stood at either end of the bar blowing a cooling breeze across the room. After the ubiquitous heat of the desert tarmac, this felt pretty close to heaven. A jukebox at the far end of the room played something slow and soft, and the muted conversations of the groups of uniformed men and women in civilian and nurse attire played an almost whispering accompaniment. Several tables were composed of men in suits and ties, reporters from the look of them, but Penny had no desire to go over and break the ice with any of them. If there was a story here, she'd nose it out herself. Reaching inside her purse for her cigarettes, she'd just removed one from the silver case when a large hand appeared in front of her. It held a silver lighter.

"Allow me," a burly looking man with a short gray beard said. His thumb snapped over the wheel igniting the wick. Penny nodded a thank you as she leaned toward the flame. Tossing her head back to free her hair from her shoulders, she looked at the man more closely.

"Say, aren't you?" she started to ask.

"D. Phillip Stringer, at your service, ma'am," the man said, sliding into the stool next to her and lighting his own cigarette. "And you are, I must say, the closest thing to a breath of fresh air since these two fans got here, Miss Cartier." Stringer grinned, showing her a row of straight, but somewhat discolored teeth.

"You know who I am?" Penny asked.

Stringer held up two fingers to the bartender who immediately brought him a shot glass and a beer.

"Of course I know who you are," Stringer said, emitting a low chuckle. His thick fingers gripped the shot glass and he downed the whiskey in one gulp. "Ahhhhhh. Nothing like that first shot after a long, hard day in front of the typewriter. Right?"

"I agree," Penny said. "But you still haven't answered my question."

"Question?" Stringer said, picking up the stein and taking a copious sip. The foam covered his mustache. "What question was that, my dear?"

"How you knew who I was."

"Oh, that." He took one last pull on his cigarette and stubbed it out. "Why wouldn't I recognize the most famous reporter of the *New York Times?* I read your by-line, even out in these parts. I even enjoy it sometimes."

"But my picture isn't with my by-line."

"True, true," he said, bringing the glass to his lips again. "But then again, it's not every day that the world renowned Doc Atlas arrives in some fly-on-the-map little airbase like this one, either."

"Oh, so that's it," Penny blew out a cloudy breath. "I should have known."

Stringer grinned at her sardonically.

"So, you could at least return my compliment by saying that you liked my books."

"Was that a compliment?" she set her cigarette in the ashtray between them and picked up her martini with both hands. After she took another sip, she turned to look at him. "But actually, I did enjoy *A Feast of Fools.*"

"I'll bet you did," Stringer drained his stein. "It's a love story. All women like those." He held up two fingers again and the bartender brought him another pair of drinks.

"So what brings a world famous author like you to this little fly-on-the-map air base?" Penny asked.

"The same as you," he said after downing the whiskey. "The possibility of beings from another world."

"And what conclusions have you drawn?"

"Conclusions?" Stringer slammed the shot glass down on the bar. "The damn army's being so close-mouthed about everything that we might as well be back at the front reading censored dispatches. But it's a might more interesting now that you're here." He grinned again and dropped his hand onto Penny's thigh. "Right!" He gave her leg a quick squeeze.

"Wrong" Penny tilted her glass so that the clear liquid poured out onto the front of Stringer's pants. He leapt up swearing and waving his arms. "You're lucky I didn't order hot coffee," she said.

Before Stringer could say anything else, he felt a strong set of fingers grab his shoulder.

"Trouble, Penny?" Assante asked, his hand still on the author's upper arm. Deagan's large hand curled around Stringer's other arm, letting him feel the slumbering power in the grip. Captain Rod Seals stood behind them looking somewhat concerned.

"Nothing I couldn't handle, Ace," Penny said. "Do you need me to introduce Misters Assante and Deagan, Mr. Stringer? And who's your handsome friend in uniform?"

Captain Seals stepped forward and introduced himself to Penny.

Stringer's lips curled back into a wicked looking smile and he extended his open palm toward Assante. Ace released him and shook it.

"Dammit. You guys got grips of iron," Stringer said. "Let me buy you both a drink."

"You're *the* D. Phillip Stringer?" Deagan declared. "I used to read your stuff in The *Stars and Stripes.*"

"Mr. Stringer is one of the few civilians we allow to have an almost free run of the base," Captain Seals said. "He occasionally obliges our base newspaper, the *Atomic Blast,* with an article or story."

"I remember *Dispatches from the Front* from the War," Assante said. "Good stuff. But I preferred *Blood on the Rose.* Your novel about the fall of Madrid. Were you really there for it?"

Stringer exhaled deeply. "Yeah, I'm a sucker for lost causes, I guess. Got shot up so bad they wouldn't even look at me for any active duty once America got involved."

"Hey, we was never involved in that one, pal," Deagan said. "If memory serves me correctly, Spain remained neutral, but old Franco was still playing footsie with Hitler after he kicked out all the Reds of Madrid. I didn't see nobody coming to help us out."

"Deagan," Stringer retorted. "You're an Irishman, huh? Maybe you should look at your own Emerald Isle before you go criticizing the Spanish Republicans."

"The only Emerald Isle that I come from is Brooklyn, pal. And don't you forget it."

Stringer looked at Mad Dog's expression, then blew out a boozy laugh. "Yep, Irish all the way. Put 'er there, pal," he extended his hand again.

"Of course I know who you are..."

"You're all right in my book."

But after Deagan grasped Stringer's hand, it suddenly became apparent that the author was trying to demonstrate that he, too, had a powerful grip. Deagan merely gritted his teeth and squeezed back. Seconds later Stringer's mouth snapped open and he was squealing loudly.

"Okay, okay, you've proved your point." As Deagan released him Stringer flexed his hand several times. "Hey, I make a living with these, you know."

"Then I'd watch where you put 'em," Deagan cocked his head toward Penny.

"Message received. Now, let me buy you guys those drinks, all right?" He motioned to the bartender. "Set 'em up for my friends, Fred. Anything they want."

Stringer's gesture was so expansive that he nearly fell over. Captain Seals had disappeared during the posturing, but now he re-entered the club with a small dark complected man wearing a tan chauffeur's uniform. They spoke in whispered tones from the doorway, then Seals left. The other man approached them and spoke in rapid Spanish to Stringer, who replied with equal, but somewhat slurred fluency.

"I guess it's time to go," Stringer said, his bulky form practically collapsing the small man. "But you're all invited out to my place. Not too far from here. It's called The Desert Shadows Ranch. Ask anybody where it's at. We'll have a party. A big party. Maybe you and I can go a few rounds with the gloves on." Just as Deagan and Assante were about to step in and help the small chauffeur, he yelled out, "Gordo!" A huge mustachioed man wearing a serape and a big sombrero moved with astonishing speed through the doorway of the club and grabbed Stringer's now slumping form.

"My apologies, *senõres*," the small chauffeur allowed the large man to carry Stringer toward the door.

"*De nada*," Assante said. When the chauffeur looked surprised, Ace began chatting with him in flawless Spanish.

"Your Spanish is *muy excellente,* senõr. I hope that we will meet again before you leave," the chauffeur came to attention and snapped off a sharp salute. After executing a precise about-face, he followed Stringer and the giant out of the club.

"Damn, did you see the size of that guy?" Deagan picked up the stein of frosty beer that Stringer had ordered for him. "Musta been seven feet if he was an inch."

"What did the little guy say?" Penny asked Ace.

"His name is Hector. We just talked about how *baracho,* or drunk, his esteemed employer was. Apparently he gets like this often. Has a standing order for his two *empleos* to ferry him home every time he comes on base. He called the big lug *Gordo,* which means large or fat."

"That guy didn't look so fat to me," Deagan commented.

"No, he didn't, did he?" Ace hadn't touched the beer that the bartender had set on the bar in front of him. "You know, there was something funny about the way that guy talked."

"Yeah, he was drunk," Deagan pointed to the frothy stein in front of Ace. "You gonna drink that one?"

Assante frowned. "I was referring to the chauffeur. His Spanish was …"

"Ace, the beer. You gonna drink it?"

Assante shoved the stein toward Mad Dog. "Be my guest."

"Isn't that what the famous D. Phillip Stringer wanted us to be?" Penny took out her cigarette case and offering one to Ace. "His guests?"

"Precisely why I prefer to buy my own drink," Assante extracted one of her cigarettes and took out his lighter.

In the basement of the base hospital army doctor Roland Vincent pulled open the steel drawer that housed the refrigerated body. Doc stood on the other side of the platform in the small, but densely built morgue. The refrigerated units covered virtually the entire wall, like a rectangular grid in a desk. Two other men, both in laboratory coats, stood next to Doc. Both men were substantially older than he and dwarfed by his Herculean proportions.

"All the drawers but two are empty, thank God," Vincent peeled back the sheet. Blood had seeped through the white material in several places.

Doc stared down at the twisted body, his amber eyes taking in the various injuries.

One of the men standing next to him, a short plump man with a fuzzy gray beard and hardly any hair on his head, spoke first. His accent was heavily laced with Eastern European inflections.

"Well, Doctor Atlas, what do you make of it?"

When Doc didn't answer the other man in the lab coat chuckled slightly and placed a hand on the bearded man's shoulder.

"Dr. Zimmermann, I'm afraid our esteemed colleague from New York is well known for being rather taciturn. Among other things."

Zimmermann raised his eyebrows as he watched Doc's silent examination. "But Dr. Vogel, he does speak, does he not?"

"May I see your scope," Doc asked. Vincent handed it to him and Doc peered into each of the dead man's ears, then did the same to the eyes. He stood and felt along the chest cavity down to the lower extremities, taking special notice of the pattern of lividity and bruises. When he had concluded this, he fixed Dr. Vincent with a stern gaze.

"You mentioned another body in storage. Whom might that be?"

"It's one of our pilots, John McGreggor. He crashed his P-51 the day before this man." Vincent pointed to Fielding's corpse.

"I wish to examine his body also," Doc slipped off his sport coat and hanging it on the coat rack by the desk. He began rolling up his sleeves. "Do you have a room available for an autopsy?"

"We've already done one on McGreggor," Vincent said. "These two gentlemen assisted me."

Doc looked at the two scientists.

"In the interest of saving you some time, Dr. Atlas," Zimmermann said, "you may read our official report if you wish."

"Thank you, but I prefer to conduct my own examination," Doc turned back to Vincent, "Do you have a spare surgical gown that I might borrow, doctor?"

Vincent looked at Doc's massive proportions and shrugged. "We might have to sew two of them together, but I'll see what I can do."

"Let me save you some time, doctor," Vogel offered. "We can tell you that the eardrums on McGreggor, the pilot, were ruptured just as Mr. Fielding's were. Each man apparently suffered massive internal hemorrhaging, but considering the tremendous impact of the crash, that is hardly surprising, is it not?"

"Did he have any subdural hematomas in the sclera?" Doc asked.

Vogel and Zimmermann exchanged glances.

"Yes," Vogel replied. "Just as Mr. Fielding had."

"Not a pretty thing, to see a body crushed by such impact with the ground," Zimmermann added. "But at least death must have been instantaneous."

"This man was in all probability, dead before he hit the ground," Doc stated.

"What?" Zimmermann said. "Why do you think that?"

Doc didn't answer. He just turned and accepted a large surgical gown from Vincent as he reentered the room. But before Doc could slip it on, a distant, but persistent wailing sound began.

"Oh no," said Dr. Vincent. "The sirens… The base is on alert."

"ALL CIVILIAN AND UNAUTHORIZED PERSONNEL WILL REPORT TO THE MAIN GATE AREA IMMEDIATELY," the loud speakers repeated. The base had become alive with uniformed men running between buildings and Military Police jeeps driving about in the lighted darkness. Ace, Deagan, and Penny all went outside and took in the activity.

"Unauthorized personnel," Deagan said. "1 guess that means us too."

"What's going on?" Penny asked as a soldier jostled by her slipping on a flight suit.

"Can't say, ma'am," he said hurrying off in the direction of the airfield.

"They're scrambling fighters," Ace pointed out.

"Yeah," Deagan concurred. "And look over there."

His big finger pointed to a row of distant mountains. Strange glowing lights seemed to light up the sky to the west with bright flashes against the dark horizon.

"What on earth is that?" Penny's eyes widened in amazement. Several of the photographers who had been drinking in the press section of the club began snapping photographs. But the snapping flashbulbs attracted a big MP Sergeant who meandered over with two equally huge MP's behind him.

"Okay, I'll take the film from them cameras now, gents," the sergeant ordered.

"Hey, ain't you ever heard of freedom of the press?" one of the reporters yelled.

"Yeah, but right now we're under base alert, so all of youse are subject to my authority." The sergeant snapped his fingers and the two MP's began collecting the cameras.

"Damn, I'd kill for one of those photos to send to New York," Penny said.

"You and the rest of these guys," Deagan said. "Hey, look, there's Doc."

Backlit by the illumination of the airfield and the fighter planes taking off, the powerful figure of Doc Atlas strode across the street toward them. The MP's had finished collecting all the cameras and were ushering the protesting group of reporters toward the main gate. One pressed his lateral baton onto Deagan's shoulder and told him to move.

"Hey, I'm a Lieutenant Colonel, dog face," Deagan growled.

"Yeah, and I'm Charlie McCarthy," said the MP.

"Relax, soldier," Penny interjected. "We're just waiting for Doc Atlas. He's coming now."

The MP glanced over his shoulder at the approaching figure and steered quickly around Deagan, Ace, and Penny. As Doc joined them Penny asked if he knew anything about the incident.

"They're sending some fighter planes up to check the area," Doc explained. "They feel the strange lights to the west may be cause for alarm."

"What do you think, Doc?" Deagan asked.

Doc didn't answer. His amber eyes scanned the horizon, as he reached into his pocket and withdrew a small, but extremely powerful telescope that was no bigger than a fountain pen. He studied the lights for more than a minute then replaced the telescope in his pocket. He turned back to his group.

"Colonel Blanchard has been kind enough to give us the loan of a military sedan. I suggest we make use of it now to secure proper lodging in town."

"But, Doc, what about them flying saucers?" Deagan questioned. "Ain't we gonna go after 'em?"

"In good time, Thomas, we will get to the bottom of this," Doc pointed the way to the Motor Pool. A worried looking PFC had the black Ford coupe waiting for them with their luggage already stowed in the trunk. After thanking the young soldier the four companions entered the sedan. Doc drove toward the Main Gate area where a long line of autos containing reporters and other civilians was being directed out through the raised barrier by two MPs. Penny and Ace were in the back seat looking through the windows as another pair of fighter planes screamed upward from the runways.

"Those are P-51's," Ace said. "Mustangs. What I wouldn't give to be going up in one of them right now."

The scream of the twin propellers of the P-51 was suddenly drowned out by a new syncopated beating.

"What's that?" Penny strained to lean across Ace to look out the window.

"It's one of those new Sikorsky's," Ace replied. "A helicopter. Doc, Mad Dog, and I ran across one of them at the tail-end of the War when we tackled that Von Strohm thing. Remember?"

"I remember you thinking you knew how to fly it," Deagan chuckled. "St. Christopher, be my guide."

"I'm better now," Ace said.

"It's good to see you two getting back to normal," Penny smiled.

Doc had scarcely gotten on the road to town when he heard a new wailing sound. Seconds later he glanced in the rear vision mirror and saw the red lights of a Military Police jeep fast approaching. As he pulled to the right, Doc noticed another pair of red lights trailing the jeep. An ambulance shot around them going at a high rate of speed. He pulled out his pocket telescope again and surveyed the area.

"It appears that there's been another crash," he jammed the Ford into gear and peeled away from the gravel shoulder. Doc followed the fast movements of the ambulance in and around the line of traffic. At times the speedometer reached such a high reading that the needle was beyond the imprinted scale. But Doc hung behind the ambulance, leaving the other traffic trailing far behind. The military vehicles slowed and made a left turn at a juncture heading north. The road was reddish dirt and seemed to travel farther out into the desert. Doc slowed the Ford somewhat due to the dust being stirred up by the preceding vehicles. Then twin columns of black smoke became visible against the velvet sky.

Doc slowed appreciably and veered to the right, away from the crash site.

"Doc, where are you going?" Ace asked. "It looks like they went down over there."

"The ambulance is en route to assist them, Ace. I thought I caught a glimpse of something over here."

Doc steered off the gravel road and onto the bumpy desert floor. Except for tough shrubbery, cactus, and occasional areas of brush, the going wasn't too bad. The others strained their eyes to try and see where Doc was heading, but only the expansive desert landscape seemed to loom in front of them. Then suddenly the front of the vehicle bounced over a dip in the earth and headed down an old dry arroyo. Ahead, to their right, a craggy expanse of rock jutted upward. The headlights shone on something white.

"There," Doc pointed to the fluttering silk of a parachute tangled at the top of the jagged cliff on some protruding rocks. Beneath the tattered chute a man in an olive drab flight suit dangled from the taut strings perhaps thirty feet above the ground. The outcropping of rocks seemed to be poised around him like deadly talons.

Doc pulled the sedan close to the bottom and they all piled out. The pilot appeared to be unconscious, his arms and legs twisting slowly.

Bloody trails dripped from his face, and his left leg appeared to be twisted at an unnatural angle.

Without speaking Doc ran to the base of the rocks and sprang upward, catching one of the jutting stones. Using the momentum of his swing the Golden Avenger seemed to scale the outcropping with amazing agility and speed. In scant seconds he was edging toward the top next to the injured airman. Gripping the harness of the parachute in one hand, Doc raised the unconscious body as easily as if he were lifting a sack of groceries.

"His left leg is possibly fractured," Doc called out. "And he may have internal injuries as well."

"You want to let him down, Doc, Ace and me will catch him," Deagan yelled.

But Doc was already reaching into another pocket of his shirt. He withdrew a small folding knife. Looping the parachute strings into a makeshift clove-hitch knot, Doc let the injured man dangle freely. Using the knife to sever sections of the upper portion of the parachute, Doc quickly twisted the collection of nylon cords into one thick cable and secured them with a second knot. Tightening his grip on the end of the twisted cords with his right hand, Doc braced his powerful legs against the rocks.

"Here he comes, brothers," he slowly lowered the pilot with a deft hand-over-hand motion. "Watch his left leg in particular."

"Gotcha covered, Doc," Deagan affirmed as he and Ace reached upward to gently but firmly take hold.

After seeing that the pilot was safely placed on the ground, Doc descended just as rapidly as he had gone up. He immediately knelt next to the injured man and began examining him.

"We'll need something to immobilize his leg. The lid of one of Penelope's suitcases should do." Deagan immediately began moving toward the car. "Thomas, use one of our halo flares to summon assistance also."

"Roger, wilco, Doc," Deagan reached in his coat pocket for one of the compact but powerful flares that Doc and his assistants always carried when on missions. Pointing the end skyward, Deagan punched the trigger which sent a small missile-like projectile streaking upward. The subsequent explosion flooded the area with an eerie white light, followed by the slow, patagial-like descent of a greenish luminescent spot.

Penny sat down and cradled the unconscious man's head in her lap.

Suddenly his eyes opened and he stared up at her face groggily.

"What? An angel," he said. "Am I in heaven?"

Penny smiled. "No, fly boy, you're still here on good old mother earth, but you're in the best of hands right now." She looked over at Doc.

Over breakfast the next morning in the hotel dining room, Doc detailed assignments for Penny and Deagan that involved interviewing the local witnesses of the recent Unidentified Flying Objects sightings. Penny winced as Deagan clapped his hands together. "Lemme at them Martians." He spoke loud enough to elicit a round of muffled laughs from the other patrons, many of whom were reporters who were trying to grab something to eat while waiting for a free phone to call in their stories on the crash. Penny had already phoned her editor in New York about their rescue of the downed flier. She took a sip from her coffee as she perused the morning edition of the *Roswell Daily Record.*

Looks like this UFO thing isn't going to go quietly into the night," she spread out the paper to display the headline: *Gen. Ramey Empties Roswell Saucer.* "They're even reporting seeing them in Iran."

"They got a lot of desert over there, too," Deagan mentioned. "Think there's any correlation?"

"Only if you correlate all the sand between your ears," Assante jibed.

"Aww, you just don't know how to put two and two together unless you got some list of case laws to tell you how to think," Deagan fired back.

Ace turned to Doc. "So what do you make of last night's crash?"

"At this point I don't have enough information to render an informed opinion," Doc answered. "The pilot stated that after the glass in his cockpit shattered, he was somehow thrown from the plane moments before it began its descent. He remembered hearing and seeing strange noises and lights immediately prior to the explosion."

"But if he'd been hit by some kind of round wouldn't we have heard the report?" Ace queried. "And what kind of gun could bring down a P-51 at night with one shot?"

"Want to know what I think?" Deagan sopped up the yolks of his eggs with a triangle of toasted bread. "I think this whole thing's starting to smell funny."

"What, your eggs?" Assante smirked.

"Naw, this whole flying saucer thing," Deagan elaborated. "Like maybe Old Butch knows more than he told us."

"That's a distinct possibility," Doc nodded.

"So where do we go from here then?" Penny took out a cigarette but didn't light it. "And how's interviewing these local yokels going to put us any closer to the truth if it's the military that's stalling?"

"It's my hope that I'll be able to reason with Colonel Blanchard myself this morning," Doc told them. "But in the meantime, we can't depend totally on his version of the events. We need to corroborate the events ourselves."

"And that's where Mad Dog and I come in?" Penny began fishing for her lighter, but Ace reached out with his and lighted her cigarette. He then took out one of his own and did the same.

"What would you like me to do, Doc?" he asked.

"I've taken the liberty of contacting the local mortician, Ace. He'll accompany us to the base where we'll secure your friend's body. It's time his family had some closure on that part of this."

"Thanks, Doc."

"Take the time you need to assist Mrs. Fielding in making the funeral arrangements. I have some other business that may take me out of the area today, but I expect to meet back here tonight at 1800 hours. We'll designate this to be our temporary headquarters."

Penny glanced up through the smoke at Doc, who was now rising.

"Thomas, if you will take care of the bill with our expense money," he strode toward the door.

"Major Atlas, I just wanted to thank you personally for all you and your associates did last night," Colonel Blanchard leaned across his desk to extend his open palm toward Doc. They were alone in the Colonel's office. "If you weren't so observant, that man probably would have perished before any search party could have found him."

"We were glad to help, Colonel," Doc shook the older man's hand. "And my appreciation as well for your assistance this morning in seeing to the release of Mr. Fielding's body. My friend Ace Assante was particularly grateful."

Blanchard nodded and sat back in his chair.

"But perhaps you could do me another favor," Doc continued. "I'm concerned about the entirety of the incident."

"You and me both, Major," Blanchard said. "I've lost three planes in the past two weeks, not to mention that civilian crash. My pilots are beginning to get afraid to take off."

"And what was your opinion of those mysterious lights in the sky?"

Blanchard pursed his lips before answering.

"Why, nothing more than heat lightning. We've been having a lot of storms sweeping the region lately."

Doc's amber eyes stared straight at the man. Blanchard looked away.

"I'd be curious to know why the base went on alert status last night," Doc said. "That seems an extreme measure for heat lightning."

"Dammit, man," Blanchard banged his fist on the desktop. But when he saw his show of belligerence had no effect on Doc, the Colonel sighed.

"All right. I'll lay my cards on the table. I received a call from Secretary Forestall this morning and he wants this matter of this UFO crash put to rest as soon as possible. Thus, I've been authorized to offer you a plane to fly to 8th Army Headquarters in Fort Worth. General Ramey held a press conference there last night displaying the recovered wreckage. The Secretary thought that a subsequent statement from you might put the whole damn affair to rest once and for all."

Doc nodded, but said nothing. It was his custom to let others speak while he observed and evaluated them.

"In the meantime, he also gave me the go-ahead to bring you up to speed. It's no secret lately that a wave of hysteria has been sweeping the country over these damn flying saucer reports. While the Army Air Corps doesn't put much credence in most of them, there's always the concern that the Russians might use this as an opportunity to launch a surprise attack."

"Do you think that's feasible?" Doc asked.

"Who knows? But we didn't expect Pearl Harbor either, did we?" The Colonel flipped open a folder on his desk and handed the top sheet across to Doc. "This is a top secret authorization I'm showing you, Major. It deals with Project Mogel. I verified your security clearance this morning also."

Doc studied the paper then looked back to the Colonel.

"So you're saying that the wreckage recovered by Mr. Brazel was not a weather balloon after all?"

"That's correct. It was a high altitude research balloon that we've been testing. These balloons have special acoustical equipment designed to monitor Soviet nuclear tests. The special reflective material makes them less visible to radar waves."

"Interesting," Doc mused.

"It's no secret that there was a rat at Los Alamos," Blanchard said. "Gave away the secret of the bomb to the damn Russians. Stalin wasn't even surprised when the President told him we'd split the atom," he snorted. "We figure it's only a matter of time before they explode their own device."

"Probably inevitable," Doc agreed.

"Plus the area they captured in Germany there at the end of the war contained all the Nazi's latest research on experimental weapons and their V-6 rocket program. Who knows what kind of stuff they found there. But as it stands now, we're still the only ones with the A-bomb. And the 509th is the only base in the world with active atomic weapons." Blanchard's eyes narrowed as he stared across at Doc. "Now, sir, do you see why we go on alert at the drop of a hat?"

Doc nodded. "That is indeed an awesome responsibility, Colonel."

"So you can understand why we've got to work together to put this flying saucer crash rumor to rest? If the news got out that we were worried the Communists might have the bomb, it could be devastating for the country."

"But a campaign of erroneous information may backfire," Doc suggested.

"Then you won't help?"

Doc considered this for a moment.

"I wish to examine this wreckage myself," he stood. "After which I'll speak with General Ramey. And I'll be taking my own plane, the Pegasus, to Fort Worth."

The Sheriff of Chaves County, George Wilcox, was polite and cooperative to Penny and Deagan. But his account of the material recovered from farmer Mac Brazel two days ago shed little light on the incident. The sheriff leaned back in his chair with a cup of coffee as he spoke. "Mac whispered kinda confidential-like that he might have found one of them flying disks," he said. "I called Roswell Army Air Base figuring that they were a lot better equipped to deal with something like that than I was." The sheriff chuckled quietly. "I've got enough to do with just dealing with problems caused by folks 'round these parts without worrying about something from outer space."

"So whom did you speak to when you called?" Penny asked.

"I got ahold of Major Marcel. He was attached to group intelligence." The sheriff took a long sip from the cup. "Him and another guy came right out. Was real excited, and all. Took the stuff off my hands and, frankly, I was glad to get rid of it."

"What did it look like?" Deagan asked. "Like something from outta this world?"

"Some metal struts," Wilcox said. "And some kinda shiny stuff. As best as I can recollect."

"Aww come on, Sheriff," Penny chided. "Are you telling me that somebody brought you the wreckage of a flying saucer and you didn't take the time to examine it closely?"

Wilcox laughed again, louder this time.

"Well, like I said, Miss Cartier, I'm a bit more concerned with the things happening in Chaves County. And besides, we're used to the local folk telling strange tales around here. Just like the legend of Cactus Jack."

"Cactus Jack?" Deagan repeated. "Who's that?"

Wilcox chuckled again. "Old Jack Persard. One of our local ranchers. Disappeared way back in the 30's after the bank foreclosed on his place. Went off into the desert with a team of wild mustangs. Every once in a while something somewhere will come up missing and somebody'll claim it was taken by old Jack."

"But this wreckage was something tangible, wasn't it?" Penny countered. "Did it look authentic?"

"Authentic," Wilcox grimaced. "Miss, now how the hell would I know what something from a flying saucer was supposed to look like?"

Deagan and Penny considered the sheriff's question as they tried to trace down Mac Brazel. Unable to find the farmer, who was out attending to his large herd of sheep, they sought out a married couple in Roswell named Wilmot, who had reported seeing a strange oval-shaped object over the western skies a few days prior. But other than saying that the object looked like two saucers turned upside down, Penny and Deagan got little from them.

Sheriff Wilcox had also mentioned a young man named Virgil Horn as another of the local residents claiming to have seen a flying disk recently, more than a month ago. He had made one of the first reports. Horn was stacking boxes in the rear of the local drugstore.

After going in and purchasing a map of the area, Penny smiled alluringly at the proprietor and asked if they might speak to the young stock boy for a moment. The druggist shrugged and said, "I don't expect it would hurt anything. But only for a few minutes. He's got work to do."

At first glance Virgil Horn appeared to be a handsome young man with oily reddish hair and a thin, wiry build. But as he leaned back against a stack of boxes and wiped his forehead with a red bandana, his smile seemed somehow a bit pretentious. As Penny and Deagan began questioning him, the venal side of his nature quickly became apparent.

"Am I gonna be paid for what I seen?" Horn asked.

"I work for the *New York Times*," Penny said. "We don't pay people for interviews. We're the biggest newspaper in the world, and a lot of very important people will be reading about you."

Horn seemed to consider this for a moment. "No money, then, huh?" Penny shook her head. "Well, I suppose I can tell you a little of what I seen. Maybe that way somebody will want to pay me later."

"Sure," Penny suspected that it was dubious.

"Me and my best gal Sally was up in the hills about a month ago," Horn related. "Had us a nice little campsite set up with a tent and all. Only her folks didn't know that she wasn't staying at her girlfriend's. She was just here in Roswell visiting. We was just kind of sitting there around the campfire, when all of a sudden we heard this loud noise. Like a bomb going off." Horn made a circular gesture with his hands. "At first I thought it was a lightning bolt, 'cause we been getting a lot of sudden storms this summer. But the sky was clear, except for this real strange glow coming from the south."

He paused and grabbed a bottle of pop from one of the wooden crates. Wedging the cap against the side of the crate, he smacked downward on the bottle to pop it open.

"So me and Sally hopped in my truck and started driving toward the light," Horn paused to take a drink. We must've drove for a couple of miles, then we seen 'em."

"Who?" Penny inquired.

"Martians. Little green men all laying around this silver disk and these colored light beams up in the air. Looked like they was hurt, too."

"How far away were you?" Deagan asked.

"Unnn, close enough to see they wasn't human," He leaned away from the wall and gestured expansively. "They had these big long heads with white faces, and wore these dark green uniforms."

"They were hurt you say?" Deagan pressed. "Did you try to help them?"

"Nope. We just hightailed it outta there. Sounded like a heavy truck was coming down the road, so we figured it was the Army."

"How would I know what something from a flying saucer looked like?"

"Horn!" a gruff voice yelled from the front of the store. "You telling that damn flying saucer yarn again? I hope to hell you got those boxes all stacked."

Horn took another quick swig from the bottle of pop and set it down.

"That's my boss. Gotta get back to work." He grabbed a box and moved over toward the stack by the far wall. "So when am I gonna be in your paper, Miss?"

"As soon as we can corroborate your story," Penny said. "Where can we find Sally?"

"Sally?" The boy frowned. "Why she went back to Albuquerque with her folks. Like I said, she was just here visiting."

"Could you show us where it was you saw this?" Penny pulled out her map and spread it out on the box in front of him.

Horn licked his lips quickly, then squinted at the map. He ran his finger along one of the lines. "If this here's the main highway, then it would have had to be along here somewheres." His fingers traced a section to the southwest of the Army Air Field.

As they left, Penny asked Deagan what he thought.

"Ah, I don't know. The kid sounded like he was telling the truth, but I don't know. Near that area that he pointed to was White Sands Missile Base. He coulda seen anything and just thought it was a flying saucer."

"My sentiments exactly," Penny nodded. "And I'm not about to use it without a second source. Not for something as outlandish as a flying saucer report."

Deagan looked at his watch. "What do you say we grab some lunch? This Martian hunting has made me hungry."

"Is there anything that doesn't?" Penny smiled.

Ace Assante drove the military sedan along the main highway from the Fielding ranch. He lighted a cigarette and blew some smoke out the open window as he ruminated about the morning. His old friend's widow, Mary, had been grateful for Ace's help in securing her husband's body and helping with the funeral arrangements. And Ace was grateful that she'd been pretty much under control. She'd only broken down once, toward the end, when Ace had mentioned how her husband had saved him on that mission.

"He always said you were the bravest out of all of them," she said through tears. "Wealthy enough that you could have gotten out of the dangerous fighting, but you were always right in the worst of it. He loved you like a brother."

The wake would be tomorrow, with the funeral to take place the day after. Hopefully, he could persuade Doc and Deagan to be pall bearers also. He was sure they would agree. Ace was also anxious to tell Doc about the widow's statements about seeing "lights in the sky all around Roswell the last few weeks." Although be wasn't sure if it was factual or just some sort of general hysteria. After all, he thought, this flying saucer craze seems to be sweeping the nation. But he was sure that Doc would find it interesting.

His ruminations were snapped as a truck came barreling up behind him. It was a large vehicle with a heavy canvas tarp securely fastened over the bed. As the truck drew along side of him Ace noticed two swarthy faces behind the windshield. One of them was the large man called Gordo.

Ace nodded as the truck passed. The giant's face showed surprise as he returned the greeting, and the larger vehicle shot around Ace's sedan. The rear end of the truck was also covered with the folds of the heavy tarp, and Ace wondered what it was they would be carrying in it that merited such secrecy. As the larger vehicle swerved in front of him. Ace caught a glimpse of Stringer's chauffeur, Hector, in the side-vision mirror.

There was something that bothered Ace about the man's Spanish. It had been very rapid, the words almost running together instead of separately enunciated. Certainly not at all like the classical lisping of Spain. South American maybe?

His curiosity piqued by the sight of the truck, Ace began to accelerate slightly, keeping it in sight. This continued for several miles, but finally the other vehicle slowed and executed a left turn onto a gravel road perpendicular to the highway. Ace slowed as he passed the point at which the truck had turned and saw a sign posted at the juncture.

DESERT SHADOWS RANCH
ABSOLUTELY NO TRESPASSING

"Shall I tell you my theory about all this?" D. Phillip Stringer set down his coffee cup and leaning forward.

"I'm sure you will regardless," Penny dumped a teaspoon of sugar into her coffee.

Deagan grinned slightly at the drollery of Penny's quip.

"Something went down over the desert out here. Something from up there." He pointed his thick finger skyward.

"Yeah," Deagan said. "We all know that."

"Please, sir," Dr. Zimmermann chided. "Let Mr. Stringer elaborate."

Deagan grunted and shoved his empty plate forward so he could lean his elbows on the table. To hell with manners, he thought. And to hell with D. Phillip Stringer.

Upon entering the diner, Penny and Deagan had barely sat down and ordered when Stringer walked in with the two scientists, Zimmermann and Vogel, in tow. The writer immediately invited himself and his party to eat with Deagan and Penny, and the after dinner talk had gradually shifted to the subject on everyone's mind: Unidentified Flying Objects.

"Yes, Mr. Deagan," Professor Vogel chimed in. "Let the man speak."

With an acknowledging grin, Stringer continued, using his big hands for expansive gestures.

"Let's just say, for argument's sake, that some craft from outer space did crash in the desert out here. It goes without saying that such a craft would probably have been occupied, does it not?"

"Not really," Deagan argued. "The Gerries were sending a lot of drones over to England there at the end, remember?"

"Ah, spoken like a true military man," Stringer sneered. "Always see every overture as an attack. But what if the occupants of such a craft had peaceful intentions?"

"Then why would it land out here in the middle of nowhere, instead of New York or Washington D.C.?" Penny asked.

"Another skeptic," Stringer said. "And such a comely one at that." He grinned and patted her arm condescendingly. "But your question has merit. Why indeed? Professors?"

"Yes," Zimmermann echoed.

Vogel said nothing. He merely squinted from behind his thick spectacles. "You were both part of that momentous project that started several hundred miles north of here at Los Alamos, and culminated in Alamogordo, correct?"

Zimmerman's eyebrows raised, but he gave no answer. The burly author removed a thick cigar from his pocket and continued.

"I'm referring to what was known as The Manhattan Project," he withdrew a silver lighter and popped back the lid. His thumb flicked the wheel, striking the flint and igniting the wick. "So why indeed, Miss Cartier? Why indeed?"

"So you're saying that all these strange reports have something to do with the atomic bomb?" Penny queried.

Stringer rotated the end of the cigar in the yellow flame, puffing copiously as he spoke.

"Fat Man and Little Boy. The prototype was first exploded out here. What if this attracted the attention of another world? One much more advanced than ours. Perhaps they would decide to send out an exploratory craft to gauge the degree of our civilization."

He blew out a prodigious cloud of smoke.

"Mind if l use your lighter, bud?" Deagan took out one of his own cigars.

"Certainly," Stringer handed it to Mad Dog.

Deagan quickly snapped a light for himself, then closed the lid with his thumb. He paused, as if admiring the lighter, and looked closely at the inscription. "What the hell kind of writing is this?"

"Just a gift from my time with the Spanish Loyalists," Stringer plucked the lighter from Deagan's fingers.

"You make these flying saucer sightings sound like something from that old Orson Welles radio show," Penny said.

"Actually, his theory has merit," Zimmermann stated. "We know that the residual radioactivity from the explosion will have a long, detectable afterlife."

"Which is an unfortunate and deadly by-product of the weapon," Vogel said. "I sometimes wonder if we made the right decision even exploding it."

"What the hell you talking about?" Deagan reacted. "Would you rather have seen thousands of GI's killed trying to invade Japan?"

Vogel looked at him with moist eyes.

"No, Mr. Deagan. But it's just that, I sometimes fear for our future now that we have unleashed this terrible power."

"Listen, buster," Deagan gestured with his fore and middle fingers. The big cigar was between them and spraying ashes over the top of the table. Penny quickly covered her coffee. "Just be glad we got to the finish line first. If the Japs or the Gerries woulda got the A-bomb first, they woulda used it against us in a heartbeat. And I'll bet they wouldn't have stopped, either."

"Hot damn," Stringer laughed. "I'm beginning to like your attitude more and more, Mr. Deagan. The flag, apple pie, and Doc Atlas."

"You're damn right," Deagan continued. "And I'll tell you something else. Whatever it is that's going on out here in the desert, Doc'll get to the bottom of it. You can take that to the bank."

Deagan was about to say more when he suddenly straightened up and felt his side. Penny looked at him expectantly as he reached down and removed a small black metal device from a clip on his belt. The device vibrated in his hand, and a small red light flashed on top.

"What on earth is that?" Stringer asked.

"A special radio transmitter," Deagan replied. "We all carry 'em for when Doc wants to get ahold of us." He got up from the table. "Excuse me. I gotta make a call."

As he was leaving the waitress came and brought them more coffee. "How does he know where to call?" Stringer dumped sugar into his cup.

"It's pre-arranged," Penny explained. "By the number of flashes. That particular one directed him to call the hotel, which was designated our temporary headquarters." She withdrew a cigarette and held it up. "Doc thinks of everything. He always covers all the angles."

Stringer immediately took out his lighter.

"An amazing man," he held the flame over toward Penny. "And a very formidable foe, I would imagine."

"I certainly wouldn't want to go against him," she exhaled a cloud of smoke.

"Nor would I," Zimmermann mused. "The man's mind is ingenious. Tell me, Miss. Did Dr. Atlas invent that little radio receiver?"

Penny nodded.

"But it's so small," said Vogel. "How did he do it?"

"Hendrick," Zimmerman offered, "remember at Los Alamos when we were having problems trying to figure out how to scale down the compression trigger, and Oppie called someone for consultation?"

The other man nodded, then suddenly looked surprised.

"But I thought Dr. Atlas spent the war on the front lines? I read about his exploits in the newspapers."

"Doc was on the front," Deagan returned to the table and resumed his seat. "In both theaters. He figured he could best serve out there where the action was."

"But he was constantly being called for other things, too," Penny added and then, turned to Deagan. "What's up?"

"It was Ace at the hotel," Deagan said. "Doc left a message for us. He had to fly to Ft. Worth, but he wants you, me, and Ace to meet him on the base at twenty-hundred. He should be coming in about that time in the Pegasus."

"That sounds important," Stringer pocketed his lighter again.

"Where Doc's concerned," Deagan drew heavily on his cigar, "it usually is."

The special press conference and meeting with General Roger Ramey at 8th Air Force Headquarters in Fort Worth, Texas had taken longer than Doc had anticipated. Now it was growing dark and he automatically switched to instrument guidance to maintain his heading back to Roswell. The edge of the sun was descending below the distant mountains on the horizon and Doc thought about the events of earlier that afternoon.

Ramey had taken particular care to explain to all the reporters present that the items recovered from the Roswell area crash were from a high-altitude weather balloon, not a flying saucer. The items were spread out on a carpeted floor, and Ramey and Colonel Thomas Dubose held up the shiny foil and metallic struts. "Sticks and tinfoil," he explained, used to track the balloon by radar. He then permitted some photographers to snap a few pictures. Ramey was grateful that Doc had agreed to stand silently off to the side to tacitly endorse the General's statements.

Ramey also went on radio to emphatically deny that the wreckage was from outer space. He stated that the previous report issued by the public relations officer at Roswell had been erroneous. All seemed to be going as planned until some of the photographers complained that they weren't allowed to get close enough. A second press conference was hastily scheduled, at which time some of the reporters claimed that something was amiss.

"Hey, this ain't the same stuff we saw yesterday," one of them said. "It's the old switcheroo."

Ramey denied any switching had occurred. The reporters began to ask Doc for a comment.

"Obviously, this material is from some sort of balloon," Doc said. "Other than that, I have no comment at this time."

Grumbling about an army cover-up, the men from the various newspapers began to make their trek back to their hotels to work on their stories before phoning them in. One of them grumbled that after today the story would probably fade. But Doc was sure that the current wave of hysteria would be further exacerbated by this governmental conspiracy theory that some of the reporters had espoused. But he expected no less, and told the general so.

"Misleading the press was not prudent."

"Well, dammit, Major, I can't very well say the wreckage was from a spying instrument that we're going to use to monitor the Soviets, can I?" Ramey asked heatedly.

"My only point, General," Doc had answered calmly, "is that a deliberate campaign of misinformation can, and usually does, backfire eventually."

"Well, as long as it holds together long enough for us to fashion this new bomb, I'll be satisfied. We're racing the Russians on this one, believe me. That's why this Project Mogel is so damn important. We know they're working hard on producing an atomic bomb. There'll be no stopping Stalin if he succeeds. Who knows where he'll pop up."

"Ironic that only a few years ago we considered him our ally."

"War makes strange bedfellows, doesn't it?" the General smiled. "I've no doubt that as we speak, he's trying to come up with ways to steal our designs and material. And with Oppenheimer backing out of working on the superbomb, we're at the mercy of eccentrics like Zimmerman and Vogel. You worked with them at Los Alamos, didn't you?"

"Not directly," Doc corrected. "I spent most of my time overseas."

"I know that," Ramey said. "I remember you dropping behind enemy lines and delivering back tremendous amounts of intelligence. I don't know how you were able to do it."

"My fluency in German helped And my knowledge of the European Continent. I'd traveled extensively there before the war."

The General straightened in his chair and looked Doc straight in the eye. "Major, I know what kind of man you are, and I know I couldn't be talking to a greater American. But understand this. We have to safeguard our atomic secrets at all costs. It's imperative. And I don't trust those scientific types. Not after Los Alamos. That espionage there was never cleared up to my satisfaction."

General Ramey's words kept ringing in Doc's memory as he scanned the darkened horizon. If, as the General suggested, the wreckage was nothing more than a high-altitude balloon, albeit an experimental model from Project Mogel, where did the hysteria about lights in the sky come from? And what was causing so many planes to go down? Something was definitely amiss. And before he and his companions left New Mexico, he would have to find out what it was.

Glancing at his instrument panel, Doc picked up his radio mike and began transmitting.

"Calling Roswell Army Airfield. This is Pegasus One, over." An indistinct, static laden reply came back over the radio.

Doc estimated that he was just out of radio range. He waited another few minutes, then rebroadcast. This time the reply was perfectly audible.

"Come in, Pegasus," the air traffic controller said. "We read you loud and clear. Over."

"I am approximately ninety kilometers south, southeast of your location," Doc gave his heading. "My estimated time of arrival is approximately twenty-minutes. Over."

"Roger, Pegasus," the base confirmed. "Do you have further orders? Over."

"Negative. I'll advise prior to final approach. Over."

As Doc replaced the mike he saw something flicker in the distance. A bright flash of luminescence appeared to the northwest, and then it was gone. His eyes continued to scan the velvet sky. Had he imagined it? Perhaps it was a reflection of some sort. The hazy cloud cover could create conditions ripe for that. But these explanations evaporated when the eerie light appeared again, longer this time, before vanishing. Doc adjusted his course slightly, heading for the area of the light. His strong fingers grasped the mike once again.

"Roswell tower, this is Pegasus, over."

"Pegasus, this is Roswell. Over."

"Do you show any other aircraft in the vicinity?" Doc gave his coordinates.

"Negative, Pegasus. Over." The controller's voice sounded tight and brittle.

"I'm seeing something directly ahead," Doc reported. "I've adjusted my heading to try and intercept. Over."

"Roger, Pegasus. Can you identify the other craft? Over."

"At this time it appears only as a bright yellow light in the sky." Then, before he could elaborate further, he heard his starboard engine begin to miss its cycling. Doc quickly glanced out the right window. The engine began to sputter and go out. Suddenly the port side engine quit too. With both engines out Doc gripped the yoke and tried to glide into the wind. But a horrible humming sound, like the scream of a banshee, seemed to whip through the cockpit.

"Roswell, this is Pegasus," Doc wrapped his arm around his head to shield his ears. "I'm in trouble. Both engines out. Some sort of—"

Before he could finish the glass surrounding the cockpit shattered smacking Doc's face with the impact of a sledgehammer. Reeling from the impact, Doc lowered his arm, suddenly feeling an enormous pressure engulfing his head. Placing both hands over his ears, Doc unhooked his safety harness and stumbled back into the plane. The howling pain continued, seeming to increase with each passing second. Away from the now open cockpit, the sound lessened somewhat, but Doc fell forward as the floor seemed to slant abruptly into a downward sloping angle. The fuselage began a slow roll over, and Doc suddenly knew the plane was going into a spin. A "deadman's spin" they called it. A spin from which it was non-recoverable.

The plane rolled over again, almost lazily this time, but Doc was thrown violently around like a buoy caught in an unruly surf. Grasping the seats, Doc's mighty arms pulled him upward toward the closed compartments where the emergency parachutes were stored. If he could only get one on in time, he might be able to bail out.

The plane rolled again, just as Doc grasped the storage locker handle. Ripping the metal door open, Doc thrust his hand inside and felt for the heavy canvas container. He found one.

The plane rotated again, quicker this time and Doc knew now that the centrifugal force would be tremendous. Slipping his right arm through the loop of the parachute, Doc went hand-over-hand toward the exit door. The plane's descent steepened. Bracing his powerful legs against the seats, Doc strained upward to open the door. He estimated that he had less than ninety seconds before he would hit the ground. For what seemed like an eternity the hatch would not budge. Then suddenly the door popped open, caught in the vortex and was ripped from its hinges.

The momentum violently tore Doc out of the plane, his hands reaching, searching for the straps of the parachute as the spinning fuselage suddenly began to whirl toward him from out of the darkness.

Penny, Deagan, and Ace sat at a table in the Officer's Club, but instead of drinks, only three empty cups of coffee sat in front of them. Deagan was drumming his fingers on the table and Penny looked up at him.

"What time is he supposed to get here?" she asked.

"The message said by twenty-hundred," Deagan glanced down at his watch. "Or twenty minutes ago."

"I was told that Doc and Ramey hosted another press conference, then they had a meeting afterward," Ace forced a smile as he touched Penny's hand. "Try not to worry. Doc could make a flight like that one in his sleep."

Just as she was about to answer, the post siren began an ominous wail. Uniformed pilots began getting up immediately and hurriedly rushing out of the building.

"Sounds like another alert," Deagan said.

"Maybe we'd better go check this one out," Ace's smile faded.

The lights near the twin airstrips were lighted, and they saw several P-5l's positioning for takeoff. An ambulance and two MP jeeps also began zooming toward the front gate. Deagan grabbed a soldier who was running toward one of the massive hangers.

"Hey, what's going on?"

"A plane went down southeast of here," the soldier said.

"What plane?" Penny asked. "Was it Doc's?"

The soldier stared at her momentarily, then tried to pull away from Deagan's powerful grasp.

"I dunno," the young soldier said. "Honest. Now, please, sir, let go of my arm."

Deagan released him and exchanged glances with Ace.

"Come on," Assante said. "Blanchard's billets are over there."

Finding no response at the Post Commander's Quarters, the three of them moved to the Orderly Room. A worried looking Lieutenant Colonel sat behind a large desk and spoke in hushed tones on the phone. Deagan pushed past an MP guarding the door and stopped just short of the officer's desk.

"We need some answers, bud. Where's Butchie?"

The Lt. Colonel hung up the phone and eyed Deagan nervously. "Colonel Blanchard is not currently available. I'm Lt. Colonel Hopkins. May I help you?"

"That ain't what I asked," Deagan barked.

"The Colonel's on leave. I'm the Operations Officer."

"We heard a plane went down," Ace stepped forward. "We're friends and associates of Doc Atlas."

"Was it his plane?" Penny asked.

The Lt. Colonel's mouth opened slightly, but no sound came out. Finally, he spoke. "I'm told that it was. We have a search and rescue team headed to the area at this very moment."

Deagan and Ace exchanged glances.

"Where's it at?" Ace asked. "Was there any communication from Doc?"

"He radioed that he was in trouble," Col. Hopkins licked his lips. "Then his transmission was cut off."

"We need a plane," Ace said calmly,

"Are you crazy?" Hopkins gasped. "I can't spare any planes right now. There's a storm front moving in, and we're expecting a plane load of VIP's later on tonight."

"The man asked you for a plane, bud," Deagan repeated. "And he was a lot more polite than I'm gonna be."

"You can't threaten me."

"I ain't," Deagan quickly smacked his large right fist into his open left palm. "I'm promising you."

"Look, give us anything," Ace said. "But let us go assist with the search." The Lt. Colonel lowered his eyes.

"I can't," he said. "We've got..." His voice trailed off. "We're doing everything we can at the moment."

"Please, Colonel," Penny pleaded. "Doc could be out there... hurt."

Ace had strolled over by the window and looked out. The airfield activity seemed to have slowed somewhat. "Give us one of those Sikorsky's," he suggested. "They're just sitting over there. No one's using them."

"You can fly a helicopter?" Hopkins asked.

"This guy can fly anything," Deagan said.

"This is highly irregular," the Lt. Colonel said slowly.

"Desperate times call for desperate measures, Colonel." Ace picked up the phone on the desk and held it out toward the other man. "Make the authorizing call, sir."

The Lt. Colonel hesitated slightly, then took the phone from Ace. "This is Colonel Hopkins. Get the Sikorsky ready for take off."

Penny stood next to the oval section of asphalt as the large rotors of the helicopter began whirling. Through the glass windshield she saw Ace pulling back on the stick, causing the Sikorsky to rise up almost vertically. He smiled and gave her a "thumbs-up" sign, but it did little to ease her racing heart.

What if Doc's hurt? she wondered. *Or even worse. No,* she thought. She would not allow herself to even consider that. But the thoughts kept worming their way into her consciousness like stubborn parasites. What if...

What if he's dead? And I've never even told him how I feel about him.

An MP jeep coasted by her and the soldier yelled for her to get off the airfield. Turning away, she began strolling absently toward the hangar area.

The wind had begun to pick up, and a crooked streak of lightning exploded across the western sky. The storm they'd been talking about was coming. Penny hoped that it would not hamper the rescue search. The heel of her shoe twisted in a slight pockmark in the cement and she stumbled slightly. Catching herself, Penny felt a sudden pain shoot through her ankle and went to lean against the ribbed wall of one of the large hangars in front of her. The numerals 51 were painted in black over an adjacent door. Removing her shoe, she rubbed her ankle, thinking how nice it would be for women to be able to wear comfortable shoes.

But I'll only wish for one miracle at a time, she thought. *And this one's that Doc is okay.*

The voices coming from the window distracted her from her reverie. The words came quickly, a mixture of soft sibilant sounds. What was it? She moved closer to the slightly open window. Inside she could see the beams of flashlights as forms moved stealthily in the darkness. Moving to the door, Penny's hand grasped the knob and twisted. It was not locked.

Slipping through a sliver of an opening, Penny positioned herself behind a row of lockers and removed both her high-heeled shoes. The rough cement felt cold against the soles of her feet, but she ignored it and crept forward. The flashlight beams seemed to be bouncing upward near a large military truck. She heard a grunting effort, then her eyes adjusted enough to the darkness that she could see a large box being lifted onto the rear bed of the truck. The man lifting it was the huge servant who'd helped Stringer out of the bar. Gordo, she thought, remembering the name.

"Now you're certain this will fulfill our bargain," a voice said in English. Accented English. Penny peered around a large wooden box and saw two men standing in the shadows near the truck.

"But of course, *herr doctor*," the second man said. "I assure you it will."

She recognized this man's voice without having to see his face. She'd heard it often enough pontificating in the last two days. It was D. Phillip Stringer.

"My family," the other man said. "When can I expect them?"

"Dr. Vogel," Stringer said. "We have not yet accomplished our task here. You must have patience."

"Patience!" Vogel cursed. "You hold my loved ones hostage and you speak of patience. I despise you, and all you stand for."

"Yes," Stringer watched the giant's progress as he worked the heavy metallic box back farther into the truck. "Sometimes I despise myself.."

"You speak of your family being held hostage, senõr," another man said, appearing from the side of the vehicle. "Yet my *pais* has been under the tyrannical rule of the imperialist Americans for almost half a century."

Penny saw Hector, the small chauffeur, step into sight. He was dressed in military fatigues and seemed to be holding something long and tubular in front of him.

"And now, Dr. Vogel," Stringer said. "It's time for our departure. And yours as well. Get in the truck, old man."

"What? I cannot leave," Vogel protested. "My involvement in this will be found out. You guaranteed secrecy."

Stringer's head lolled backward in a subdued, but still braying laugh.

"I lied. Now get in there, dammit, or I'll have Gordo break your legs and carry you in."

Hector moved forward and whipped the long tubular object across the scientist's temple. Vogel collapsed to his knees. Hector hit him again and Vogel fell the rest of the way.

"Careful," Stringer cautioned. "Don't leave any bloodstains."

Hector replied with something in Spanish.

Penny whirled around, trying to get back toward to the door. Something was terribly wrong here, and she knew she'd have to flag down the first MP she saw. But as she began to run she dropped one of her high-heeled shoes which she'd been carrying. It skittered across the floor and she was sure they'd heard her. Increasing her pace into an all-out run, Penny dashed forward. The door to the hangar was only a few feet away now, but she could hear voices and movements behind her. With three more steps she made it to the door and pushed it open. Just as she did this she ran into someone. The impact knocked both of them back, and she saw it was Captain Seals, the MCI officer.

"What? Miss Cartier," Seals looked at her startled.

"Oh, thank God," Penny regained her balance and pointed to the hangar. "There's some spies in there."

"Spies? What are you talking about?"

"Come on, I'll explain later. We've got to get out of here now. We need the MPs."

"I think not," Seals quickly swung his arm in a looping, overhead movement. A heavy leather sap grazed Penny's temple, but it was still enough to send her down in a heap on the sidewalk. Seals glanced around quickly, then stooped and picked up her unconscious form. A breathless D. Phillip Stringer appeared in the doorway moments later and stopped.

"Hold that damn door open for me," Seals grunted as he carried Penny inside. "Get her damn shoes."

Stringer smiled as they went past, looking down at Penny's firm neck and long, dark tresses hanging downward.

"Now that ain't any way to treat a lady," he said.

Doc wasn't sure where he was when he regained consciousness, or how long he'd been out. Because of this, he was careful not to move or show any other, outward signs that he was awake. Instead, he kept his eyes closed and let his other senses provide input. He knew he was lying on a hard surface. The ground, probably. A few feet away he heard stirring movements and someone whistling a song. A western song that he'd heard in an old Gene Autry movie: *Don't Fence Me In.* The whistler stopped and swore. Doc's nostrils detected something burning, and on his skin he could feel the heat from what he inferred was a bonfire. His wrists and ankles felt free and unbound. With slow and cautious deliberation he opened his eyes.

The yellow whirl of a campfire licked at a bloody carcass of some small animal on a rotating spit. An ancient looking metal coffee pot sat at the base of the fire on two sticks over some glowing embers. An equally ancient looking man, replete with whitish hair that had been looped back into a ponytail, hunched over the fire. When Doc sat up the old man glanced over and the light played over a set of craggy features and an enormous gray mustache.

"I was wondering ifn' you was gonna wake up sooner rather than later," the old man said. "Never thought you'd make it after the way you fell outta the sky like that, but you must be made of cast iron."

Doc said nothing. The old man shrugged and went back to his cooking tasks. Perhaps twenty feet away several horses tied to a long piece of wood weighted by several stones, snorted and stamped.

"What's your name, young fella?" the old codger asked. "You do speak English, don't ya?"

"Michael G. Atlas."

The old man seemed to consider this for a moment, but if he recognized Doc's last name, he didn't show it.

"Jack Persard. But folks 'round these parts just call me Cactus Jack. Them that knows me, that is, and they ain't but a few. You with the army or something?"

"I was during the War," Doc flexed his fingers and busily checking himself for injuries and possible broken bones. He remembered nothing of his freefall after exiting the Pegasus. "What happened to my airplane?"

"That was yours?" Cactus Jack shook his head. "Looked to be a damn fine plane at one time. Not much left of it now, though."

"How far are we from the crash site?"

"Oh, probably 'bout ten, twelve miles. Me and old Apache Joe found you out in the desert. Saw you coming down. Joe thought you was a spirit or something." He chuckled softly. "We used a lean-to to bring you here. Your head was banged up some."

Doc's fingers were already tracing an expanse of cloth that had been wound around his temples.

"Old Joe's all excited about that fancy piece of cloth you floated down to earth in," Cactus Jack said. "Says it'll make a swell tepee. He took it to the reservation. Hope that's all right with you. Thing feels like it was made out of silk."

"It is," Doc said. "And he's welcome to keep it." He stretched his arms, then his legs. Nothing felt broken or sprained, but he did have a variety of contusions and lacerations. They ranged in severity from minor to severe, but Doc didn't think that any required immediate medical attention.

"That's mighty generous of you," Cactus Jack grabbed a pair of old metal cups and handing one to Doc. "Here, have some of this." He poured a stream of dark liquid into Doe's cup, and the odor of strong coffee assailed his nostrils.

"Thank you," Doc let the coffee cool before trying a sip. "I have some friends who will probably be worried about me. Where's the nearest telephone?"

The old man laughed as he brought his own steaming cup to his lips.

"Where'd you say you was from? New York City?"

Doc nodded, even though he hadn't mentioned his origin.

"Ain't no phones out this way, that's for sure," Cactus Jack eyed Doc with an appraising squint. "You must be pretty rich to have had your own airplane. You ain't connected with any of them dadburned banks, are ya?"

"No."

"That's good," Cactus Jack said with a resounding nod of his head. "Damn bankers foreclosed on my ranch back in the Depression when times was hard. I lost everything. Settled out here in the high desert, just me, a few remaining Indians, and a couple of herds of wild mustangs." He took another sip from his cup and looked wistfully out over the bleak terrain. "I ain't complaining though. Not like I didn't see it coming."

Doc tried a small sip from his cup. The bitter liquid burned his tongue, but he showed no reaction.

"Like it?" Cactus Jack asked.

Doc made no comment, but took another drink. The old man grunted.

"We must be close to the air base," Doc looked at the sky.

"Not too far. Is that where you'll be wanting to go once we've ate?"

Again Doc did not reply. Instead he asked, "You've lived out here for a long time? Tell me, Mr. Persard, have you noticed any strange lights in the sky recently?"

"You're dern tootin' I have," Cactus Jack took a more copious swig of his dark brew. "Let me tell you, I seen some things out here lately that would curl the toes off a goat. Especially by my old spread."

"I would appreciate hearing about them," Doc allowed himself a rare smile. "And I will have some more of your coffee, please, sir."

Penny awoke to more voices. Her head felt like it had twin sledgehammers inside it banging away, and she was suddenly conscious that her hands were tied behind her back. Blinking her eyes to try and focus them, she saw Professor Vogel lying a few feet away from her. He was also bound, and a streak of dried blood had wormed its way down the center of his forehead. They were outside, but under some sort of porch roof. Penny could see a lighted ranch-style house a few hundred feet away on a macadamized road. The structure above them seemed to be connected to a larger, barn-like building. The sky was a myriad of bright stars sprinkled over black velvet.

Penny tried to rouse Vogel by wiggling closer to him and nudging the unconscious scientist with her shoeless foot. But all this elicited was a few faint moans.

They must have really clocked him good, she thought.

Turning her attention to the immediate area around her, she began looking for something she could use to free herself. The sharp edge of a broken bottle, or perhaps a loose nail. *That was what they always used in the movies, wasn't it?* She thought. But nothing was available. Her thoughts suddenly turned to Doc and she wondered if Deagan and Ace had found him.

Oh, God, I hope so. At least please let him be alive and safe.

"No, I'll take my share now," a voice said from inside the barn.

Another voice spoke up. Penny couldn't quite understand the words, but she was sure it belonged to Stringer.

"Look, comrade," the first man said. The words were redolent of contempt. "I've fulfilled more than my part of the bargain. And after helping you sneak the box off the base tonight, there's no way I can possibly go back. So if you don't mind, I'll take my money and be off to Mexico." She recognized the speaker now. It was Captain Rod Seals, from MCI. The creep who'd belted her with that blackjack.

"Spoken like a true capitalist," Stringer said. "What did you say your job was in the War? A rear echelon file clerk?"

"Ask your Red friends. That's where they recruited me."

Stringer laughed. "A small price to pay, I suppose. All right, you'll get your money tonight, but only after we load the U-235 and tie up a few loose ends."

U-235 Uranium! Thought Penny. That was the stuff they'd used to build the atomic bomb. And Seals had called Stringer "comrade." Suddenly it all made sense. Stringer writing about fighting with the Loyalists during the Spanish Civil War. The Loyalists had received help from the Soviet Union. She remembered Deagan questioning the inscription on Stringer's Zippo lighter. At the time it had looked familiar to her, but she couldn't place it. But now she'd bet that it was written in Russian.

"Senõr Stringer," a new voice said. "We have little time to position the *macqina.*"

It sounded like the diminutive chauffeur.

Stringer replied in Spanish.

"Speak in English," Seals said. "So I know what you're saying." Stringer laughed again.

"And you're planning on retiring to Mexico?" he spoke again in Spanish to Hector.

"Mr. Persard, have you noticed any strange lights in the sky recently?"

"What was that?" Seals asked.

"He said you are a typical capitalist opportunist," Hector said in his heavily accented English. "A man who betrays his country for thirty pieces of silver."

"Oh yeah! Well if I'm a Judas, what does that make you? Aren't you selling out too?"

"I am a Puerto Ricano," Hector shouted back. "My country will soon be free of your Yankee imperialism. With the help of others, who are the true enemies of fascism, we will strike the fascists of your government until you give us our freedom. *Libertad o muerte.*"

"You're living in a fool's paradise, greaseball, if you think the Soviets give a damn about your tiny little island in the sun," Seals said. "This was all about what's in that lead box. Now give me that briefcase you showed me earlier."

"You think you can insult me and get away with it, gringo?" Hector yelled. "Gordo!"

Penny closed her eyes and wished that she could close out the terrible screams that filtered out of the window from the barn. Then suddenly, the noises stopped after a hideous sounding crack.

"I wish he hadn't done that yet," Stringer said. "Having a front page murder of a military officer is going to attract attention."

"As if the theft of the uranium will not?" Hector sneered. "Come, *mi compadre.* We will bury him out on the *deseirto* once we have shot down the plane carrying the American Generales and el Secretario."

"Have Gordo load the uranium onto the plane, and tell your men to turn on the runway lights as soon as I give the signal," Stringer directed. "I want Dimitri to be able to take off in our plane as soon as they scramble their Mustangs. One plane among many. It will be the perfect subterfuge for us."

Shoot down? Penny thought. She renewed her efforts to free herself, working her wrists raw straining against the fight ropes.

Vogel groaned again. His head moved slightly. He seemed to be waking up. After trying unsuccessfully to get up, Penny spoke gently to him, explaining that they were both being held captive.

"Where are we?" he asked weakly.

"I'm not sure. It seems to he someplace away from the base. Stringer seems to be setting up some sort of gun to shoot down a plane."

"Oh no, we are at his ranch," Vogel realized. "Secretary Forestall and a group of generals were due to arrive tonight. He's going to use the vortex cannon. They are probably already tracking them on Stringer's radar device."

"They've got radar here?" Penny asked. "And what's that other thing you mentioned?"

Vogel grimaced in pain as be attempted to roll on his side to look at her. "It's a weapon devised by the Nazis. The Soviets recovered it from the German vortex technology research facility at the end of the War. It shoots concentrated sound waves capable of shattering glass and stopping engines. That's what they've been using to shoot down all the planes. It has some kind of high intensity light ray attached to it that acts as a long range sighting device. The light is filtered and reflects off the low altitude clouds causing the bright flashes that everyone's been seeing."

"You knew all about this?" she accused. "And you didn't say anything?"

"I know you must think me terrible. But you must understand. They're holding my family hostage. They told me if I helped them obtain enough enriched uranium to develop the plutonium necessary to build their own bomb…"

"They'd release your family" Penny finished. "But does that justify the deaths of all those innocent pilots?"

"Actually, you might try thinking of it in more metaphorical terms," D. Phillip Stringer said, rounding the corner. "You can't make an omelet without breaking a few eggs, can you?"

Penny scowled at the braying laugh that followed.

"Professor," Stringer squatted down next to the bound scientist and checking his ropes. "There's been a change in plans. The good part is that you're going to see your loved ones a bit sooner than you anticipated." He grinned sardonically. "But you're going to have to take a long plane ride with us first."

Vogel began a series of low sounding sobs.

"What about me?" Penny asked.

Stringer clucked, feigning sympathy.

"You present something of a problem, my dear," he swung over to test the knots on the ropes securing her also. "Your knowledge of nuclear physics is probably a bit lacking for you to accompany us, and I've no real need for a barefoot contessa. But," Stringer stood up, "I'm sure Hector will tell Gordo to make it quicker with you than he did with our late Captain. And very pretty wildflowers do tend to grow on unmarked graves out here."

"So you used that vortex ray thing to shoot down Doc's plane?" It was more of an accusation than a question.

"I couldn't afford to have your meddlesome hero blundering about now, could I?" Stringer replied. "Even though I'm sure he would have gotten nowhere."

Penny swore at him as he walked away. *If only Doc were here*, she thought. But she wasn't even sure if Doc was alive.

"Professor, we have to try to get loose," she said in a low voice. "Is there anything around you that we can use?"

"It's hopeless," Vogel said. "Do you hear that?" The sound of a heavy truck pulling something equally heavy became audible. "That's the vortex cannon. They're setting it up. They've won. There's nothing we can do now."

Penny swung her leg over and kicked him.

"Look for something sharp, dammit. Wait, what about your glasses?"

"My glasses? They must have taken them from me. But wait, I may have a spare pair in my pocket."

Penny wiggled over next to him then rolled onto her side so her hands could explore his coat. The ropes had been tied so tightly that her hands felt numb. But still she worked to feel the scientist's coat. Her fingers traced over something oval. With quiet desperation Penny tore at Vogel's lapels, reaching and straining until finally she felt the smoothness of the glass between her fingertips. Withdrawing the spectacles carefully, she clutched them under her and rolled over them several times. Finally, through tedious positioning and pressing, she managed to cause one of the lenses to break. Gripping the shards she went to work on the ropes. The broken glass cut into her flesh and soon the fragment of glass was slipping from between her blood-covered digits. Several times she thought about stopping, but she considered the alternative and kept going.

"How are your hands, Miss?" Vogel asked quietly.

"I'm not so sure I'll be able to type out this story," Penny said between grunts of effort. "But I think I may be getting somewhere."

With a few more attempts, Penny sawed through the rope. Suddenly the drone of a large airplane became faintly audible.

"That must be the plane with the generals and the Secretary," Vogel said. "They were flying up from Fort Worth. You've got to get behind shelter. Even on the ground, being too close to the ray without protective equipment will incapacitate you."

"Incapacitate? How?"

"Nausea, vertigo ... Prolonged exposure causes rupture of the small blood vessels and organs. Eventually heart failure and death."

"Swell. Come on, professor, roll over and I'll cut you loose."

"It's too late for me now, Miss. Save yourself. Go. Run. Hide in the desert."

Realizing that Vogel was a lost cause, Penny got to her feet and ran around the corner. A large open barn door yawned before her like the maw of a huge inert creature. The barn was massive, extending at least fifty feet. Above her dim lights burned from a series of suspended light bulbs, washing over a horribly broken and twisted body. It was Captain Seals.

Putting her horror aside, Penny knelt by the body to see if he had a weapon or perhaps some car keys. The dead man's eyes seemed to stare up at her from his head's unnaturally twisted position. Trying to put the stinging from her lacerated fingers aside, Penny quickly went about her task, finding what appeared to feel like a set of keys in his right front pants pocket. Struggling to force her hand inside, she felt the ragged ends of her fingers brush the flat metal. Working her hand in deeper, she was finally able to snare the keys and pull them out. But just as she did so, an engine at the far end of the barn seemed to rumble to life. Twin beams of headlights switched on, and the lights enveloped her. Standing quickly, Penny turned to run into the fading shadows, but she smacked into someone. Two gloved hands grabbed her wrists, and as she glanced up she saw a long, white slate of a face with two large, dark oval eyes glaring down at her. Some kind of strange looking metallic helmet flared out from the strange head, and secured into a metallic collar set over a dark green suit. She fought unsuccessfully to free herself of the thing's grasp, when suddenly the entire area was illuminated by a powerful burst of white light.

For the third time Deagan and Assante picked through the wreckage of the Pegasus. The plane had hit the desert floor with tremendous force, breaking apart like a shattered bottle and scattering debris over several hundred yards. With so little left of the fuselage, they felt certain that had Doc survived he would have been in the vicinity. They hurried back to the helicopter and got inside. Both men had grim expressions on their faces as the large overhead rotor began its initial twirling.

"Dammit, where could he be?" Deagan uttered as the copter began to lift off.

"I think we have enough fuel to circle the area a few more times," Ace said. "Perhaps he was thrown clear or he wandered off."

"I don't know, Ace," Deagan's eyes welled with tears. "I think if Doc was alive, he woulda found some way to signal us already."

"Still we're not giving up until we're sure."

"You're damn right," Deagan surreptitiously wiped at his cheeks. Then, as he looked in the distance his eyes popped open. Quickly grabbing Assante's arm in an iron grip with his left hand, he pointed with the other. "Ace look over there. Is that what I think it is?"

Ace's eyes scanned the darkened horizon and saw the bright star-like light slowly floating downward and he grinned broadly.

"Looks like a halo flare to me," he said.

The big truck began rolling forward toward Penny and her captor. As she struggled she saw another long, white slated face with slanted oval eyes through the windshield. The gloved hands that gripped her wrists felt like rubber, and she was able to pull one of her wrists, now slick with blood, free. Lashing out with her foot, she aimed a kick at the man's shins but her toes glanced off. She suddenly felt herself being twisted down into the dirt as the front bumper of the truck continued to come at her. The tires stopped about three feet from her and the driver got out. His hands went to his face and began a twisting motion. Suddenly the white face rotated to the side and snapped off like a diver's helmet. The man said something foreign sounding and the one standing over her lifted his arms in a shrug. Reaching back inside the truck, the driver's gloved hand reappeared holding a large barreled revolver. He stepped down from and walked over to Penny.

The man spoke again, and this time Penny recognized it as Spanish. Very rapid Spanish.

"Who are you?" she asked.

The two men exchanged glances and the one holding the pistol shrugged again. He gripped the weapon with both hands and pointed it directly at Penny's face. Her hands covered her eyes. There was no mistaking the intention that was evident on the man's dark visage.

Suddenly the man's evil smile turned into a grimace as the point of a projectile pushed out the front of his rubberized suit. Seconds later Penny heard a clopping sound that sounded like horse's hooves. The man holding the pistol slumped forward and the second man bent quickly to retrieve the gun. But as he did so Penny saw a sight that she would never forget. Two men on horseback riding flat-out toward the barn. One was an old cowboy and the other was Doc. He was holding a long bow beside the horse's flaring nostrils.

The pistol in the cowboy's hand flashed and the second man lurched back against the truck's front bumper, a bloody hole in the side of the green suit. He straightened slightly and began reaching for his comrade's pistol, but Penny pushed his arm away. The man smacked her with his gloved fist, splitting her lip open. The horses reigned in about twenty feet away and the gun in the old cowboy's hand flashed again.

"Hey, varmint," he yelled. "Looks like you could use a lesson in manners."

Doc leaped from his horse and ran forward, sweeping Penny up in his arms. Tears streamed down her face as she felt his embrace.

"Oh, darling you're alive," she gasped.

"Yes. Thanks to Cactus Jack. And you? Are you injured?"

"I'll survive. But you've got to stop them. Stringer's a Communist spy and they've got stolen uranium. And there's some kind of sound cannon that they're going to use to shoot down a military plane."

Doc nodded as she spoke and turned to the old cowboy.

"Jack, watch our flank."

The old man dismounted and nodded.

"It'll be a pleasure, pardner."

Doc pried the pistol from the dead man's fingers and immediately checked its cylinder. He then handed the weapon to Cactus Jack and withdrew another arrow from the leather quiver.

"He's damn good with that thing," Cactus Jack said. "Must have some Injun blood in him somewheres."

Penny couldn't help but smile, despite the dire circumstances. She watched as Doc crept around to the side of the barn and fitted the arrow in the bow.

"Please be careful," she cautioned, but doubted that Doc heard her. She felt the old cowboy pulling her toward the shadows of the building.

Doc saw a group of four men loading something into a twin engine Cessna approximately fifty yards to the south on what appeared to be a small dirt airstrip. One of the men appeared to be a giant. The pilot was out rotating the propellers as the other three lifted the box inside. Perhaps thirty feet to his right Doc saw three other men sitting around a large truck. A huge cone-shaped device protruded from the bed of the vehicle. The cone was aimed skyward and seemed to be glowing with some sort of eerie red light. A fourth man sat behind a metallic shield as he looked up through some sort of viewfinder. His gloved left hand was on a throttle and his right was wrapped around a trigger assembly. A beam shot skyward and the cone began an incremental thrumming sound. Doc ran back to the fallen men in the green suit and ripped the helmet off the ground. Slipping it on, he ran around the side of the barn and pulled back the bow string.

The first arrow flew straight into the right side of the man holding the trigger. He lurched backward in an arc, screaming silently inside his oversized helmet. One of the men on the ground looked up as the gunner fell, then glanced over to see Doc running toward them. This second man reached immediately to signal the others, and then hopped up to man the vortex cannon.

Still on the run, Doc strung another arrow and fired. This arrow met its mark too, striking the second would-be gunner squarely in the chest. He slumped to the ground and before the others could react, Doc was upon them. Lashing up with a tremendous kick, Doc felled one of the remaining men, then whirled striking the other with a powerful backhand. Both men crumbled like clay pigeons and Doc hopped up to the controls of the sonic weapon. Suddenly he heard the sounds of gunfire behind him, coming from the barn. It only took Doc a few scant seconds to locate and set the safety on the weapon. Then he turned his attention back to Penny and Cactus Jack. A group of four men were advancing on the barn firing rifles as they went. Doc jumped from his position, pulled out three arrows and jammed them into the red dirt. He twisted off the helmet and tossed it down. He nocked the first arrow, raised the bow and fired. It soared, striking one of the riflemen in the neck. The man dropped instantly. Doc reached down and grabbed a second arrow, but before he could string it he was hit across the back with what felt like a two-by-four.

Rolling forward to minimize the impact, Doc swiftly regained his footing. But just as he did so, the huge Gordo swung the thick board again, striking Doc's left shoulder. Once more Doc rolled with the blow as the white hot searing pain shot through his arm. Gordo swung a foot up with surprising agility for a man of his size. But Doc twisted slightly causing the kick to miss its mark. Snaring the giant's leg, Doc rose up from his crouch and pushed.

Gordo lurched backward, but recovered immediately with an almost ursine grace. He grunted and gripped the board with both of his ham-sized hands, as if he were holding a baseball bat.

The two combatants circled each other warily. Doc held his arms slightly elevated, ready to ward off another blow. Gordo's eyes flashed moments before he lashed out allowing Doc to avoid the crushing swing by a fraction of an inch. As the board sailed past, Doc encircled the giant's forearms with his right arm.

Pivoting, Doc attempted to shift his weight to his left, but he realized too late that he'd underestimated Gordo's substantial mass. The bigger man stamped down with his right foot, negating Doc's attempted throw. Rearing backwards, Gordo whipped Doc's body into the side of the truck with a resounding thump. The impact was cushioned by the iron musculature of Doc's mighty back, but he was still momentarily stunned. The Golden Avenger felt his grip on the giant's forearm slipping. Reaching out, Doc managed to grab the end of the board, but Gordo transferred his pull downward and snapped the board loose. Doc felt the sting of slivers of wood embedding themselves deeply into his palm.

Raising the board above his head, Gordo lurched forward delivering a forceful stroke, but Doc swiftly leaped to the side. The board struck the metal fender of the truck and bounced upward. Seizing this opportunity, Doc brought his right foot up with stunning force striking the giant's chest. He then moved to the big man's left and delivered a combination of powerful punches. Gordo seemed unaffected, and he tried to swing the board around at Doc's head. Doc leaned back, away from the arc of the swing, then stepped forward again, smashing a powerful left into the giant's face.

The end of the board skittered across the red dirt as Doc followed up with another series of incredibly rapid punches to Gordo's head.

Dropping the board, Gordo lurched forward and wrapped his arms around Doc, sealing him in a powerful bear hug. Leaning backward, Gordo attempted to apply bone shattering pressure, but Doc shoved with his feet sending them both down in a heap.

As they struck the ground, Gordo's hold was momentarily broken and Doc quickly tried to regain his footing, knowing that the giant outweighed him by at least a hundred pounds. But as he rose, the huge hands snared his head and neck. Gordo grunted attempting to apply the same death lock he'd used earlier to break the neck of the army officer.

Doc's powerful hands grasped the giant's wrists. Twisting, both men struggled on their knees, their breaths coming in rasping gasps, each knowing that the battle was nearing its climax.

Doc grimaced as he braced his powerful neck, staving off the fatal twisting motion that the giant sought to apply. Slowly, inexorably, Doc managed to pull Gordo's huge right hand away. Still gripping the other wrist, Doc managed to pry that one from around his neck. Rising, Doc held the bigger man's arms outstretched. The gleam in Gordo's eyes foretold defeat as Doc twisted the bigger man to the ground and managed to encircle his neck. But the giant made one last ditch effort to throw Doc down. The twisting motion was almost successful, but the Golden Avenger swung his legs in front of Gordo and, still maintaining the iron grip on the big man's neck, flipped him over on his back. Gordo fell with an enormous plopping sound. He attempted to get to his feet, but saw only stars as Doc's fist smashed into his jaw.

Glancing upward, Doc looked in horror as the remaining riflemen were closing in on the barn. A burst of flame shot from one of the barrels into the open doorway. Doc looked quickly for his bow, but saw that it had been crushed during his battle with the giant. Then, just as he was contemplating a suicide charge, he heard the syncopated rhythm of a helicopter approaching. He reached in his pocket for his final halo flare and fired it in a trajectory over the barn. After the initial brightness faded, the slow parachuted descent of the illumination lit up the area. Doc heard a loud whooping yell, followed by the staccato burst of machine gun fire. Seconds later the Sikorsky helicopter swooped in a downward arc, with Ace Assante at the controls and Mad Dog Deagan hanging out the other side of the chopper firing a Thompson submachine gun. Doc felt a surge of relief as the remaining riflemen advancing on the barn fell. He waved at his passing friends but was doubtful that they even saw him.

Suddenly the helicopter's rotors were replaced by another sound. Twin propellers. Doc remembered the Cessna and Penelope's statement that Stringer had stolen some enriched uranium. Glancing to his right, Doc saw the Cessna already beginning its takeoff down the red dirt airstrip.

Picking up the discarded helmet, Doc slipped it on as he leaped aboard the truck. Doc swiveled the base of the vortex cannon toward the direction of the ascending plane. The cannon vibrated beneath him. Gripping the throttle, he adjusted it to a low frequency setting, sighted through the viewfinder, and gripped the trigger. A pinpoint of brightly colored red light seemed to dot the Cessna's starboard wing. Doc squeezed the trigger and the plane's engine immediately sputtered and faded. This occurred just as the Cessna was lifting off into the wind, and the small plane canted downward, the wingtip brushing the ground, sending off a burst of sparks. The wing tore away from the fuselage with savage force, sending the plane into a pell-mell rotation, bouncing on the ground twice before bursting into a flaming inferno.

The Sikorsky helicopter swung over the burning wreckage, Deagan still hanging halfway out of the glass enclosure. It hovered about fifty feet in the air.

Stripping off the helmet, Doc glanced back to see Penny and Cactus Jack emerging from the barn. The old cowboy methodically went over to each of the fallen riflemen and kicked them. Penny rushed to Doc and he put one arm around her.

"Thank God you're safe," she said.

Doc squeezed her gently, his right palm leaving a bloody imprint on her arm.

"Was Stringer in that plane?" Penny asked.

"I assume he was," Doc said. "I saw him loading a metal box on it earlier."

"That must have been the uranium," she guessed. "At least we won't have to worry about that madman Stalin getting the Bomb."

"For now. But I fear it's only a matter of time now that the atomic genie has been let out of the bottle."

"All of them sidewinders is down for the count," Cactus Jack came up to them. "Say, you look like you been wrestling with a mountain lion yourself."

"Perhaps a grizzly bear would be a more appropriate metaphor," Doc nodded his head over toward the fallen giant.

"You guys arrived just like the Lone Ranger and Tonto," Penny said. "But how did you know where to find us?"

"All the credit goes to Mr. Persard," Doc smiled. "He was aware of the strange goings on here, and told me. I realized that it was most probably connected to the sabotage of the planes, especially after they shot down the Pegasus."

"Yes siree," the old cowboy chuckled. "This here spread used to be mine, Miss. And I guess I never did lose my knack for hiding out in them fading shadows 'round here. Saw that old bearded guy Stringer bringing in all kinds of equipment and illegal aliens. Figured he was up to something."

"Well, you certainly saved my bacon, pardner," Penny extended her hand toward Cactus Jack.

The old cowboy grinned as they shook.

"Well, shucks, it was my pleasure, ma'am."

"I guess I'm supposed to say, 'smile when you say that,' right?" Penny asked.

As the big military DC-9 transport plane taxied to the end of Roswell Army Air Field in preparation for takeoff, Doc and Company fastened their seat belts. Penny twisted around slightly so she could look out the window.

"I don't know about the rest of you, but I'm sure not going to miss this place," she said.

"Oh, I don't know," Deagan said. "It brought back a lot of old memories, right Ace?"

"Yes, and not all of them good, either," Assante leaned forward resting his hands on his cane as his eyes swept around the massive fuselage compartment. "You know, Doc, this is almost as roomy as the old B-19's I used to fly. We ought to consider getting one of these to replace the Pegasus. We could go anywhere in the world then."

"It's something that I've been contemplating for some time, Ace," Doc admitted. "We'll have to look into it when we get back to New York."

"Hey, Doc," Deagan said. "Do you think old Cactus Jack will take you up on your offer to buy back his ranch for him?"

Penny glanced at Doc.

"You offered to do that for him?" she asked.

"Yes," Doc said. "After all, he did save my life, and yours as well."

"Hey, I'm not arguing," she clarified. "It's just that he seemed like such a strange character."

"Just like some of them in your books, huh?" Deagan said.

"Actually, he already declined my offer," Doc said. "He told me that the life he's established out on the plains suits him at this particular time. But he is interested in opening a dude ranch in the area and might be in need of some financing. He intends to call it the Desert Shadows Rancho Mirage. I told him the offer stands indefinitely."

"Cactus Jack," Deagan said. "What a guy. As eccentric as they come."

"Actually, he reminds me of you," Ace said. "Too long under the hot sun to think straight."

"Oh yeah, wise guy?" Deagan shot back. "Well, just whose idea was it to commandeer that helicopter that saved the day?"

"Why, I believe it was mine," Ace answered.

"Yours! We'd still be debating with that blown up butterbean officer if it wasn't for me." He smacked his huge right fist into his open left palm. "And if I hadn't had the presence of mind to grab that Tommy gun…"

Before the exchange could continue, the propellers increased their speed and the plane began to taxi down the runway.

"See, even the pilots are anxious to get us back to New York," Penny pointedout. "They're probably afraid they'll have to listen to you two argue all the way there." She turned to Doc. "Darling, do you think we've heard the last of this Roswell flying saucer business at least?"

Doc considered the question for a moment as they all felt the plane rising from the runway.

"Sometimes legends take a long time to die," he smiled. "And I have a hunch that this particular one will persist for a long time to come."

THE END

THE GREEN DEATH

February 12, 1948
Somewhere in northern Brazil, along a remote tributary to the Amazon River

Maku watched through the trees as the *mapinguari* came again, followed by the army of white devil men. He had only been a child when they first appeared a little over three years ago, advancing behind a web of fire. His father and the other warriors moved to meet the advance as the white men crashed through the burning jungle in their giant rolling, metal monsters and strode boldly into the camp ... Their strange spears spitting fire and death ... Maku remembered seeing his father and some of the other tribal elders fall ... The shaman yelling for everyone to run for the forest as he tossed handfuls of holy dirt toward the advancing monster ... Maku's mother grabbing him, pulling him toward the trees ... He looked back and saw the fire sticks spitting more death and destruction. When those who had run finally returned hours later, they found many dead, and many more missing.

The white devils returned several times over the intervening months. Never with a regular pattern but always with the *mapinguari*. How had these white men mastered the *mapinguari*, the huge man-monster and spirit of the forest? Their power was great. Greater even than the shaman's. Even he was helpless before them. He spoke in hushed tones around the secretive fires in the forest about how a hero was needed to combat these masters of evil.

"Fear not, for one day such a man will come," the shaman had said. "He will be pure of spirit and help us fight the evil white demons and the *mapinguari*."

Maku held on to this belief even through the darkest of days. Time and the periodic raids continued. Today's raid had taken them completely by surprise. The warmth of the sun had barely begun to creep down through the trees and the *mapinguari* appeared at one end of the camp throwing fire from his arms. When they ran, the white devils appeared at the other end and began their customary pillaging, shooting some, capturing many others. Maku had barely made it to the safety of the trees when glancing back, he saw one of them strike down the shaman. He heard his mother's screams and then she disappeared too, leaving him alone. Certain the *mapinguari* and death were right behind him, he ran with all his strength toward the river and there he found what he knew was a sign: a canoe. He got in and began paddling. Farther down the river he saw an enormous canoe filled with white devils shouting and yelling. They were herding many of his tribe into the bottom of the vessel. Maku paddled into a section of overgrown roots and waited. Finally, the big canoe began making a loud noise and turned, going up-river. Maku waited until the big canoe had passed, then began to follow at a safe distance, keeping close to shore. He didn't know where they were going, but he would follow. He would follow them to the edge of the world

New York City
The Empire State Building
Doc Atlas Headquarters

The short, squat man walked past O'Bannion, the doorman at the Broadway entrance of the Empire State Building. O'Bannion was used to Doc Atlas and his crew coming and going at all hours, normally they were friendly and good natured. But today the short man looked very dour and preoccupied. Nevertheless, O'Bannion smiled and said, "Good morning, Mr. Deagan."

Deagan merely nodded. His big hand reached out and pulled the door open so quickly O'Bannion was afraid it would pop off the steel hinges.

O'Bannion knew Deagan and the rest of the crew normally used this entrance because it was closer to the special elevator that was the only access to the headquarters and living quarters of Doc Atlas on the 86th floor.

Something bad must be eating him, O'Bannion thought as Deagan disappeared inside. Something real bad.

Deagan went to the elevator on the far side of the entrance. It had no button to press, only a slot into which he inserted a key. The doors opened and he got in and pressed the button. This particular elevator was closed to public use and went directly to Doc Atlas' office and headquarters. Deagan

"Fear not, for one day such a man will come."

heaved a sigh and lowered his head, waiting as the elevator car ascended. It came to a quick stop and the doors opened. Deagan started out, but suddenly stopped when he noticed someone in front of him. His head shot up and he saw Polly St. Clair, Doc's chief secretary and head of his office staff. She was also Deagan's girlfriend. Deagan looked at the lighted display and saw that the car had stopped at the 85th floor, where the secretarial pool was located. His mouth turned upward into a smile. Whenever he saw Polly he felt like he'd just picked a bouquet of four leaf clovers.

"Hiya, Sweetie," he pursed his lips as he reached out to kiss her.

Polly leaned back and held up her hand. "Hold your horses, buster." She pointed to the camera lens in the upper right corner of the elevator car. "What would Doc and Ace say if they saw us kissing in the elevator?"

Deagan grimaced because he knew she was right. There was a special alarm system that was activated every time someone used the elevator and Doc or someone upstairs was usually watching on the closed circuit television monitor. "Ah, Doc wouldn't say nothing. He seldom does. And as far as that shyster, Ace, it's nine o'clock in the morning. He probably is just rolling over in bed."

"Nope, you're wrong," Polly said. "He's upstairs. So is Penny. She brought over a bunch of newspaper files Doc wanted."

"Her I can understand, but him ..." He took off his hat and held it upward blocking their faces from the camera's view. Then he pursed his lips again. "Let's give him something to look at. How about that smooch?"

Polly looked at him, canted her head, then gave him a quick kiss, followed by a light tap with her palm on his cheek.

"What was that for?"

"Just because, you big lug," she smiled getting in the elevator and waiting for the doors to close. "What are you doing here? I thought they invited you down to Washington to lecture on military combat tactics?"

"I had to cancel." Deagan frowned and shoved his hat back on his head. "I wanted to talk to Doc about something. A favor."

Polly looked at him and canted her head. "Oh oh, I think he's got something planned. He had me look up a bunch of newspaper clippings from the newspaper office this morning."

Deagan felt a sinking feeling. "Aww, shucks. That'd be my luck all right."

The doors opened again and they stepped out in the hallway that led to Doc's living quarters. Before they got to the door it opened and a handsome face, a dead ringer for Errol Flynn's, peered out between the door and jamb with an ear-to-ear grin.

"Shame, shame, shame," Ace Assante rubbed his thumb over his forefinger. "Kissing in the elevator like two school kids."

Polly blushed and gave Deagan a rueful, I told you so look.

"Ah, just like a typical shyster," Deagan said. "Always putting your nose in where it shouldn't be."

Ace held the door for Polly, who entered first then quickly removed his hand as Deagan got there. As quick as a panther, Deagan reached up and grabbed it, the frown still etched on his face. "Where's Doc?"

Assante's eyebrows rose. He obviously noticed that his good friend was preoccupied and wasn't in the mood for their constant, yet good natured ribbing.

"He's in the library, I believe," Ace replied.

Beyond him Deagan could see Penelope Cartier, the stunningly beautiful brunette who was a renowned reporter for the *New York Times* as well as Doc's girlfriend.

If she was here something must be up, Deagan thought. He hoped he'd be able to talk to Doc and ask that favor before the man decided to go off gallivanting on some adventure at the far corners of the earth.

"Hey, Mad Dog," Penny greeted, "I thought you were in Washington D.C.?"

"I was. Came back early."

Penny shot a quick look at Polly who shook her head slightly. Penny shrugged and reached into her purse and withdrew a pack of cigarettes. Ace saw her and took out his own pack, quickly holding it toward her so that several smokes extended outward.

"I think we smoke the same brand," he smiled.

Penny smiled back and reached for one. Suddenly the door from the inner office opened abruptly and Doc Atlas strode in. He was a magnificently proportioned man over six feet with blond hair and amber colored eyes. His high cheekbones and handsome features gave his face a regal cast.

"I'd prefer that you'd abstain from any tobacco usage at this time," he glanced toward Ace and Penny. "I should like to have a meeting in the library." He turned to Polly and handed her a stack of newspaper clippings. "Would you be sure these get delivered back to the morgue at the *Times*?"

Polly took the clippings and nodded. As she turned she smiled at Deagan.

"Doc, I wonder if I could talk to you privately first," Deagan interrupted.

Doc Atlas stopped and looked at him, then said, "Certainly." He turned and walked toward his private office.

Penny and Ace exchanged glances. She withdrew one of the cigarettes from his pack and held it to her lips.

Ace took one also and flipped open his lighter. "I guess we do have time for a smoke after all." He held the flame to the tip of hers.

"What's eating Mad Dog?" Penny sucked in some of the tobacco smoke. "Any idea?"

Ace lighted his own smoke and shook his head. "Whatever it is, he looked like he was rather upset."

Inside his office Doc watched as Deagan lowered himself slowly into the leather chair in front of the big mahogany desk. The desk had belonged to Doc's father and Doc usually sat behind it to formally receive visitors and clients. The two men sat in silence, neither apparently wanting to begin. Deagan wrung his big hands together with a pained expression on his face.

"You seem preoccupied, Thomas," Doc remarked. "Is something troubling you?"

Deagan sighed. "Doc, I feel like a heel coming here to ask you a favor, but this is really important."

Doc stared at Deagan, not speaking, which was his custom.

Deagan blew out a heavy breath. "Aww, Doc I'm embarrassed." He stopped.

Doc waited, still not saying anything.

Deagan compressed his lips. "As you know, I got no reason to complain. I get a good pension from the army, and I've been picking up a bunch of speaking engagements the past couple of years. That brings in a lot of extra dough."

Doc's amber colored eyes focused on his friend.

"I just put a down payment on a sweet little place on Long Island," Deagan continued, "just in case one of these days Polly and me decide to settle down." He wrung his hands again.

Doc finally spoke. "Thomas, you're being rather evasive. I do have an urgent matter pending so it would be better if you got to your point."

"Yeah, Doc, sure." He made self-conscious clucking sound. "You see, I'm kinda short of cash right now, and something came up. I gotta go to South America real quick. To help somebody out."

"Does this have to do with your friend from the military, Reese Manning?"

Deagan looked shocked. "Yeah, how'd you know?"

Doc didn't answer.

"Doc, you remember how that Reese saved my bacon in the War?" His face took on a pained expression. "And how he lost his right hand doing it."

Doc nodded.

"Well, Reese sent me a telegram from someplace down in Brazil," Deagan clucked again. "He didn't say too much. Just asked if I could shoot down there right away and help him out. He didn't come right out and say so, but he's gotta be in some kind of a jam." He looked at his big shoes, then back to Doc. "I was gonna ask you for a loan."

"Would that be Mancopa, Brazil?" Doc inquired.

Deagan did a double take. "You know, I think it was something like that."

"Then it won't be necessary for me to loan you any money, Thomas. I was about to ask you and Ace to accompany me down to Brazil regarding another pressing matter. It most likely dovetails with Manning's request as well."

"Huh? It does?"

"Yes." Doc opened a file on his desk and removed a photograph which he handed across the desk to Deagan.

"Is this Mickey Vankeller?" Deagan asked.

Doc nodded again. "As I'm sure you know, he disappeared three weeks ago somewhere in the Brazilian rainforest. I believe your friend Manning was sent down there to look for him."

"Huh? By who?"

"By Mickey Vankeller's father. He called me this morning. It seems he does not feel that Manning is making sufficient progress."

Deagan nodded. "Yeah, it makes sense. Since he was forced out of the army Reese's been making his living as a soldier of fortune. So I guess Vankeller's old man hired him to go down there to nose around and see if he could find him, huh?"

"Mr. Vankeller, Mickey's father, was a close friend of my father's," Doc explained. "He's made the same request of me. I had Ace filing our flight plans earlier. I was under the assumption that you would want to make the trip as well."

Deagan's face lit up. "Gosh, that would be swell. Sorta like killing two birds with one stone, so to speak." He stood up and extended his hand across the desk. "Thanks, Doc."

Doc shook his friend's hand and stood. "Thank me later. I have a feeling that this trip may be fraught with unforeseen dangers."

He walked toward the door. Deagan followed.

Doc put his hand on the knob, but stopped. "And I still have to tell Penelope that she will not be able to accompany us."

Deagan emitted a low whistle and a grin. "She ain't gonna like that."

Penny lit up her cigarette, took a long drag, and blew the cloud of smoke up toward the camera lens on the ceiling of Doc's special elevator. The car continued its rapid downward descent.

Of all the nerve, she thought. *Telling me this trip was too dangerous. Too dangerous, after I've been half-way around the world traipsing through jungles and such with him on his capricious adventures. Too dangerous … With this missing Mickey Vankeller being the son of one of the richest SOBs in the country. This could be a Pulitzer story.*

She took another drag. The elevator had reached the first floor and the doors opened. Penny strode out and briskly walked to the exit.

Just because I'm a woman, she thought. *Too dangerous.*

O'Bannion, the doorman, tipped his hat to her and said, "Good morning, Miss Cartier. It's a fine, fine day, isn't it?"

"It is if you're a man," she motioned for him to get her a taxi.

O'Bannion waved down a cab, but his expression was a bit perplexed. He held open the rear door as Penny got in.

"And how's the good Doctor Atlas doing this morning?" he asked.

"Why don't you ask him yourself?" she gave the driver the address to the Times. "And make it snappy."

O'Bannion's eyebrows rose like twin caterpillars and he stepped back from the curb.

As the cab pulled away Penny took another drag on her cigarette but it tasted flat. She tossed it out the window. One of these days she was going to have to quit smoking, like Doc wanted.

Like Doc wants, she thought. *It's always like Doc wants. I got a chance for a great story here, and he's excluding me from getting it, just because I'm a girl. It's not fair, it's just not fair.*

She continued to mull on the conversation she'd just had with Doc in his office.

"We'll be going down to some uncharted territory," he'd said. "Vankeller was purportedly down there checking into some locations for some of his family's rubber plants to be built. It's said he went inland along the river and into the rain forest. It's an immense jungle and a very savage place."

"I've been to savage places before," she'd said. "Look at our trip to Mexico."

Doc smiled. "If my memory serves me, you arrived after the situation had been stabilized. And you were not in the uncivilized sections."

"It was still no picnic. Plus, I had to find my own way down there."

"Against my orders," he recalled. "I strictly forbade you to accompany us due to the inherent dangers, and I'm doing so again."

That had really sent her fuming.

Him, forbidding me, she thought.

"You look like you got something on your mind, lady," the cabbie said. He looked like a twin of Tony "Two Ton" Galleno. "Have a fight with your boyfriend?"

Her eyes flicked toward him, but she didn't reply. She saw his wide grin reflected in the rear vision mirror.

"Yeah, I figured as much. You look just like my old lady when I roll in after hoisting a couple at Murphy's Bar. So what'd your sweetie do? Forget to send you flowers or candy for your birthday, or something?"

Or something, Penny thought. She still didn't reply.

"My old lady, I just tell her, when it's you out there making the money, then you can decide how to spend it." She saw his grin broaden. His fat face looked like a catcher's mitt with crooked teeth. "You gotta admit that sometimes you broads can be downright unreasonable. So, the quicker you realize how right I am, the quicker you'll be back all lovie-dovie and he'll probably be buying you them chocolates and flowers."

Penny smiled and leaned forward. "How about you make like a clam and concentrate on driving? And don't take the long way there, either. You're already down to a nickel tip."

The cabbie's grin turned into a frown and he quit talking.

Penny's thoughts turned back to Doc. *Him, forbidding me*, she thought. *Well, I'll show him. I made my way down to Mexico last time he pulled this, and I can sure as hell get down to Brazil myself. And when the story breaks, it's going to be headlines under my byline.*

✪✪✪

Doc's newest plane, a DC-7 he'd named the Athena, circled high above the city of Mancopa, Brazil. He pointed to Ace, his co-pilot, to the long, winding river that twisted away from the metropolis and into the verdant rain forest to the east.

"It looks very formidable, doesn't it?" Doc asked.

"It certainly does," Ace replied.

"They call that tributary Verde Morte," Doc said. "River of the green death."

Deagan appeared looking over Assante's shoulder. "I wonder if that Vankeller kid is down there somewhere in that maze."

Doc and Assante exchanged looks. "And if he's alive," Ace added.

"That remains for us to find out," Doc picked up the radio and began speaking in Portuguese to the airport located south of the city. After receiving clearance to land, Doc turned to Deagan and Assante.

"Keep in mind our primary mission here is to find Mickey Vankeller. Also keep in mind that the political situation in this country is a bit unstable at the present time. We must do nothing that would provoke the indigenous population."

"Ain't they friendlies?" Deagan asked. "They backed us against the Krauts, didn't they?"

"If you call sending a token force to do nothing backing us up," Ace flipped a few switches that changed the fuel mixture on the engines.

"Well, at least it was something," Deagan retorted. "More than those damn Swiss."

"There's a high concentration of expatriate Europeans living down here south of the equator," Ace said. "Including a lot of Germans."

"As I said," Doc interrupted, "the situation is a bit unstable. We have to be on guard not to raise undue attention to ourselves after we land."

With that he reduced their airspeed and began the descent to toward the landing strip.

Once the Athena had been secured in a hangar Doc was not surprised to see a police vehicle waiting for them outside. One of the uniformed officers walked up and whipped a sharp, palm-outward salute toward him.

"Doctor Atlas," the policeman said in accented English. "Welcome to Macapa. I have been instructed by *Capitain* Rudolfo Reyes of the National

Policia to escort you and your associates to his office."

"We'd prefer to check in to our hotel first," Doc said. "Perhaps we could then see the captain."

The man shook his head rather emphatically. "No, *sehnor*, that is not my *instrucciones*. You will please come with me now. I will see to it that your baggage is taken to the hotel."

"Listen, bud," Deagan started to say.

Assante clamped the tip of his black cane onto Deagan's toes. The other man grunted.

Ace smiled rakishly. "What my friend was about to say was, we're delighted at your hospitality." He turned toward Deagan and added, "The last thing we wish to do is upset the local police."

Deagan took a deep breath, pursed his lips, and nodded.

The ride into the city took a solid fifteen minutes, made longer by the lack of consistently paved roads and the presence of many ox-drawn carts stacked with various harvested crops that crawled past the occasional ramshackle shacks. Finally the lush undergrowth gave way to a series of successively taller, well-constructed buildings and the vehicle pulled up in front of a solid brick building with a *POLICIA* sign on the front. Two uniformed guards holding rifles came to attention and saluted as Doc and the others followed the first policeman inside.

"I ain't seen so many high-balls whipped on me since my retirement ceremony," Deagan declared.

Ace grinned. "Just be glad you don't have to salute back."

The office of Captain Rudolfo Reyes was a rather small room off to the left of the high countered waiting room filled with a group of peasants. Inside it was stifling hot and the smell of human sweat hung in the air. Reyes, a heavyset man with a mustache, sat behind a large, paper-strewn desk fanning himself. The sweat had seeped through his tan shirt in various places, making the sea of medals he had on his chest look like an island surrounded by wetness. His eyes darted toward a thin, swarthy man who had a partially disassembled electric fan spread out on some newspapers on the floor. Reyes said something in Portuguese to the man, who nodded. He turned back to Doc and smiled as he stood up extending his open hand.

"It is a pleasure to meet the famous Doc Atlas," he fanned himself some more. "I apologize for the heat, *sehnor*, but it is, after all the summer."

Doc shook the man's hand.

"Please, please, sit down," Reyes indicated the row of chairs in front of his desk. Deagan looked at Doc who nodded. All three of them then sat.

Reyes canted his head and smiled. "Ah, that is better, no?" He continued fanning himself for a moment then cleared his throat. "As I'm sure you know, my country is run by a military junta, but we are in the process of establishing it into a democracy."

"I have heard that is Presidente Dutra's intention," Doc said. "A noble goal for a great country."

Reyes smiled again. "Good. Very good. Then you also must know that as *estranjer*—- as foreigners, in my country, you must show respect our laws and customs."

"Of course," Doc said.

"Good, good." Reyes waved hand in front of him and glanced toward the thin man working on the electrical fan. "Mario, how much longer are you going to be working on that?" he said in Portuguese.

"I try my best," the man answered.

Reyes frowned then gave Mario's haunch a kick. "Get out for now, you idiot. Go find me a new one."

The man got to his feet, glanced at Reyes, then turned and left, pausing to nod at Doc and company.

"*Pardone*," Reyes fanned himself some more. "I am surrounded by incompetence. These *idiotas* cannot even fix an electrical fan." The telephone on his desk rang and Reyes smiled as he picked it up. He spoke in Portuguese for several seconds, listened, then stared at Doc. He barked a few orders into the phone and slammed the receiver down. After a few more fanning gestures, his obsequious smile returned.

"Doctor Atlas, my men at the airfield have informed me that they have discovered several pistolas in the luggage of you and your friends. Can you explain this?"

"What right did you have to search our stuff?" Deagan said, half-rising from his chair.

Doc shot him a quick glance and Ace placed a restraining hand on Deagan's forearm.

"We are planning a trip into the interior," Doc answered. "We felt the weapons would be appropriate should we encounter any wild animals."

Reyes squinted, nodded contemplatively, and then shook his head. "Absolutely not. It is forbidden for *estranje* —- for foreigners to carry such weapons. I cannot allow it."

"Listen, bud," Deagan argued. "We've carried weapons all over the world. When did this stipulation come into effect?"

Reyes held up his hand. "I am sorry, but most recently we have had, shall I say, a bit of trouble with some Americans being armed and causing trouble"

"Americans?" Deagan echoed. "Was one of them named Reese Manning?"

Reyes smiled again. "Ah, I see you are familiar with one of them." His expression took on a stern look. "There was an incident, a shooting. Mr. Manning was involved in it."

"Where is he?" Deagan asked. "He here?"

Reyes fanned himself before he answered. "At this time, he is being sought for questioning."

"If he was involved he must have had a good reason," Deagan said. "I know Reese Manning."

Reyes smiled and barked an order to a subordinate in his native language. Ace and Doc looked at each other. Deagan sat dumbly.

"Nice going, knucklehead," Assante whispered.

"What?" Deagan asked.

"I have given the order that your plane be impounded until further notice," Reyes said.

"Captain," Ace said in his most polite, but lawyerly tone, "may I ask why you have taken this rather severe measure? Surely you're aware of Doc Atlas's sterling reputation."

"Of course," Reyes gave Doc a deferential nod, "But considering your association with a wanted fugitive, I'm afraid I cannot take the chance of any more such incidents involving guns and foreigners."

Deagan snorted and smacked his big fist into his palm. Doc glanced at him, but said nothing.

"Aww, I'm sorry, Doc," Deagan apologized.

"You certainly are," Ace said.

Deagan and Ace continued to argue as the three of them walked along the dusty street. A slew of adobe huts and framed buildings lined each side.

"You really missed your calling, Mad Dog. You should have been a diplomat."

"That's a job for a shyster," Deagan retorted. "All talk and no action."

Doc continued to remain silent, but looked farther down the block. They were going in the general direction of the hotel, but he pointed to a perpendicular sign that hung suspended across the pathway that passed for a sidewalk.

"Perhaps we should stop in there for some refreshments," Doc suggested.

Deagan did a double take. "Huh? I can't read the sign, but I know a tavern when I see one. You want to go in there?"

"He said he did, didn't he?" Ace pivoted and pulled open the wooden screen door. "Shall we?"

Doc entered first, then Deagan, followed by Ace. Inside the room was stifling hot with a smattering of patrons. Several sets of wooden tables and chairs lay between them and an equally crude looking bar. Behind the bar a big, swarthy man polished glasses with a towel as he stood in front of numerous rows of bottles on either side of a filthy mirror. Some of the men at the tables looked up from their beers. Others remained oblivious. Doc strode through the tables and stepped to the bar.

"*Americanos*?" the bartender had a huge black mustache.

"Si," Doc said. "You speak English?"

"*Poco, poco.* But this," the bartender said in heavily accented English, holding his palm toward the rows of bottles, "is the universal language, no?"

"It is," Doc placed some Brazilian currency on the bar. "Give my friends whatever they want. I need to use the … How do you say it? *Bano*?"

The bartender glanced down at the money, then his yellow teeth shone from under the mustache. "Of course, *senhor.* It is out back." He pointed toward a door with a curtain composed of several strings of hanging beads.

"Wait here," Doc got up and went through the curtain. Deagan and Ace exchanged glances but said nothing.

The curtain led to a hallway which had several rooms on each side. Doc continued toward the rear door which opened into a small, fenced-in courtyard. An outhouse sat at the far end. Doc walked a few steps, stopped, and turned. He waited in the center of the yard as a man slipped through the doorway and into the yard. It was Mario, the same man who'd been working on Captain Reyes's electrical fan.

"I figured we could talk with more privacy out here," Doc said.

Mario smiled. "You saw me following you, eh? You ask a lot of questions, *senhor.*"

Doc nodded. "I'm in need of some information."

"And me, I'm in need of something too." Mario reached into his pants pocket and pulled something cylindrical out. He held up his hand and the silver blade of a knife flipped outward with a snick. "*Dinero. Americano dinero.*"

Doc stood impassively, watching as Mario stepped forward, holding the long-bladed knife out in front of him with his right hand.

"You have on a money-belt, American pig?" He moved closer, but Doc still kept his arms at his sides. "Open your shirt and show Mario, eh?"

Doc moved his hands to his chest, as if to begin unbuttoning his shirt, then Doc's left hand shot outward and seized Mario's right wrist, twisting it back in one quick motion. The knife fell to the ground and Doc's powerful thumb rotated the man's hand backward until he rose up onto his toes

"As I mentioned," Doc said, "I need some information."

Mario grunted with pain. "Please, *senhor*, please. If you are looking for *sehnor* Reese Manning, I can take you to him."

Doc did a quick search of the man and found a small revolver in his back pocket. He tucked the gun into his belt and pulled his shirt out to cover it, then recovered the switchblade and pocketed it. After a brief lecture, he marched the skinny man back inside. Mario followed Doc's instructions perfectly, looking straight ahead with a smile on his face.

Ace and Mad Dog swiveled their heads in surprise. The bartender had just set the two beers on the bar.

"Time for us to go," Doc said.

Deagan and Assante exchanged quizzical glances. Ace nodded at Mad Dog and followed Doc. Deagan grabbed his beer, took a huge sip, and tossed a few coins down beside it. "Keep the change, buddy."

They walked down the cobblestone street away from the center of town. Deagan took the left flank as Doc walked along Mario's right side. When Doc was sure that no one was watching, he removed the revolver and handed it across to Mad Dog. A wide grin burst across Deagan's face. He poked the gun into Mario's ribs just for emphasis and then put his hand and the gun in his jacket pocket. Ace dropped further behind to scan the street and watch their backs.

After a few minutes, they approached a large two-story wooden building with the words *Pousada Anjo* painted above the door. "This *ees* it," Mario whispered. He was completely drenched in sweat. "The Angel Inn. Can I go now?"

"When we see our friend," Doc replied in Portuguese. "Is there a back door so no one will see us enter?"

Mario's face showed surprise that Doc spoke Portuguese. "*Si,*" he led them to a rickety stairway behind the building.

"Doc," Deagan asked as Ace joined them. "What's going on?"

"We are either going to find Reese Manning, or we are walking into a trap."

"Wouldn't be the first time." Ace grinned. "Right?"

Deagan grinned too.

"Ace," Doc said. "Stay here and guard the stairs."

Assante twisted his cane and slid the inside sword out an inch from the hilt and nodded.

"Thomas, let's go up." Doc pushed Mario up the stairs, holding him by the collar. At the top landing the rotted door opened easily and they stepped into a dark, sweltering hallway. Mario pointed to the first door on the left.

"Open it," Doc whispered.

"No, *sehnor*, he will shoot me. There *ees* a *passhword* and *especial proceedhure*."

"Then proceed," Doc ordered.

Mario knocked eight times. Then he said, "Did you call for the room *servicio*. I have the strawberries and the best champagne."

They heard the sound of the door being unbolted from the inside. Doc moved to the side as Deagan rested the gun on Mario's shoulder.

"What day is it?" a voice asked from inside the room.

"The day after yesterday," Mario replied.

The door opened slowly. It was dark inside but they could see the outline of a barrel-chested man standing in the shadows.

"Reese, is that you?" Deagan asked.

"Mad Dog?" the man in the shadows said, moving into the light.

He was Caucasian and in his late thirties, with thinning sandy hair and a Government Model Colt 45 in his left hand. Deagan pushed past Mario and burst into the sparsely furnished room.

"Reese, you old son of a gun, how have you been doing?" He started to thrust his arm out to shake hands , then stopped. Manning smirked and extended his right arm, the silver hook at its end.

"Forget about this?" he reminded his old friend.

Deagan made a clucking sound and looked at the floor. He cleared his throat. "Reese, you remember Doc." Deagan cocked his head toward the door just as Doc ushered Mario into the room.

"Sure. Who doesn't know Doc Atlas?" A wry smile twisted Manning's face. "I'd offer you someplace to sit, but as you see, they didn't give me the penthouse this time."

Doc looked around. "Do you have anything to tie this man up?"

"No need for that. Mario's jake as long as you pay him good." Manning turned to Deagan. "I just knew that if anybody could find me, it would be you, old buddy. But I didn't think you'd bring the famous Doc Atlas along."

"Well," Deagan looked over to Doc, who simply nodded. "Turns out we're all on the same mission. Mr. Vankeller was, ah, worried he hadn't heard from you so he asked Doc to look into it. So, we're really all here for the same reason. To help you find that Mickey kid."

"Yeah," Manning sat on the edge of the bed, "who'd a thought finding some snot-nosed playboy would be so hard. He couldn't get lost on the Riviera or the casinos in Cuba. No, he has to get lost while looking for new oil deposits in the jungle."

"Is that where he is?" Deagan asked. "Your telegram was kind of vague."

Manning snorted. "I had Mario bribe the telegraph operator to get out of the office so I could send it myself. You can't trust anybody around here."

Deagan's eyes shot toward Mario who was standing quite still next to Doc.

Manning laughed. "Like I said, he's okie-dokie, but don't trust the cops. Mario set me up with a local priest named Father Henkel. He got us set up with a boat ride up river."

"Us?" Deagan said. "You got someone helping you?"

"I started out with a team of two. A Frenchman I worked with a couple times before and an old army buddy, Hal Gordon. He went missing up river." Manning shook his head. "Frenchy and me came back to resupply so we could go back and look for him, and he was gunned down. I barely got away. Someone was waiting for us. Now the cops are looking for me, saying I killed Frenchy."

Deagan glanced at Doc who was listening intensely. "So, why did you stay?"

"Hell, Mad Dog, I gotta job to do. I finish what I start. Plus, I owe it to Hal to find out if he's still alive, and to Frenchy to find out who killed him." He shook his head. "All over finding some run-away rich kid. Even if I only find the playboy's bones, I'm gonna finish the job."

Deagan patted Manning's shoulder. "Well, Doc, what's our next move?"

"We're not on good standing with the police ourselves," Doc said.

"I can help, *sehnors*," Mario said. "I know a river boat *capitan* who can sneak you all out of town and down the river. He takes the padres to the *nativos* with clothes and medicine. He can get you away from here and into the jungle."

"Do you have any supplies?" Doc asked Manning.

"Yeah, that duffel bag has guns and ammo and maps. Those other two hemp sacks have food. Maybe enough for a week."

Deagan motioned at Mario. "What do we do about him?"

"Trust me, he's fine," Manning repeated. "He was in the process of setting up the boat ride for me. But I'm a little short on dough."

Deagan and Doc exchanged glances, then Doc nodded.

Manning grinned. He was missing a few important teeth. "Mario can book the passage for you to go up river tomorrow morning. You guys can pick me up down by the second bend." He looked at Mario, who was also grinning like a schoolboy who had just been given a reprieve by the principal. "And you keep your mouth shut, understand?"

"Si, *sehnor* Manning. You know *mio*. Mario, he can be trusted."

"Yeah," Deagan sneered, "I'll bet you can, as long you ain't been paid in full yet."

The next afternoon the train from Bailique, where she'd flown from someplace in French Guiana, and prior to that, from Havana, was slowly rumbling to a long, slow stop. Penny glanced out the window and saw the lush countryside quickly become littered with a series of ramshackle shacks. Half-naked, dirty children played in the dusty street that ran parallel to the tracks, and gradually the buildings became bigger and the area more built up. She felt like she had been rolling around in dust for eight hours and then poured sand over herself just of good measure. The only thing she was glad about was that she'd learned, from all her trips with Doc, was the ability to stuff everything she needed into a small suitcase. But getting this story, and proving herself, was more important than looking glamorous. Plus she had no support on this trip. No one to smooth the way. She figured anonymity was her best ally. She had to blend in with the local population. Call no attention to herself. Luckily, the population of Brazil seemed to have a plethora of various physical types, various races and hair colors. Even so, she was way too white. Most of the populace was tan, or naturally dark complected. And very poor, from the looks of things. So she quickly secured her stylized brunette hair under a large bandana and put on a floppy straw hat. Not that she'd had the time or the inclination to concentrate much on her make-up, but she figured a heavy foundation would give her a tan look. On one of the water stops she'd bought a loose fitting tan peasant dress and a pair of sandals. So as she stepped down off the train, and onto more dust in Macapa, she hoped she looked like any other Brazilian peasant woman returning from a trip. All her belongings were in a straw basket that she purchased on the train from a dirty-faced lad who was more than happy to also take her 5th Avenue suitcase as part of the bargain.

But there was no faking the language. She picked out a sympathetic looking clerk in the railroad station and asked directions to the Church of Santa Maria. The man looked like he half-understood what she was asking, but replied in a mixture of Portuguese and halting Spanish that the church was several blocks away. He pointed down the street and then hooked his hand in a gesture she assumed meant several blocks.

So much for blending in, she thought, and began walking, careful to keep her head down. Dust accompanied her every footstep.

Several minutes later she reached the town square and looked up to view the most ornate building in this simple little city. It was not overly large, but it dwarfed everything around the square. The church was neo-gothic, its spires reaching up towards heaven. According to the phone call she made to her colleague, a correspondent for the *Times* in Belem, she should avoid the local *policia*, who were notoriously corrupt, and seek information from the padres of the Deutsche Christen missionaries. They were a missionary branch of the Catholic Church and would surely help her.

"But be careful," the colleague had warned. "It's a very dangerous place, especially for a woman."

Too dangerous. Not safe for a woman, she thought as she pushed back the huge wooden door to enter the church. He sounds as bad as Doc.

She paused and dipped her right hand in the onyx bowl of holy water and quickly made the sign of the cross not able to recall when the last time it was that she did that. Her sandals clicked as she made her way up the center aisle past the worn wooden pews toward the Communion rail that separated the congregation from the stone altar. The gold tabernacle sat squarely in the center flanked by several candles. Penny stood there taking in the simplicity and subtle majesty of this place of worship.

"*Eu posso ajuda-lo?*"

The voice from the shadows startled her. Turning, she saw a man in a brown robe approach from her left. As he entered the natural light of the church, a myriad of colors washed over him from the stained glass windows. Despite the prism of light, she could make out his short cropped salt and pepper hair and his high cheek bones. He was a handsome man about 5 feet 6 inches tall.

"I'm sorry ... I just ... I'm looking," she stammered in English.

The priest smiled. "Do not worry, *senhorita*. All people are welcome in God's house." His English was tinged with a European infection. "I am Padre Henkel. How may I help you?"

Padre Henkel? That sounded German. What was a German-named, English speaking priest doing in a country that spoke Portuguese?

He smiled again. "Yes, my child. I can sense that your first question is how I came to be ministering to the people of this region, so far from my home. The Church survived the persecution of that madman Hitler. In our thanks to God, we have been spreading his word in Africa and South America. The Sisters of the Precious Blood Ministry are establishing a mission in Manaus even as we speak. God's word does not recognize national boundaries." He looked at her expectantly. "And, now ... how may I be of assistance?"

Penny smiled for the first time since she left New York. Finally, a friendly face. "I'm looking for some friends. I, ah, got separated from them."

Father Henkel nodded, the smile still locked on his face. "You were to meet them here in Macapa?"

"Yes," she said. "They probably arrived here yesterday."

The priest nodded. "And what was their business here?"

"They're trying to find someone. Another friend."

The priest's eyebrows rose. "Another friend? And who might that be?"

This wasn't turning out the way Penny had hoped, but perhaps the best tactic would be to lay her cards on the table. This guy was a priest, after all. "Have you heard of a Mickey Vankeller?"

Henkel's small-boned hand rubbed his chin in thoughtful contemplation. "No, *senhorita*, I do not believe so." He gestured for her to sit in the pew. Penny moved to sit down. Henkel stopped, turned, genuflected facing the tabernacle, and after making the sign of the cross joined her. "But the jungle is a very dangerous place. Do you think he is in some kind of trouble?"

I never said anything about the jungle, she thought. *He must know more than he's telling, but why? Maybe he doesn't know if he can trust me.* "I'm not sure, Padre. And my name is Penny."

"Well, Miss *Penny*," He smiled again, as if the overall picture was becoming clear to him. "If you tell me more then perhaps I can ask my parishioners if they know anything about your friend, *senhor* Vankeller."

"It's not just him, I need to locate. The other ... friends I have to find are already down here." She bit her lip. Dropping Doc's name was usually a trump card to gain entrance and information anywhere she desired. But

So much for blending in, she thought

it would also tip her hand. But this guy was a priest, after all, and it might get him to trust her. "Have you heard of Doc Atlas?"

Henkel's brow furrowed. "Doc Atlas," he said slowly. "He is a doctor who works with the *nativos* along the Amazon?"

She looked away, trying to formulate a new tactic to find out something about Doc's whereabouts. A huge shadow moved in her peripheral vision and an extremely tall monk, cloaked in his brown robe with the hood covering his face, stepped out from the sanctuary to the side of the altar. The several large sacramental candles he held in his hand looked like burning twigs in his oversized hands.

"Do not be startled," Henkel said. "It is only Brother Franscico."

Penny smiled and said hello.

"Ah, forgive him that he does not reply," Henkel said. "He has taken a vow of silence."

A vow of silence? A fat lot of good he would be. But that was okay. The big monk kind of gave her the creeps, if you could think of a priest as creepy. She turned back to Padre Henkel. "You would have noticed Doc. Did anyone new, foreign—-American, come in to Mancopa the last several days? He would have had two men with him."

Henkel considered this and shook his head. "I am afraid not, but I am kept very busy with maintaining this parish and my missionary work with the *nativos*. There are many days that pass that I do not even ..."

Penny had stopped listening to Padre Henkel and instead focused on Brother Francisco, who crisscrossed right in front of the altar replacing the candles. It seemed he was obsessed with getting the heights matched perfectly with the burnt ones that were to remain.

Something's wrong with this picture, she thought. *But what?*

It was then that she realized that the monk was not stopping to genuflect before the tabernacle when he passed in front of it. Every Catholic knew it was a sign of reverence to genuflect when passing in front of the tabernacle that was the symbolic vessel of God. Especially a priest. *Something's very, very wrong here*, she thought as she felt a sudden chill creeping up her spine.

Henkel was no longer speaking. He was studying her, then followed her gaze toward the altar. Penny faked a quick smile and started to stand. "Thank you, father, but I've really got to be going. You've been a big help."

His hand grabbed her arm. "Dammit," Henkel said. "Francisco, get down here now, you idiot." The huge monk dropped the remaining candles and lumbered down the steps, pulling his robe up to vault the low

Communion railing. Henkel uttered another profanity and yelled, "Get her!"

A priest swearing in church ... A monk not genuflecting ... What the hell had she stumbled into? She had to get out of this place now.

Penny swung her straw bag squarely against Henkel's head as he attempted to stand up. He fell back releasing his grip on her. She turned and quickly edged out of the pew then took her first running steps toward the door. The sandals slipped on the tiled floor, not giving her much traction. A few more steps ... Heavy breathing behind her ... Right behind her. She felt a powerful hand reach out and grab her shoulder. She tried to shake it off, then the oversized monk bore down on her, his other hand seizing her hair, his massive weight bearing down on her back, forcing her downward. The floor seemed to rush up and smack against her face. That was the last thing she remembered as a curtain of darkness descended.

The morning sun hung over the jungle canopy like a hot coal as the thirty-foot boat navigated the twisting river. On either side of them the jungle was a verdant mass of hanging leaves, thick trees, and twisting vines that seemed to form a solid wall. As they progressed the cacophony of birds and insects along the river bank suddenly ceased, replaced by a foreboding silence. Ace was on the foredeck, conversing in Spanish with Eduardo, one of the two crewmen. Doc, Deagan and Manning sat in a circle on the flat area behind the captain's perch, a map spread out on the deck. Below them was a capacious cargo hold. Jose, the skinny crewman with the ragged straw hat, huddled in the slim shade in front of the wheel house.

"As far as I know," Manning kept his voice low, "this guy McGuire is legit." He brought a cigarette to his lips and the tip glowed brightly as he drew on it. "He takes stuff up river all the time for the missionaries, but that don't mean he doesn't work both sides of the fence."

"You said you'd traced Mickey Vankeller to this region?" Doc indicated a section on the map. "Is that where your friend was killed?"

"Yeah." Manning's face took on a grim expression as he took one last drag on his cigarette, then threw it over the side. "We'd rented a motorboat and tied off at this clearing. Our guide was saying how we'd have to travel inland and try to establish contact with the forest people. Indians. Hal and the guide went down the pathway to reconnoiter a bit, then we heard shots."

"Who was it?" Deagan asked. "Indians?"

Manning shook his head. "Don't know. Bullets stated raining down from all over. Frenchy and I ran down there to help, but there was no sign of either of them. Then more shots. We tried to return fire but we only had two pistols between us and ran out of ammo." He snorted. "Aww, we couldn't even see who was firing at us. We were lucky to get back to the boat. We kept calling to Hal and the guide, but they didn't answer. I hated to leave them there, but it was all Frenchy and me could do to get the boat untied and get outta there." Manning rubbed his face with his left hand. "They deserved better from me."

Deagan placed a hand on Manning's shoulder. "Sounds like you did all you could."

"Did you ever see your assailants?" Doc asked.

Manning shook his head. "It was like they were invisible. It was like they knew we were coming ... Right where we'd be."

"Mind if I join you, gents?" a voice intruded as Captain Thomas McGuire lowered his considerable bulk down the ladder from the captain's perch. "I've got Eduardo spelling me at the wheel. It's a pretty straight stretch for a bit, and I thought I could be using a smoke." He grinned showing bad teeth as he pulled out a pipe and started packing it with tobacco.

"So," McGuire belched as he sat down beside Deagan. "I take it you'd be looking for that rich explorer who got himself lost in this jungle." He cracked a wooden match with his thumb and held the flame over the bowl.

"We never said that," Manning said.

McGuire flashed his decrepit smile again and took off his cap, exposing a shock of thinning red hair. "Well, that you didn't, but your little friend, Mario, told me you wanted to go up the *Flor Escura* branch. It's common knowledge that your rich American was out that way too." He puffed on the pipe to get it going. "Looking for lost gold or treasure, he was. Hell, there ain't nothing up that way except a bunch of small villages and savages. They call it the Black Flower River."

"So, you've been up the Flower River before?" Deagan asked.

"Sure, plenty-o-times. I take the missionaries up that way every couple-o-weeks. Not that it does those savages any good, showing them the way of the Church." He drew copiously on the pipe and blew out a cloud of smoke.

"Are the Indians receptive to foreigners?" Doc asked.

"Some more so than others." McGuire laughed as he drew on the pipe again. When he spoke his words were mixed with smoke. "But I guess that'll depend on whether you can find out if the head of that rich explorer boy of yours is still attached to his body, or decorating the mantle of some pagan altar, won't it?"

Penny wasn't sure of just when she regained consciousness, but the incessant noise of propeller blades was unmistakable. So were the voices. Two men and they were both speaking German. She opened her eyes a crack and saw them, Father Henkel and Brother Francisco.

Those two jokers are no more priests than I am, she thought.

They sat side-by-side about ten feet in front of her in some kind of pilot's compartment, an instrument panel and two yokes in front of them, the cloudless blue sky visible through the windshield. She looked around some more. Metal walls and a metal floor ... boxes stacked against them, secured by canvas straps. They were inside a plane, all right, and from the bumps that came a few seconds later, she knew they had just landed somewhere.

Henkel turned and looked down at her. "Ah, you are awake, my dear. I was beginning to worry that the amount of chloroform that Brother Francisco administered was too much."

"Spare me," Penny said. "And can the Brother Francisco malarkey. Who are you guys really?"

Henkel smiled. It was a smile full of malevolence. "We are soldiers, Werner and I."

"Soldiers? In what army?"

Henkel laughed as the plane coasted to a stop. He didn't answer.

They exited the plane and Penny heard the side cargo door sliding open. Brother Francisco, or Werner, grabbed her with his huge hands and pulled her out, slinging her over his shoulder like a sack of potatoes. He began walking, the ground seeming to bounce up at her with each step. She twisted her head to the side —- A solid wall of verdant trees and bushes. But beneath her was a smooth, macadamized stone surface ... Obviously someone had built an airfield landing strip in the middle of nowhere. After about two hundred feet they entered a built up area with various wooden framed buildings and a few of brick and mortar. She heard a knock, then a door opened and they all stepped into a large room full of lab tables and test tubes.

Werner stopped and Penny could hear Henkel talking again in German. He said something that sounded like "*Sieg heil.*" What the hell was going on?

"Untie the female and let's have a look at her," a voice said in English. It was tinctured with a German accent. She felt Werner bend and then her worn sandals were on the ground. In a few seconds her balance came back to her and she saw a short, stout man with frizzled gray hair and gold, wire-rimmed glasses in front of her. He scanned her face with an appraising look.

"Yes, yes, she is very comely," the man said. "I shall get much enjoyment out of her."

"Enjoyment?" Penny repeated. "Who are you guys?"

The stout little man's head cocked to the side, then he came to mock attention. "Forgive me, *frauline*, for not introducing myself. I am Herr Doctor Fritz Rhinnemann of the New Third Reich."

"New Third what? You've got to be kidding me."

"I assure you, I am quite serious." Rhinnemann stepped aside and gave her an unobstructed view out the expansive window. Penny could see several good-sized buildings had been constructed, and numerous trucks were being unloaded by a bunch of Indians being guarded by more uniformed soldiers. "As you can see, we are well under way to rebuilding the Third Reich into prominence and power once more."

"Looks like you're as big a hit with the local population as you were in Europe," she said.

"These people are ignorant and superstitious. Meant to be ruled by a strong hand, and easily manipulated to suit our purpose."

"Your purpose?" Penny asked.

"Cheap labor for our construction projects," he lifted his hand toward the expansive array of buildings, "and a good supply of research subjects as well."

"How nice," Penny said. "Since you don't have the luxury of other misfortunate people, like all those Jews you bastards murdered."

Rhinnemann smirked. "A fortuitous substitution. They prove useful. For the benefit of science." He reached forward and touched her hair. Penny tried to move away, but Rhinnemann grabbed a handful and pulled her back toward him. "And a woman as lovely as you will prove useful as well. It gets very lonely here in the jungle, and the supply of Indian women grows tiresome. You have some degree of cultivation and breeding, for an American, that is."

"You just wait till Doc Atlas gets here. He'll make you eat those words."

Rhinnemann laughed. "Your outmoded and ersatz hero, Doc Atlas. How pathetic you Americans are, clinging to invented myths popularized by your pathetic movies and pulp magazines. Did you think we did not know of your hero's arrival? I have already prepared a special reception for him." Rhinnemann's head swiveled at a knock on the door as another soldier in a gray uniform came through the doorway. "Herr professor."

They spoke in German again. Penny felt like she'd been transported into some pre-World War II nightmare. Were these guys some Nazi hold-outs here in Brazil?

Rhinnemann turned back to her, smiling again and holding his hands in front of his chest in an anticipatory gesture. "All of your questions will be answered in due time, my dear. But right now, I'm afraid I have to attend to the completion of one of my experiments." He looked at Henkel and spoke in German again. Werner grabbed Penny's arm and pulled her out of the room. They walked her across another crushed stone surface, almost like a cobblestone street, toward a solid looking brick building. A uniformed guard with a rifle stood by the door, and Henkel said something to him as they approached. The guard turned and unlocked the heavy door. They went inside and down a short, dimly lit hallway to another set of doors, these just as fortified as previous one. The guard again used his keys and pushed the door open. It was dingy inside and poorly lighted from an encased bulb high on the ceiling and a tiny set of windows.

"Until we meet again," Henkel said, and shoved Penny inside the room. The door slammed behind her and she stumbled to the floor. As she got to her hands and knees she felt another set of hands on her shoulders. Screaming, she shook them off.

"Don't touch me!"

"Sorry, miss," a man responded. "I didn't mean any harm."

The voice sounded American. Penny turned and saw an incredibly filthy man standing there with stringy blonde hair and several weeks' growth of beard. His face had a familiar cast to it.

"Who are you?" she asked.

"My name's Mickey. Mickey Vankeller."

Deagan and Ace stood on the port side watching the slow progress as the steamer crawled along against the current, slowing down every hundred yards or so to navigate sharp turns as the river wound through the thick, steamy jungle.

"This damn thing winds around like a carelessly dropped ribbon," Ace swatted at a mosquito on his neck.

Deagan grinned. "At least we got some shade coming up, more or less." He pointed to the piercing shafts of light through the canopy of trees and vines. The steamer made another sharp turn then came to an abrupt halt.

"Hey, why we stopping?" Deagan yelled. "We ain't there yet, are we?"

"This is the worst part of this damn river," McGuire called down from the wheelhouse. "You got to stay right in the middle and watch out for those tree stumps and logs floating 'round. Jose, get up to the bow and take a look."

Jose grunted, got up slowly from his nook in front of the wheel house, and shuffled up to the front of the boat.

Ahead the dark stretch of river was blanketed by a canopy of trees and intertwined branches. The tributary itself had narrowed to less than sixty-feet wide. It was even narrower as the shoreline was littered with fallen and half submerged tree trunks poking their twisted stumps above the waterline. Instead of a discernable river bank, the landscape sloped sharply on both sides.

"This reminds me of our trip to Burma, don't it, Doc?" Deagan asked.

Doc surveyed the area. "The erosion of the shoreline is most likely caused by the rainfall flowing into the river." He pointed to the flecked canopy stretching above, the branches and vines winding in a supportive embrace forming a dense alcove that virtually blocked out the sun. "This has also caused the trees on both sides of the river to list towards each other."

McGuire yelled down from his perch. "Keep a look out for any bulwarks floating by that could scuttle us."

As the steamer slowly resumed its journey, the dark shadows crept over the water. Some of the heavily entwined branches hung only twelve feet overhead almost scraping the roof of the wheel house. Manning joined Deagan on the port side.

"That clearing where Hal disappeared wasn't much farther up river." His face was covered with sweat.

"We got to get there first," Deagan said.

They continued to scour the murky water for half-sunken trees, Doc was carefully scanning the foliage above.

"Doc," Ace called out, "there's something up ahead."

"Canoe coming," Jose said from the prow.

Deagan and Manning joined Ace on the prow while Doc surveyed the foreground from a vantage point farther back on the deck. Approximately thirty yards ahead he saw a young Indian standing in a wooden canoe clad only in a breach-cloth. His dark hair hung down to his neck and he was holding a primitive looking spear. He yelled something and pointed upward before letting the spear fly. It sailed in a high arc, skimming the limbs of overhanging tree branches, and skittered loudly on the deck of the boat.

McGuire reached down and stepped out from the wheelhouse brandishing a Thompson submachine gun. The weapon roared and bullets stitched over the water and splayed across the back of the canoe, filling the air with tiny shards of bark. Doc pushed past Manning and grabbed McGuire, throwing him down hard to the deck.

As Doc turned to check on the boy, his peripheral vision caught a sudden movement from a thick cluster of heavy branches above. A huge snake slithered downward over the prow of the boat, coiling around Jose like an endless spool of impending death. It slammed into the man's shoulders and quickly wrapped around his body. It kept coming, a thick greenish coil twenty-four inches in diameter, dropping down from above and enveloping the struggling man. The thirty-foot olive green and black spotted anaconda had departed its ambush spot and now slid into the brackish water.

Doc dove head first into the churning water. As he split the surface of the river, he reached down into his boot and withdrew the six-inch combat knife from his boot. Straining to see in the murky water, Doc saw the large anaconda coiling its two-foot thick body around the struggling man. He knew that anacondas were more at home in the water than on dry land and that the snake, though non-venomous, would sink its teeth into its prey to hold it in place while it continued to constrict its entire body and slowly crush the life out of its victim.

The snake began its underwater dance of death, twisting and twirling to make its prey expunge their last breath of air; all the time tightening its suffocating grip on the drowning victim. Doc swam right up to the head of the huge snake, reached out and grabbed its thick neck in his left hand. He raised his knife, but the spiraling motion of the massive creature had rotated them closer to the shore and Doc slammed into a submerged tree trunk and lost his grip on the knife.

The snake's head shot toward him, its jaws agape. Instantly, Doc locked both hands around the snake's neck and slammed it into the tree trunk as hard as he could. Then he braced his legs against the trunk and propelled himself to the surface, dragging the snake with him. The anaconda was loosening its grip on Jose and now coiling its enormous body around Doc, dragging him under the water. They spun madly as Doc could feel the pressure increase around his ribs and waist. He had one chance. His legs were still relatively untangled as he had never stopped kicking and climbing through the coils of the giant snake. He kicked furiously to catch the slow current and drive them both into the middle of the river.

Just as the boat swerved overhead, Doc gauged the position and depth of the propeller. Summoning all his strength, he thrust the head of the giant anaconda up until the blades nicked its head. The spinning blades then came within inches of Doc's hands and face as he was spun upwards. Suddenly he spiraled downward and was squeezed tighter by the rolling reptile. One last thrust was all he felt he could manage. The thick scaly body tightened incredibly and the snake twisted faster. As the enormous snake's head began to shake vehemently, Doc made one last thrust. The anaconda's head was sliced in two by the rotating propeller blades.

Doc reached out, placed one hand on the bottom of the boat and pushed himself downward away from the propeller. His lungs were bursting as he ripped at the giant snake and unraveled himself from the coiled constriction. He broke the surface of the river and gasped for air while pushing against the rigid coil of the muscle memory that still caused the massive snake to maintain its grip.

"Mad Dog," Ace called out, "there's Doc."

Deagan grabbed the rusted grappling hook that was part of the junk that littered the back of the boat. He cautiously extended it and hooked the thick girth of the headless snake and pulled Doc close to the side.

"Reese, get over here," Deagan barked. "Hold this."

Deagan handed him the pole, which Manning tucked under his right arm and gripped with his left hand. Mad Dog shoved some rope aside and picked up an even more rusted machete. Leaning over the side of the boat, he began to hack away at the anaconda. After a few yards of the snake were slit, Doc burst free of its grip.

"Take my hand," Deagan said, holding down his arm.

Doc shook his head and pointed to the floundering Jose. "Help him first. I'm going to check on that native boy."

Doc took a few gasping breaths and swam over to the sinking canoe. Inside, the Indian boy lay bleeding as the river rapidly poured into the bark canoe. Doc grabbed the boy and swam back to the steamer waiting a several yards away.

After handing the unconscious boy up to Deagan, Doc hoisted himself on board. McGuire glared at both of them. Deagan began performing artificial respiration on the boy. Doc quickly went to Jose, who was writhing at the bow of the boat.

"Several of his ribs are broken," Doc said. "He may have internal injuries as well. Keep him immobile."

"I got him breathing, " Deagan said. "How you doing steering this thing, shyster?"

"It's a cross between driving a car and flying a plane," Ace called out from the wheelhouse adding, " Nice work."

The Golden Avenger moved deftly to the back of the boat grabbing the small medical bag from the floor of the wheelhouse as he passed it. He nodded at Ace who nodded back, knowing that Doc had signaled him to keep an eye on the captain and his mate. Ace then made eye contact with Manning and cocked his head towards McGuire and Eduardo. Reese nodded and flipped open the leather latch on his holster. At the rear of the boat, Deagan huddled over the Indian boy who was shivering and bleeding from several small wounds and splinters in his leg.

"I think it's mostly flesh wounds, Doc," Deagan said.

"Thank you, Thomas, I'll take it from here."

As Deagan got up to leave, the boy reached out and grabbed his military jacket tightly.

"On second thought, perhaps you should stay," Doc said with a hint of a smile.

The door slammed shut and the dark shadows seemed to envelop both of them. The smell in the room was awful. Penny felt like gagging.

"You're Mickey Vankeller?" Penny asked. "We came down here to find you."

"Who's we?"

"Doc Atlas. He brought his associates too." She tried to muster as much optimism as she could. "Don't worry, they'll find us. These Nazis can't keep a place like this secret."

"I'm afraid they've been doing a pretty good job," Vankeller said. "Did you see any other prisoners when they brought you in?"

"Some Indians unloading a couple of trucks."

Vankeller shook his head. He was barely visible in the low lighting. "No, not those poor wretches. There's another American prisoner here. Hal Gordon. The guards took him out a little while ago."

"Took him out? Of where?"

"Here." Vankeller's hand moved through the single beam of sunlight shining in through the small window. "I'm afraid this isn't the Waldorf."

Penny's eyes had grown more accustomed to the low lighting. She saw two neatly rolled blankets and a pot with a lid on it. The odor of human waste emanated from it.

"Did Rhinnemann say anything to you before?" Vankeller asked. "About Hal?"

Penny shook her head, suddenly dreading the total lack of privacy and hope.

Vankeller moved toward the wall with the window. It was about eight feet above them and only six inches in diameter. "Come over here, Miss."

Penny hesitated. What did he want?

"Please. I'll boost you up so you can look out the window. Tell me what you see."

After a moment's hesitation she complied, and Vankeller squatted and told her to stand on his shoulders. She did and he said, "Use your hands to steady yourself as you move up the wall."

Penny did and felt the cold, rough surface scrape her palms. Vankeller straightened up and soon she was able to see out the window. "Too bad this isn't big enough to fit through," she said.

"Believe me, we thought about it many times. What do you see?"

She looked out and saw a group of armed soldiers standing in a circle. One man was in some sort of rubberized suit with a full hood and a horizontal glass plate across the front and a small tank on his back. He opened the door and entered a small wooden structure about seven-foot square with no windows. One by one, he pulled out three men. Two were Indians and one was a white man.

"That's got to be Hal," Vankeller said as she related it to him. "What else is happening?"

"Rhinnemann's there. He seems to be holding a stop-watch."

"Oh, God, no," Vankeller said. "I hope this isn't what it sounds like."

"What's that?" But before he could answer the three men began screaming and convulsing. Penny continued to watch in horror as one-by-one, the deadly dance continued until they fell to the ground, clutching at their throats and then stiffening with a sudden jerk. Rhinnemann held the watch upward and exclaimed something in German. He seemed ebullient.

"Let me down," Penny demanded. "I can't watch this anymore."

"The men," Vankeller said, "are they …"

"They're all dead. What's going on?"

Vankeller slowly squatted as she moved down the wall. "It one of Rhinnemann's little Nazi terror experiments. He calls it the green death."

The late afternoon sun sliced through the thick jungle foliage overhead. The native boy skillfully weaved his way through the underbrush and tangled, untamed growth of the Amazon forest. McGuire, toting his Thompson machine gun, was puffing yards behind him. He had argued vehemently about accompanying them to the village, but Mad Dog forcibly made the point that Eduardo could guard the boat and McGuire would come along as insurance. Manning, Deagan and Doc carried the duffel bags of guns, ammo and food. Doc, Ace and Mad Dog trailed slightly behind as Assante did his best to traverse the uneven terrain with his cane and a Browning rifle.

"Hey, shyster," Mad Dog paused for a moment and grinned, "Let me take that rifle. I don't want you to accidentally shoot me."

"And here I thought monkey hunting season was over." A wry smile of acknowledgement crossed Ace's lips as he handed the rifle forward. "So, Doc, what did you get from your conversation with the native lad. I take it his spear was meant for the big snake back there on the river?"

Doc paused so that the three adventurers were together. "His name is Maku. He speaks a combination of indigenous dialects. They refer to the snake, an anaconda, as the mother of the river." Doc glanced around, as if he'd heard something. "He recognized Manning from his hook as one of the men who were attacked by what he calls the white demons. Maku's village seems to be one of many that has been pillaged."

"Pillaged?" Ace said.

"Yes, by a group of white men led by a one-eyed monster who throws fire from both hands." Doc paused again, then continued. "Local legend calls it the *mapinguari*. It's accompanied by a great beast that roars out of the jungle, trampling trees and huts. It then spits out white demons who take the natives away on a mighty canoe."

"Giant beasts, white demons. And what is a mapin – gooey?" Deagan asked.

Doc frowned. "Thomas, before we left I urged everyone to read the folders that I reviewed on the Amazon."

"Yeah, I read about the Mapinguari," Ace shot a grin at Mad Dog. "One of the folders contained clippings of a 1937 report mentioning the *mapinguari* or roaring animal described as a huge biped with one eye and crocodile skin that emitted a frightening shriek."

"That's correct, Ace," Doc said.

Deagan looked down at the ground and heaved a sigh. "Sorry, Doc."

"Maku has been living in the jungle since his parents were killed," Doc continued. "He keeps an eye on his village, but is afraid to return because of the *verde muerte*."

"The green death," Ace whispered.

"What's that?" Deagan asked.

Doc shook his head. "He described it as something magical caused his tribesmen to scream in pain and, if I translated it correctly, explode in blood and then die."

"What in blazes is going on down here?" Deagan grumbled.

"Things are definitely not what they seem." Doc replied. But before he could continue, Maku had stopped. Doc bolted ahead.

"Here, fly boy," Deagan handed the rifle back to Assante. "Try not to shoot yourself in the foot."

"And you watch out for amorous baboons," Ace smirked.

Deagan joined Doc, Manning and Maku behind a slight ridge that was crisscrossed with rotted tree trunks. , McGuire stood in back of them, a bored expression on his face. Doc pointed through the high trees and wild grass toward a huge clearing with a crushed stone surface that had a dozen new brick buildings of various sizes, a large water tower, and several rows of primitive straw and mud huts. A group of large, tarp-covered crates sat off to the side of the smallest building. Beyond it lay a macadamized landing strip with a shiny twin engine aircraft. The setting sun was casting long, ominous shadows on the incredible scene. Ace and Deagan crawled up beside Doc who was using his binoculars to survey the camp.

Deagan emitted a low whistle. "Looks way too advanced for an Indian village."

"That's scary," Ace grinned. "I find myself agreeing with you."

Doc spoke in a low tone. "The four large buildings must be the barracks for approximately forty people. They have generators and there are several rows of outhouses behind each one. That rectangular building on the perimeter of the air strip must be where their vehicles are stored." He surveyed the site a bit longer. "There is the shadow of a fuel tank on the side of the structure. The building in the center has several small chimneys at the far end. Most likely it's the mess hall."

A wisp of smoke trailed upward from the chimneys.

"Shucks," Deagan said. "It looks like we missed dinner."

"The small building by the runway must be the command center," Doc surmised. "You'll note the long antennae stretching up from the roof. Obviously they've got radio communication with someone. I can see a guard leaning up against the wall of that small square bunker on the far right perimeter. It could be a detention area"

Manning had just begun to focus his binoculars as the Golden Avenger finished. "My God, you've figured that all out already."

"Course he did," Deagan winked as he slid up next to Reese. "He's Doc Atlas, my partner."

Reese squinted "What's that flag in front of that building by the air strip?"

"That, brothers," Doc said, "appears to be a Nazi flag."

"Nazis in Brazil?" Deagan cursed. "What the hell?"

"There is a large German population here," Ace pointed out. "Perhaps they established a safe haven."

"Well, I didn't sign up for this," McGuire bawled. "I'm heading back out-o-here."

"Keep your voice down," Doc snapped.

"I ain't keeping nothing down." The big Irishman jumped up drawing back the top bolt on the machine gun. "Now everybody toss all-o-them guns back there behind you. Then get on your knees and put your hands in the air."

Before anyone could react, Doc said. "Do as he says, brothers."

Begrudgingly, all three men tossed their guns away and raised their hands.

McGuire grinned, showing his bad teeth again. "Ha, the great Doc Atlas. Ain't so great now. You had no idea what you were getting into."

"I shoulda flattened you when I took that Tommy-gun away from back on the boat," Deagan said.

McGuire laughed again. "You should've been so lucky. My Nazi friends know your coming. Me man, Eduardo radioed them after we left. So, you're

"Local legend calls it the *mapinguari*."

going to march on down there so they can lock you up with the others."

"What others?" Manning asked.

"That millionaire sissy and your pal and some lassie reporter from New York." McGuire sneered. "It's going to be real cozy in that cell."

"Thank you," Doc calmly stood up and took a step forward.

"Hold it," McGuire shouted, "or you'll die right here."

Doc took another step forward. "I think not."

Doc kept walking. McGuire squeezed the trigger but the machine gun didn't fire. McGuire pulled it again. Nothing. Doc grabbed the end of the gun with his left hand and threw an arcing right hook into the big Irishman's jaw. The blow sent him flying back several feet, hitting the ground unconscious.

As Doc's three compatriots scrambled to their feet and retrieved their weapons, Manning shook his head. "You got guts, Atlas, I'll say that. But you were sure lucky that the Tommy-gun jammed."

"Not luck, Reese. Just a bit of planning. I've had my suspicions about Mr. McGuire for some time. The radio on board his boat was the confirmation I needed. I switched the ammo clip on his weapon before we left the river. He didn't have any bullets in his weapon and I have the spare magazine."

"What about the radio?" Deagan inquired.

Doc smiled. "I also removed the tube from his radio. It's in that bag. I apologize for letting this charade proceed, but I had to let him think he had the upper hand to determine the extent of his deception."

Deagan began trussing up McGuire with Maku's help. "This couldn't happen to a nicer guy," he shoved a rag into the Irishman's gaping mouth and tied it behind his head. Then his face grew serious. "But, Doc, he mentioned something about a lassie reporter. Are you thinking what I'm thinking?"

Doc's face had taken on a grim expression.

"Who else do you think it could be?" Ace shook his head. "Doc did warn her to stay away. If they have Penny down there it complicates things."

"This SOB ain't going nowhere." Deagan stood and cocked his head at McGuire. "Do you have a plan, Doc?

"A plan?' Manning's face creased with skepticism. "How the hell are we supposed to take on dozens of Nazis?"

"We've faced bigger odds," Ace said.

"You'd need a small army to tackle that place," Manning shot back.

"Brothers," Doc's eyes narrowed and he looked down at Maku, "I believe we already have one." He nodded at the boy, who made a strange, trilling sound with his mouth.

Deagan and Ace grinned as Manning's head swiveled around. The jungle foliage parted in several dozen places and natives, their bodies streaked in red and black designs, appeared holding an assortment of spears, bows and arrows. Maku smiled up at Doc and pointed to a man in breechcloth with an ornate headband. He said something in his native dialect.

"That man is the medicine man," Doc explained. "The shaman. He's the official leader of the tribe at this time." He slowly approached the shaman, Maku by his side.

They began a conversation that was accentuated by many hand gestures. Gradually, more of the tribesmen joined the circle around the Golden Avenger.

"Well," Ace smiled. "Like Doc said, I think we've got our army."

The door suddenly swung open to the small cell.

"Good afternoon," Father Hans Henkel said with a malevolent grin. He was now dressed in his Nazi major's uniform and holding a huge flashlight that illuminated the interior.

Penny put her hand up to shield her eyes. "Nice to see your true colors."

Henkel smirked and stepped aside as the huge Werner crouched down to get through the six-foot doorway. Penny saw he was holding two pairs of metal handcuffs as he strode across the floor and grabbed Vankeller. He spun him around. "*Giff* me your hands now." His English was heavily accented.

"I see he's broken his vow of silence," Penny said.

"Werner never could shake off the accent of his youth," Henkel said. "I, on the other hand, found I had a talent for mimicking foreigners. It engenders trust. The real Father Henkel, I'm afraid, found it so trusting that I had no problem slipping into his identity."

Werner slapped on a pair of handcuffs over Vankeller's wrists then turned to Penny. "*Giff* me your hands."

The huge ham-like hand grabbed her shoulder and spun her around, tearing her flimsy peasant dress. Werner held both her wrists together with one hand as he cuffed her tightly with the other hand.

"Watch it, buster! You'd better not break any nails."

"Ah, American humor," Henkel said from the doorway. "Make all jokes you wish. Your overconfidence will be your downfall. Soon, I'm afraid, it will be time for tears."

"Yeah," Penny shot back as they were pushed out of their cell, "just like the ones you guys shed when we kicked you out of Europe."

Within minutes they were escorted across the compound and ushered into one of the larger buildings lit by the harsh, flickering light provided by a generator outside. Vankeller was weak and began to stumble. Werner reached out, grabbed him by the collar and dragged him along. Penny quickly surveyed the interior. They were ushered through a small ante room and into a larger area with two operating tables. The other side of the room had several wooden tables strewn with microscopes, Bunsen burners, vials, and dozens of boxes marked with dates on the side, some going back to 1944.

The heavy cloth curtain that cut off the back of the room parted and Dr. Rhinnemann appeared, looking like a mad scientist out of a horror movie with his lab coat, sinister black goggles and his shock of frizzled gray hair. He carefully removed the goggles so as not to break his gold wire rimmed glasses. He looked at them and smiled, then told Werner "Put him on the table."

Werner picked Vankeller up like he was a rag doll and dropped him on the metal slab. Then he shuffled away and disappeared behind the curtain.

Henkel, who was standing close behind Penny, leaned into her ear. "Miss Penny, you may have beaten that mad little paper hanger in Germany who was obsessed with parades and sending young soldiers to their death, but you have not yet witnessed the true might of the New Third Reich. We have succeeded in merging science and superstition. This time we will triumph."

"Yeah, when pigs fly," Penny spit out, trying to sound brave.

"That would not help us at all, *frauline*," Rhinnemann smiled as he approached the table. "But this – this is the crowning achievement of my life's work. I started this when working with Dr. Von Strohm. But it was here, in this outpost that the Reich established during the war, that the New Third Reich will rise. It is all because of the green death. It is time to test it on this pathetic American. It worked well on the healthy, strong American we captured. Let's see how quickly it will kill this man in his weakened state."

"Let him go, you monster." Penny screamed. Henkel jerked her back as she tried to rush forward.

"Ah, *frauline*, you are a spirited one. *Das ist gut.*" Rhinnemann smiled as his eyes swept over her. "Now, behold my genius at work. Watch how I command death. And remember that if you are not, how do you say it, friendlier to me, then you will be next."

Rhinnemann moved over to the lab tables and pulled the cover off of several large, glass terrariums. They looked like they were full of plants or tree branches. Turning to his left, he picked up a vial of murky liquid and a huge syringe. Slowly he inserted the needle through the cork at the top of the vial, held it up to the shimmering overhead lights and withdrew the mixture into his hypodermic needle. A spurt of liquid shot out of the needle as he depressed the plunger.

"Werner," Rhinnemann said, "have you prepared yourself?"

"*Ya*," a voice said.

Penny gasped as the drape parted at the far end of the room and Werner stepped towards her. Again Penny thought that she was trapped in a horror movie as he was wearing a heavy suit of some sort of canvas banded by metal strips. His hands were encased in large gloves of the same material and under his arm was a metallic helmet with a slit of glass face plate. He stopped, grinned, and placed the helmet over his head.

He looked like a huge Cyclops as he ambled over to the terrarium, pried the lid off and slowly reached into the pile of bark and leaves that covered the bottom of the tank. His huge gloved finger poked through the foliage until he found what he was searching for and he gently removed something that looked like a thick green worm. Werner lumbered over to the table where the Rhinnemann waited, the reflection of the flickering ceiling lights filling the hood's rectangular face plate and the circular frames of the doctor's glasses.

"This, *frauline*," Rhinnemann said, "will bring the world to its knees and establish the New Third Reich for a millennium."

Penny stared at the green worm in the big man's gloved fingers. It was segmented and covered with bristly looking hairs. "It's, it's just a caterpillar."

Carefully, Werner positioned the caterpillar between his thumb and forefinger and held it toward the doctor. Rhinnemann leaned over and inserted the needle into the caterpillar. It stiffened and curled as he withdrew all the fluids from its tiny body

He turned to Penny, a sinister grin twisted across his small, shadowed face.

"You're going to conquer the world with fuzzy caterpillars." She summoned up her most sarcastic tone. "After all this time in the jungle, I think you've gone buggy."

"*Nien*," he yelled taking a step towards her. Penny instinctively flinched, only to bump against Henkel who grabbed her shoulders. "I am now death itself. I have been working for years in this secret outpost to prepare the way for the new Reich." He smiled as he pointed to the emerald insect that still writhed between Werner's gloved fingers. "*Lonomia Obliqua*. They are known throughout the country as the fire caterpillars. Their sting keeps the blood from coagulating, and death results from internal hemorrhaging." His smile was evil looking as he turned and cast an admiring glance at the little green insect again. "They are primarily found in the southern part of the country, but I have transplanted them to an entirely new environment to do my bidding."

"You're insane," Penny screamed. "You'll never —-" She didn't finish her sentence as the lab was rocked by two nearby explosions.

"*Was ist das*?" Henkel shouted as he pushed Penny forward to Rhinnemann. "*Werner, ergreifen sie den flammenwerfer.*" The giant Nazi turned and moved back to the open terrarium holding his hand inside and brushing the caterpillar back into the foliage.

Reverberations from another explosion wracked the room.

"Hurry up," Henkel switched to English. He moved to the window. "It looks like the Indians are attacking us."

"What?" Rhinnemann's face froze in an expression of puzzlement. "They do not have the sophistication for such devices."

"Come see for yourself," Henkel raised his Luger and fired off several rounds.

Werner practically tore the door off of a metal cabinet in the corner of the room. He quickly strapped on two horizontal metal tanks with a long steel cable with a cone-like end that ran from the bottom. Penny had seen them on the newsreels during the War: a flame thrower. Werner ambled towards the open door where Henkel stood with his Luger in his hand.

"Go, Werner," Henkel commanded, "burn them. Put the fear of the *mapinguari* into them."

"*Ya*," Werner's muffled voice replied.

Penny watched in horror as the hulking monster looked down adjusting the knobs on the side of the cone attached to the cable. As he reached the doorway a pair of powerful looking hands grabbed the giant's left arm and he suddenly flew several feet through the air, landing on the crushed rock outside.

Henkel stepped toward the door and raised the Luger. The strong hands seized the sleeve of his black uniform jacket and ripped the pistol from his grasp, then backhanded the butt of the weapon into Henkel's face.

The Nazi dropped to the floor.

"Doc," Penny exclaimed as the Golden Avenger stepped into the room.

"Halt, *Amerikaner*," Rhinnemann shouted as he grabbed Penny and held the syringe just inches from neck." Take one more step and the *frauline* dies."

Outside, the rest of the compound resembled a hornet's nest set ablaze. The three pronged attack, with Deagan, Ace, and Manning each leading groups of natives had struck with sudden and unexpected effectiveness catching the complacent Nazis off guard. Deagan's group had blown up the fuel tanks on both sides of the motor pool and barracks, while Manning's crew had started from the other side. With the two barracks on fire at the rear exits, the soldiers coming out were easy targets. Assante and Deagan had taken up positions opposite each other behind solid cover. Ace, a rifle marksman, was set with three Browning automatic rifles and one native they'd showed how to reload them. A quick shot from Ace took out the lone guard and the communications shack. Deagan had three submachine guns and Maku, who never left his side, was reloading as fast as he could. The Nazis, choked by smoke, could only dash into the center of the compound into the crossfire outside.

As soon as Manning and a few natives saw the fire begin to grow in the barracks, he tossed two grenades into the small command center adjacent the airstrip. Manning's group quickly rushed the large wood shed that housed jeeps, trucks, a bulldozer and the halftrack with a plow welded on its front. The natives froze in terror and shrieked when they saw the half-ton vehicle and would not enter the shed. Manning assumed that they had a bad experience with the beast and signaled them to stay outside and keep watch. He entered the shed and saw a uniformed man crouching by the halftrack. The man raised a pistol but Manning flattened against the side of the truck and brought his own weapon up and fired. The Nazi slumped to the ground.

Manning looked around the garage and wry smile twisted across his lips. Carefully, with his hook and his good hand, he opened the duffel bag and took out a grenade and moved towards the large fuel tank. He held the grenade in his left hand and managed to snare the pin with his hook. As the pin slid out, Manning felt the sweat drip from his brow. An underhand toss with his left arm, his only good arm, would allow him scant seconds to run from the ensuing explosion. More shots rang out and he knew what he had to do. Taking several running steps forward, he threw the grenade at the fuel tank and sprinted in the other direction.

The resulting explosions, separated by a few seconds, sent a concussive wave over the entire compound.

The Indians, buoyed by the shaman's prognostication of the "man pure of spirit" who would come and help them fight "the evil white demons and the *mapinguari*" began attacking with their arrows and spears, their ferocity not tempered by the brutality and torture they had received at the hands of their repressors.

The last group of native warriors, led by their shaman, stormed the mess hall and dispatched their one time oppressors with savage efficiency. They then joined their fellow tribesmen behind the two barracks to dispense jungle justice to any Nazis who braved running through the fire to escape or tried to drop from the narrow, ceiling-height screened windows along the side of both buildings.

Looks like we ain't gonna be taking any prisoners, Deagan thought as he watched the butchery. But then again, he knew the Nazis to be low on compassion for their enemies as well. As ye sow, so shall ye reap, he added mentally and continued to fire.

Inside the laboratory Doc stepped over the seemingly unconscious German on the floor, leveling his revolver at the Nazi madman who now held Penny hostage. In a commanding tone he said, "I suggest you release her immediately."

The madman in the lab coat smiled. "I think not, *Herr* Atlas. Yes, I know who you are, and I know this *frauline* is very special to you, yes?"

Doc cocked back the hammer on his weapon, evaluating the chances of a successful brainstem shot.

"Shoot me and she will die a painful death right in front of you. There is no antidote." The madman pressed the tip of the needle to the whiteness of Penny's neck. "Now, drop your weapon."

"I don't think so," Doc said. Suddenly, the man on the floor scrambled to his feet, took a look around, and bolted out the door. The Golden Avenger scanned rest of the lab. A curtain covered the back of the room. Mickey Vankeller struggled to free himself from an operating table. Penny and the madman were still about ten feet away.

The Nazi smiled. "We shall make a trade. My freedom for the *frauline*. Now, place your pistol very slowly on the floor."

Doc held his revolver straight out in front of him. His eyes caught Penny's. She had seen that look many times before: the look of a tiger ready to pounce.

She twisted away from the needle and with one violent motion, she thrust her manacled hands between the open folds of the madman's lab coat and squeezed. The doctor howled in pain and recoiled back just as Doc squeezed the trigger. The bullet hit the Nazi in the right shoulder and sent him reeling against the lab tables. He rotated again, this time trying to regain his balance but put his hand down into the open terrarium. Suddenly his eyes bulged and his mouth twisted downward.

"No!" he screamed, as he held up his bloody hand that was covered with green caterpillars. "*Nien, nien.*"

The madman took a few halting steps, stopped, and keeled over.

"No antidote, creep," Penny reminded, looking at him.

The Golden Avenger holstered his revolver and strode over to her. "Are you all right?" he asked.

She looked into his eyes, then toward the floor. "I think so. They didn't have time to hurt me."

Doc grabbed the chain on the cuffs securing her wrists.

"Oww," Penny squealed. "Please don't break my arm trying to save me." She smiled up at him.

Doc ignored her and his powerful hands yanked the cuffs apart. Doc then moved over to the lab table where Vankeller still struggled trying to free himself. The muscles in Doc's arms bulged like steel cables and he once again pulled at the handcuff chains, causing them to separate with a resounding pop.

"Did he inject you with the poison?" Doc asked.

Vankeller shook his head. "He was about to, but you got here first."

Doc nodded again and helped Vankeller assume a sitting position.

"I'm afraid I'm too weak to walk far," Vankeller admitted.

Doc turned to Penny. "Help him to the door." He then turned to look at the fallen madman who writhed in pain on the floor.

"Help me," Rhinnemann said, his voice cracking. "I am a scientist. I can help you save the world."

Doc shook his head and stepped on the syringe that the madman had been holding. The glass crunched on the floor under his boot. Satisfied that the madman was no longer a threat, Doc turned back to the others.

Just as Penny began helping Vankeller off the lab table the giant in the fire-retardant suit lumbered through the doorway, the cone tip of the flame thrower blazing.

Penny screamed as the hulking Nazi sent a deadly stream of flame across the lab.

The Golden Avenger rolled away from the lab table as a ball of fire burst against the wall. Glass vials exploded as the rear wall was engulfed in flame. Doc rolled across the floor for the cover of the second metal operating table, a ribbon of fire trailing close behind him. Grabbing the leg of the table, Doc tipped it forward as the heated stream of death scorched the metallic surface. The giant took several clumsy steps forward in his bulky suit as the rear of the lab was quickly becoming an inferno.

As Penny reached the door she looked back at Doc. She had to get out of the lab, but didn't want to leave him. Vankeller signaled her to stop and pointed toward the floor. She looked down and saw it: the Luger that Doc had taken from Henkel. Leaning Vankeller against the wall, she stooped and picked up the gun.

"Give it to me," Vankeller said.

She handed it to him and as he raised the gun his arm slumped downward slightly. Penny reached out and pushed him upright.

"Are you sure you can shoot that thing?" she yelled over the crackling of the fire.

"Never shot one in a burning Nazi lab before." His voice was a low wheeze. "First time for everything." He squeezed off a round and the jointed arm flipped up signaling the weapon was empty. Werner lurched forward, then awkwardly spun around. The hulking Nazi sprayed a burst of fire a few feet in front of the pair, torching the floor. Penny, with Vankeller in tow, tumbled out the door.

Doc sprang over the table and jumped forward, grabbing the gun housing as the giant turned back. A stream of pure flame shot toward the ceiling and Doc felt the searing heat too close to his face. He extended his arms and brought his foot upward, delivering a powerful kick to the giant's midsection. The massive Nazi staggered but did not fall. Doc threw another kick, but the bulky suit seemed to be absorbing much of the force. Doc held the arm with the nozzle of the fire gun with both hands at arm's length. A gigantic gloved hand closed around Doc's throat and almost lifted him from the floor. Another cascade of fire shot out from the nozzle and more of the laboratory burst into flame. The monster, protected by his flame retardant suit, held his ground in the center of the conflagration.

Doc shifted his weight and twisted the giant around. A small stream of liquid was gushing out from where Vankeller's shot had punctured the fuel tank. Doc twisted once again, still holding the giant's wrist with both of his hands. Doc delivered another powerful kick and pushed the giant back. He then bolted for the door as the fire leapt upward from the floor along the stream of fuel pouring from the tank. The entire laboratory exploded behind him just as Doc made it through the doorway. He glanced back toward the inferno, then, satisfied that no threat existed there, looked at Penny and Vankeller who were crouching a few feet away. The sound of gunfire and screams were beginning to taper off throughout the camp.

"Darling," Penny said, "I'm so glad you found us in time."

Doc gave her a stern look and made no reply.

Deagan inserted the final magazine into his Thompson and stood. The fighting and the dying had all but stopped and the smell of burning buildings and the dead bodies within began its terrible wafting over the compound. He motioned for the Indians to move away from the fire which threatened to overtake their position.

Once the jungle starts on fire it'll burn till it gets to the river, he thought. He made his way over to Ace's position.

"I don't like the look of this," Ace pointed toward the wall of advancing flames.

"Me neither," Deagan agreed. "Where's Doc?"

Ace shrugged. "He went to the lab to find Penny and Vankeller." His handsome face changed into a smile. "Look, there they are."

Deagan glanced over and saw Doc and Penny. Doc was carrying a man in his arms. His head cocked toward the airfield.

"Looks like Doc wants us to move to the airfield," Ace said. The Indians were already beginning to scatter. "That plane we saw is our ticket out of here. Come on."

"You go ahead," Deagan gave Ace a pat on the shoulder. "I'm gonna go round up Reese."

Ace gave him a solemn nod and began moving toward the airstrip.

Deagan started walking and suddenly Maku was beside him, pulling on his sleeve and pointing in the direction of the river. The boy's anxious face showed he was aware of the impending danger from the fire.

"No," Deagan shook his head. "You go." He pointed.

Maku looked at him and shook his head.

"Go. Now," Deagan urged.

The boy looked up at him.

Deagan frowned. "Dammit, that fire's gonna get us both if we don't start moving." He pointed to himself, then in the direction of the airstrip.

Maku nodded and started to turn. He stopped and removed his necklace and handed it to Deagan. Deagan took it and smiled. The boy began to move away and Deagan yelled, "Hey." Maku stopped and Deagan took off his wrist watch and tossed it to him.

"Something to remember me by," he grinned. "It kept good time all through the War."

Maku grinned too, then his face froze in shock. A Nazi in a gray uniform, bloodied and bruised, had appeared out of nowhere pointing a pistol at Deagan.

"You *haff* not beaten the Riech, *Amerikaner*," the Nazi growled.

"Hey, Father Henkel," a voice yelled from behind them. "Remember me?"

The Nazi whirled and fired his pistol. Beyond him Deagan saw Reese Manning grab his chest and topple over. As the Nazi turned back Deagan was already sending a spray of forty-five caliber bullets from his Thompson. Major Henkel's dream of a new Reich ended as he crumpled to the jungle floor.

Deagan dropped the empty machine-gun and rushed across the matted jungle grass and skidded to a stop next to Manning who was face down and not moving.

"Reese, Reese," he slowly turned his old friend over and cradled his head. A sliver of blood leaked out of Manning's mouth. "Hang in there, pal. You're gonna be okay."

"Hey, Mad Dog, did you get him?" Manning coughed, sending a spray of blood into the night air.

"Yeah, Reese, I got him. Thanks to you."

"I woulda shot him but I was out of ammo." He coughed again. More blood seeped from his mouth.

Deagan swallowed a large gulp of air. "You saved me again, Reese."

The hint of a smile outlined Manning's lips. "Getting to be a habit." His voice was a soft gurgle.

"Yeah," was all Deagan could manage to say.

"Don't think I'll be around for round three," Manning's body stiffened and he reached up with his left hand and grabbed Deagan's arm. "Mad Dog, don't leave me here."

"I won't, Reese. Just hold on. I'm gonna get you to that plane."

Manning shook his head, coughed again, and smiled. "If I die in a combat zone —" His voice trailed off.

Deagan winced at hearing the old army marching song, his memory supplying the matching refrain with inevitable gloom: *Box me up and ship me home.*

Deagan felt Manning's grip soften and his hand fell away, his eyes fixed in a blank stare accompanied by the sound of the final bit of air escaping his body.

Tears began to run down Deagan's face as he slipped one arm under Manning's back and the other under his legs. He stood and began trotting toward the airstrip.

Don't worry, buddy, he thought. *I ain't leaving you behind.*

One week later, they were all seated around the large table in the library on the 86th floor of the Empire State Building.

Doc addressed the group. "I'm happy to report that Mickey Vankeller has made an amazing recovery. He was released from the hospital earlier today and sends his thanks."

"Hard to believe he was really sent down there by the government," Deagan said. "I thought he was just some spoiled rich man's son."

"He saved my life," Penny said. "And helped Doc too."

"Then I guess not mentioning he's a government agent in your story won't be too difficult, eh?" Ace grinned at her as he put a cigarette between his lips. A stern look from Doc kept him from lighting it.

Penny frowned at him but said nothing.

"What's that agency called again?" Deagan asked.

"The Central Intelligence Agency," Ace said. "And you know how Washington likes its acronyms. It'll probably end up being known as the CIA."

"We probably haven't seen the last of it, either," Penny predicted.

"I hope we have seen the last of your impetuous behavior," Doc said. "Do I have to remind you that I forbade you to accompany us for exactly that reason?"

Penny blushed but said nothing.

"You knew VanKeller was a spy, Doc?" Deagan asked.

Doc looked at Penny for a moment longer, then nodded. "I'd surmised as much from the newspaper accounts of his numerous exploits to various places around the globe. They always coincided with the possibility of some kind of brewing foreign dissonance. He was working undercover for the greater good."

Deagan made a clucking sound. "At least poor Reese didn't die for nothing."

"Indeed not." Doc stood and glanced at his watch. "We should be going if we want to catch that train to Washington."

"Yeah," Deagan said. "Wouldn't want to be late for Reese's internment at Arlington." He held up his arm and glanced at his big hairy wrist to check the time, and then seeing that his wrist was bare, just shook his head in frustration.

As Penny and Doc headed for the door Ace placed his hand on Deagan's shoulder. "Hey, I thought you could use this, old chum." He held out a small, cardboard box.

Deagan's brow furrowed as he opened it. Inside was an Army Air-corps pilot's watch. His head shot up and he looked at Ace.

"I can't accept this. It's the one you wore during the War, ain't it? On your bombing missions?"

"You keep it." Ace grinned and held up his wrist displaying the latest gold, self-winding Rolex. "Besides, I've got a new one."

Deagan's mouth puckered up for a moment and he held out his big hand toward Ace and they shook. "You know, shyster, you're not such a bad guy after all."

Ace smiled. "Just don't tell anyone. I have a reputation to uphold."

THE END

ABOUT OUR CREATORS

WRITERS –

MICHAEL A. BLACK - is the author of twenty books and over one-hundred short stories and articles. His latest novel is *Chimes at Midnight* and he is also writing the Mack Bolan Executioner series (*Sleeping Dragons, Deadly Salvage, Payback*). Being in this anthology fulfills his lifelong ambition to write a Sherlock Holmes story.

RAYMOND LOUIS LOVATO - loves writing pulp fiction with his lifelong friend author Michael A. Black. Ray also enjoys traveling the world with his lovely wife, Susan. Years ago, on a five-hour flight to Sint Maartin, he was inspired to draft an homage to Doc Savage, the Man of Bronze. After presenting the first chapter as a serial birthday gift to his best friend, the Adventures of Doc Atlas was born. Black wrote the first Doc Atlas novel, A MELODY OF VENGEANCE, as a tribute to the Pulp Age of Heroes.

ARTIST –

ED CATTO - A voracious reader, Ed has been enjoying pulps since stumbling across Shadow and Doc Savage reprints as a kid. His love for illustration and art has guided him through a life-long love of comics, pulps and illustrated paperbacks. As a branding and advertising executive, Ed's career has evolved to include a focus on entertainment marketing in many ways:

A founding partner of Bonfire Agency, Ed helped establish the world's first marketing firm focused on connecting brands, in authentic ways, to passionate and enthusiastic fans of comics, graphic novels, games and movies.

Ed has also shepherded the rebirth of the iconic 60s toy, Captain Action, in collectibles, books, comics and even a national toy line. An animated television series is currently being shopped for development.

A convention enthusiast, Ed helped develop Reed Pop's New York Comic-Con (now the nation's largest con) and is currently doing the same for Syracuse's Salt City Comic-Con.

Ed speaks nationally as a panelist and moderator at conventions, leading conversations on entertainment marketing and comics history. Ed has also appeared on CNBC's Squawkbox, BNN Business News Network , and PBS's Superheroes documentary.

Ed recently started teaching at Ithaca College, sharing his experiences and enthusiasm for business and entrepreneurship to both MBA's and undergraduates. As an artist, Ed also leads graphic novel classes for kids of all ages. The Adventures of Captain Graves Marks Ed's debut as an illustrator for publisher Airship27. Ed and his wife Kathe currently live in New York's State's Finger Lakes Region, enjoying the area's local comic book shops and wineries. Between consulting, teaching and drawing, Ed continues to work very hard to whittle down the teetering tower of books on his nightstand.

www.ingramcontent.com/pod-product-compliance
Lightning Source LLC
Chambersburg PA
CBHW071436260626
47170CB00008B/2736